Beyond the
Antares

Open Signal

Edited by Brandon Rospond

Beyond the Gates of Antares: Open Signal
Edited by Brandon Rospond
Cover by
Zmok Books an imprint of
Winged Hussar Publishing, LLC, 1525 Hulse Road, Unit 1, Point Pleasant,
NJ 08742

This edition published in 2016 Copyright ©Winged Hussar Publishing, LLC
Beyond the Gates of Antares is the property of Warlord Games and Rick
Priestley, produced under license by Winged Hussar Publishing, LLC

ISBN 978-1-9454300-5-3
Library of Congress No. 2017938434
Bibliographical references and index
1.Science Fiction 2. Space Opera 3. Action & Adventure

For more information on Winged Hussar Publishing, LLC, visit us at: https://
www.WingedHussarPublishing.com
Twitter: WingHusPubLLC
Facebook: Winged Hussar Publishing LLC

Beyond the Gates of Antares

Beyond the Gates of Antares lies a universe vast beyond comprehension, a universe of human endeavor stretching eons into a dark and turbulent past, a universe of embattled civilizations possessed of unimaginable power. Across millions of worlds rival empires are locked in a struggle for dominance, driven by intellects that are as much machine as human, the omniscient integrated machine intelligence of a society and a time very different to our own. This is the universe of the Seventh Age of Humanity and the setting for the game. It is called Beyond the Gates of Antares because that is where our adventures will take us. We will travel through Antarean dimensional gateways to the galaxy spanning empires of the PanHuman Concord and Isorian Senatex, and further to the myriad worlds of the Determinate and beyond. We will board the glittering space borne cities of the Vardari, the great mercantile powers of Antarean space, and we will confront foes as implacable as the Ghar and as merciless as the Renegade NuHu Shards. Beyond the Gates of Antares was originally conceived as a game and that is where our journey begins. However, this is only the first step upon a path that promises to take us to new stars and undiscovered worlds. It is a living, breathing universe, and one that we intend to realize fully in the form of novels, campaigns, background expansions and - in time - further games exploring the many different aspects of our setting.

Rick Priestley 2017

Table of Contents

An Introduction

Space is an enigma that stretches infinitely, expanding with it an endless amount of galaxies and lifeforms. While we on Earth can hardly grasp our own planet, we know that our solar system belongs to the Milky Way, but trying to contact any other living species that might exist is nothing more than a pipe dream for our technology. Even if we were to somehow communicate with some foreign species, how would we get to them?

Surely that is something that the denizens of humanity before the First Age thought as well, long before the red giant known as Antares was ever reached, before the term 'PanHuman' came to recognize offshoots of the human race, and before the need to worry about the numerous collapses of Antares could ever even be fathomed. To be limited to one small planet, one single galaxy, a race would be considered extremely primitive!

Just beyond the farthest orbiting planet of a galaxy, there is a tunnel of light known as a 'gate'. This bright circle is what connects a solar system to the red giant, Antares, that theoretically lies in the center of the universe. Countless serpentine-like tunnels jet from Antares, each leading to a different system. And it is here that the Terrans first discovered that life is larger and farther reaching than they ever believed possible. And they entered, what would be known as, the First Age.

Six ages have transpired since then. Six times the gates of Antares depowered, trapping ships and populations in whatever system they might have been in, keeping civilizations stranded from other worlds they might have controlled. Each time that the gates have fallen silent, they remained that way for hundreds of years. No one knows what truly causes the collapses, nor what brings them back to their working status.

Yet, here, in the Seventh Age, is the setting for the vast stories that will take you, the reader, through the wide birth of space, and beyond the gates of Antares.

This anthology consists of ten stories that cover tales of the different factions in the universe known as *Beyond the Gates of Antares*. Four of our authors, myself included, have already been published in other works. The other six are the first batch of hand-picked winners from a short story competition. Each story has been tailored to fit into the overall lore of the universe, having worked closely with the creators, as well as unified under my guidance to create one overarching universe for our fiction. This is but the first of many works we plan to publish in the Antares universe!

Mark Barber is the first of the six short story winners for this anthology. Barber's story, entitled, "The Greater Cause," tells of a planet that is resisting domination from the Concord Combined Command. The Concord forces are usually seen as more machine than human, relying on the IMTel more than human emotions and judgment. However, it is the C3 that are given more freedom to think and act, while still depending on the IMTel to help them with targeting, statistics, and tracking enemy movements. It is through this tale that we see the more humane aspects of the C3 as we follow Squad Leader Ryen Tahl and his squadmates as they try to assert domination for the Concord over the Prostock Militia. Meanwhile, Barber also gives us a counter-perspective from the militia's point of view, by way of Trooper Kona Reece. In war, there is always a victor, and there are always those that suffer. While people of the Concord are more machine than most of the other races, the soldiers do still have emotions, and Barber puts both opposing forces through their paces as they must fulfill their duties in this planetary war, as they must both fight for the greater cause.

Scott Washburn is best known under Zmok for his works on the series "The Great Martian War," and his own original stories. Washburn is knowledgeable about all things military related, and thus, the most apt one to explain all of the workings of the Concord military. "Gateways" is somewhat of an introductory tale for the universe of *Beyond the Gates of Antares*. It is the first day of training for fresh recruit Cadet Tamika Gatchnall, and the main class of this perspective is with veteran of combat and multiple-times reincarnated Captain Krissa. The android like figure tells the class all about the workings of space travel and the red giant, Antares; but all the meanwhile, Tamika feels torn. She is still having a hard time adjusting to life in the C3, and her feelings begin to cloud her judgment. Can the trooper change her way of thinking and accept belonging in the Concord forces, or will she be free to leave and return to being a civilian?

Tim Bancroft is a name that most Antares fans will probably be familiar with. Bancroft's works have been published by Warlord Games bit by bit over the years, slowly telling the tale of Batu Delhren and his many adventures, but this particular one was chosen as one of the fan submissions because of the unique faction known as the SITAI. While the C3 and the Isorian rely on technology more than the other races, imagine what it would be like if the machines *were* the main force. That is what Batu, and his bodyguard, Baray, encounter on their mission from the Vard. All the while, the captain of the ship they travel on, a NuHu known as the Raya, undermines Batu's every action. While "Batu Meets the SITAI" is just one of many Batu stories, it is a piece of what fans can expect in Bancroft's to-be-published Batu novel!

The Boromites are more than just big, bulky rocks, but that is the first impression one might get when first looking at them. Their size and muscle can be intimidating, but with all groups, there is always someone who leads; someone with more than just brawn. In Tim Maguire's "Aggressive Negotiations," it is a battle of wits between Guildess Matriarch Melith of the Under-Fallen and the Freeborn Commander Janus K'zana. While the Freeborn think that they have the upper hand, sold on the fact that the rock-like PanHuman are more brawn than brain, the guildess calmly sips her tea as the battle unfolds. Can the Boromite forces combat the Freeborn and find a planet to live and mine from, or will the Freeborn pirates win this facility for their vardos?

Craig Gallant is another veteran author to grace the pages of this anthology. Gallant is not a newcomer to the world of science-fiction. He has written several books for our Wild West Exodus series, as well as his own novel, *Legacy of Shadow*. In this story, Gallant flips us back and forth through several different points of view, the primary two being Freeborn Admiral Bha ko-Rhan and C3 Commander Pehn Kowroon. Both are after the notorious Freeborn pirate, Captain Rollen Stihl. As the story starts, Stihl is in a losing battle with another ship, and his demise seems imminent. However, is it at the hands of the other

Freeborn admiral, the C3 commander, or perhaps someone else? Will ko-Rhan be vaulted into the pages of glory, capturing Stihl and his ship, or will Kowroon be able to return with one less pirate on the run?

Nacen Byzantia is the recently appointed captain of the Carmine Canotila, having begrudgingly inherited it from his father. In Riley O'Connor's story, "A Fair Trade," it is one of the Carmine's first missions under Nacen, as they head to the trading hub known as the Crab. While it seems that the loyalty of the ship's crew-members is questionable, everyone must step up as the trading post is assaulted from an unknown force, and the Boromites that run security pin it on our Freeborn protagonists. Can Nacen prove his crew's innocence and find out who is responsible for attacking the Crab? Can he command the respect of both his crew-members and the Crab's personnel, or will the new captain fall short?

Many Boromite clans are forced to move from planet to planet. They often integrate with other forces such as the C3 and maintain peaceful relationships so they can continue to mine and prosper. However, many clans are often left homeless, constantly in search of a suitable planet that they must fight and claw their way to obtain. In Robert E. Water's story, "Leap of Faith," Captain Hersh Ryza and his Boromites have been banished from their clan, but they have been given a second chance - a suicide mission from their Guild Mother to find a group of missing Algoryn. Reluctant to put his squad in danger, Ryza eventually agrees to the mission, but when he discovers the Algoryn, he starts to weigh the price of rejoining the clan, thinking the mission more than he bargained for. Waters published his first novel, *The Wayward Eight*, under the Wild West Exodus series, as well as numerous short stories. His story promises to make the reader really question if Ryza's mission is worth the prize as they take a leap of faith alongside the Boromites.

One of the most interesting aspects that I always find when developing these anthologies and setting up the universes that they take place in is how the civilians act to everything that goes on around them. Dave Horobin's story, "Subversion," gives the readers insight on just what it is like to live under the rule of the Concord and the omnipotent IMTel. Ryson repeats the same actions and the same routine every day, and the IMTel gives him all the reassurance needed to go about his day feeling content. However, Ryson also partakes in a recreation known as 'stimming' that worries his family because of the IMTel using portions of one's mind. What could go wrong in this picture of perfection?

We close out the anthology with Andrew Tinney's "Into Darkness." Kale is the leader of an Algoryn AI squad, sent to the planet Ylarys to look for technology to help them find a suitable home. Kale's mission goes awry as a squad of Boromite spring upon her troops, and her unit is sealed in a cave, into darkness. Lost and cut off from communication, Kale's squad wanders deeper into the Boromite lair. Tinney depicts the Algoryn in the perfect resilient personality, helping the faction to find its perfect niche in this anthology. Can Kale find victory on Ylarys, or will they be fodder for lavamites?

Finally, we come to myself. Being the lead editor of Zmok, I have worked with each of these authors to get their stories as perfect as possible for your reading enjoyment. Besides this anthology, I have edited everything under the Zmok imprint; from the Wild West Exodus series, to All Quiet on the Martian Front, to the Starybogow novel called *City of the Gods*, and even my own fantasy novel, *Rebirth of Courage*. It has been my great pleasure to work with all of these men and women on all that we've published and accomplished over the past few years. That said, my story, "Slipstream," is about an Isorian group of phase troopers who are sent to find Fifth Age technology. Caught between the Ghar and Algoryn as they fight across the planet Pfytorus, Fenris Teyvirium must lead his squad as they stealth through the jungles, into the last remaining relic of an ancient society. Will they find the technology they seek, or have the Ghar and Algoryn already destroyed it in their battle across the foliage-covered planet?

Our writers have come together to provide readers with stories that help to add depth to an already vibrant world, fleshing out the background and broadening horizons for all of the different factions. *Beyond the Gates of Antares* has a truly spectacular and amazing community, and the submissions that we received were overwhelming. Thank you to all that contributed stories and keep writing and thinking of ideas. After all, what is a game without its loyal players to build the universe? Hopefully these tales can help to inspire some unique battles of your own to write and play, as well as commanding characters to help lead the foray.

Brandon Rospond

The Greater Cause
By Mark Barber

A fine but persistent mist drizzled from leaden clouds that sat heavily in the lime green sky above. Though slightly acidic, the trickle of moisture failed to shift the remnants of the previous week's snowfall which still clung in small patches to the devastated buildings and narrow footpaths snaking in between them. The acrid smell of burning hung in the air, permeating the sensory filters of the Concord troopers' battlesuits. Strike Commander Ryen Tahl risked a quick glance over the shattered synthecrete walls of what was once a schoolhouse, surveying the battered remains of the town square in the center of what had been dispassionately labeled 'Settlement Urban 417'. The thick, angular armor he wore marked him and his strike troopers out as humanoid, but they were no doubt terrifying to the planet's defenders.

"Squad Jai, spotter drone," he murmured, patching in to the visual sensors of the small craft which accompanied one of the five squads of strike troopers which formed his current command.

Instantly a panoramic view of the battlefield appeared in the upper left corner of Tahl's visual display, giving the company commander unparalleled situational awareness of an area some 100 yan from his current position. Exhaling gently, Tahl utilized his mental link with the spotter drone to cautiously edge forward through the smoking ruins of the edge of the town, closer toward the militia positions to the south. As the drone crested an icy ridgeline, he was able to look down into the rocky ravine at where a battery of three x-launchers lay in wait, their crews huddled over their squat, boxy projectile launchers.

An alert flashed in the forward right quadrant of the spotter drone's visual display before a fraction of a second later its view froze in place and then faded away altogether. Tahl winced as the connection was severed.

"Squad Wen," Tahl initialized a link with one of his strike squads, "enemy launcher battery about 100 yan from your position. I'm sending you a waypoint. Close and eliminate."

Before the squad leader could even verbally respond, Tahl sensed the reactions to his orders through the shard connection; the invisible field of microscopic nanospores which seamlessly connected both man and machine at every level of society, both military and civilian. The feedback from the shard was closest with his squad leaders, and he felt grim determination and purpose from one; resentment and disappointment from another.

"Squad Wen copied, we got visuals from the drone. We think there's a sniper about 50 yan west of your waypoint which took the drone out," Strike Leader Van Noor replied gruffly. "We're advancing to deal with both threats."

"Command, Squad Jai," Strike Leader Rhona called in, "my squad is closer, we're... I'm sending a waypoint now. We're good to go."

Tahl exhaled again and glanced past his visual array to his immediate surroundings, looking at the three battlesuit-clad soldiers which formed his command squad. Even without the shard feedback, he could tell their thoughts from their body language.

"Negative, Squad Jai, hold position," he ordered.

Tahl's map display showed a cluster of six green dots advance through the ruined town, made up of its archaic, rectangular buildings, and close with the waypoint he had plotted for them. He felt slightly apprehensive – nervous, even – but realized that it was feedback filtering through Squad Wen's shard to him; one of Van Noor's new boys, no doubt. It was perfectly forgivable - the Prostock Militia forces were putting up more of a fight than anticipated, certainly a lot more than had been expected from such a smaller, weaker, and less advanced civilization.

"As soon as those launchers are neutralized, be ready to move," Tahl instructed his command squad as the incessant drizzle intensified into rain.

***

Trooper Jordan Reece had not volunteered for the militia to fight. Years of threats about the PanHuman Concord coming to absorb his world along with the rest of the Prostock Alliance had seemed far-fetched, something for another generation to worry about, and so signing on for two years military service had seemed a safe bet and an easy way to impress a certain girl. Reece hunched up his shoulders as a drop of rain fell through the damaged neck seal of his body armor and rolled down his back. She moved to a different continent a week later anyway, leaving Reece in basic training with no girl to impress. He allowed himself a brief chuckle at the thought.

"Movement!" Squad Leader Vorten announced as he peered through his viewscope from his vantage point at the crest of the icy plateau, his green armored bulk hidden amidst the waist-high razor grass. "Looks like they're moving in on the launchers!"

Reece waited impatiently, but seeing no update through his eyepiece, he quickly keyed refresh on his forearm console. The map display which was projected in a ghostly blue at the bottom of his field of vision briefly froze in place, crackled, and then updated to show six red squares moving from the southern suburbs toward the launcher battery below them. Clearly they had not been quick enough in shooting the enemy spotter drone out of the sky.

"Ready!" Vorten hissed.

The ten militia men took up firing positions along the plateau and hugged their mag guns to their shoulders. Reece's eyepiece immediately married up with his weapon's scope and he scanned from left to right amongst the outskirts of the town as he waited for his first ever glimpse of an enemy soldier.

"What's going on?" Asked Gander, the only militiaman in the squad who was even younger than Reece. "I can't see them! The map says they're right there but I can't see them!"

Reece's mouth was dry and somehow, even though lying immobile, he had a stitch in his side. He had seen the propaganda posters put out by the Concord, the invitations to join the paternal care of their all-consuming empire with the unsaid threat of what would happen if they refused, but he had never really believed the hype of their invincible Strike Troopers and drone tanks. Not until this exact moment when he lay atop a hill defending his home planet against a superior enemy which suddenly seemed to have the ability to turn invisible.

"Use iron sights!" Vorten suddenly shouted, "look over your scopes!"

Reece yanked his eyepiece from his head and used his naked eye to look down the sights of his weapon, blinking and struggling to focus through the grimy rain. There – rapidly approaching the ridge above the launcher battery's ravine – six bulky shapes moved rapidly in pairs across the open ground, their armored suits perfectly color matched with their surroundings even as the backdrop changed behind them from ruined city to icy hills.

Vorten swore as the six enemy soldiers disappeared from view.

"Unor Battery, this is Guardian," he called to the battery's shard network. "You've got six Concord troopers right on top of you! They've got some sort of camouflage against our scopes and..."

A pair of Concord troopers appeared to the left of the ridgeline, a second pair to the right, and the final two were just visible at the top of the ridge. With coordination and accuracy which Reece thought to be impossible, the six Concord troopers opened fire with their plasma carbines, sending streams of blue lines stitching through the battery crewmen and dropping them where they stood before a single retaliatory shot could be fired.

"Open fire!" Vorten yelled.

Reece pulled the trigger of his mag gun. The weapon jolted back into his shoulder as the magnetic coils accelerated a projectile out of the barrel with fantastic speed, the weapon heating up and glowing softly against his cheek. Reece fired again and again. The faceless, armored enemy soldiers ahead of him were out of focus as his attention was drawn to the bucking barrel of his weapon, completely unable to tell whether his shots were anywhere near his barely registered target. An opaque purple square appeared momentarily over the shoulder of one of the enemy troopers as a shot was deflected by the Concord soldier's hyperlight armor.

There was a scream somewhere to the right and Reece realized that the heat he could sense was not solely emanating from his mag gun; pulses of blue plasma fire were piercing the air just above his head.

Reece froze. He stopped firing. At that precise moment, he realized for the first time that enemy soldiers were trying to kill him.

Next to him, Gander tensed up suddenly and rolled over without a sound, the left half of his head completely absent, and what was left of his skull now cauterized into a smoking mess of black. A hand grabbed Reece by the scruff of his neck and he was yanked from his firing position and down the far side of the plateau, stumbling until he found his feet to join his surviving comrades in fleeing.

***

The rain finally eased off shortly after sunset, and Tahl found himself caught out by the beauty of the night sky and the familiar stellar constellations as he gazed toward home, light years away. He thought of his mother, still as worried about him now after ten years of soldiering as she was on the day he left to become a recruit. The IMTel – the Integrated Machine Intelligence which amalgamated the shards of every aspect of PanHuman society into one pool of thought for the greater cause – was a constant source of comfort for every human being who basked under its paternal blanket of care. Still, even knowing that her son had been specially selected to be in the right place at the right time for his particular skill set, there was only so much of human nature which could be overridden with technology, and Tahl knew his mother would always worry.

"Commander?"

Tahl was brought back to the present, back to the company's base camp in the ruined town where his troopers held a solid defensive position alongside Drop Commander Keenen's Company. Stood in front of him, his hyperlight armor now pitch black to blend into the night, Strike Leader Van Noor nodded respectfully. The stocky man had rolled back his helmet's faceplate, no doubt enjoying the relatively rare combination of a breathable atmosphere and a location secure enough to let his guard down momentarily. A single red vertical line in the center of Van Noor's chest plate was his only badge of rank, and even that was calibrated so as to be invisible to any eyes other than those patched in to the C3 military shard. Van Noor was the company's senior strike leader and as such would normally accompany Tahl. But given the shortages of experienced leaders, Van Noor was now utilized as a squad leader once more.

"You wanted to see me?" The blonde squad leader said.

"Yes," Tahl replied quietly, "yes, I did."

He glanced around at his soldiers as they sat in groups within the shelter of the roofless houses. By and large they had formed up into squads, even in their down time, whilst they ran diagnostic checks on their weapons and armor in the light of the triple moons, their hushed conversations occasionally eliciting a bawdy laugh or terse insult.

"Good job today," Tahl said, "you and your guys. I know you've taken a few hits since we took the lead on this offensive, but your squad is the most experienced in the company and I honestly think we're nearly done here."

Van Noor nodded slowly, his dark eyes glistening.

"Forty-five days now, Boss," he finally said. "The IMTel reckoned we'd have these guys finished in less than half of that. And the IMTel doesn't make mistakes."

"Keep your voice down, Leader," Tahl said, glancing around cautiously before continuing, "I know you're frustrated, Bry, I can understand that. But don't go questioning our leadership in front of the troopers, it can't bring anything good. You've got any problems at all, you bring them to me and I'll take them forward on your behalf. I'll listen, and I'll take you seriously."

"I know, sir, I know," the veteran soldier replied sincerely, "but these men and women are living off combat stimulants and good will, and we're running out of both. We were promised some time away from the front line after Naubek and it didn't happen. The same again at Tarantell V. Now we're here and this one is dragging out; these bastards don't know they're beaten and now they're sending militia kids up against us. The guys and girls are tired, demoralized from our losses, and now that we're massacring half trained kids it's getting even worse."

"And this is cause to shake your faith in our system?"

The new voice made both men turn to face the figure which had appeared by their side. Standing a full head taller than both men, the thin, pale, wraith-like form of Mandarin

Leeoras stared at the two soldiers with cold, impassive eyes.

"Strike Leader Van Noor is merely voicing his concern over the state of the men and women under his command, ma'am," Tahl said calmly, "he meant nothing by it."

"Yet you both seem nervous," the tall, pale woman observed, her head cocked slightly sideways as she waited for his response. Tahl had not even been aware of the emotion now registering in his brain. As a NuHu, Leeoras was in many ways an evolutionary step ahead of a regular human being. With a hyper developed mental ability which facilitated a seamless link with nano-technology and shards at every level, a NuHu was able to control any machine with only a mere thought; able to read the minds of any human connected to IMTel without that person even being aware that their deepest secrets were already known.

"Carry on about your business, Strike Leader," Leeoras said passively, allowing Van Noor to dismiss himself before turning back to Tahl. "Walk with me, Commander."

Dressed in white and green robes which covered her armor, the NuHu's blossom pink hair complimented her complexion which almost gave a warmth to her appearance. Tahl noticed that the tall, thin woman walked as any human would, rather than manipulating her surrounding nanosphere to simply levitate, as he had seen other NuHu do with contemptuous ease.

"Many humans find it off putting," Leeoras replied to his unvocalised question, "but that is not what I wanted to talk to you about. Our enemy is beginning to wise up to our technology. As your company found today, we are encountering less and less of their professional soldiers and more of their militia. Their technology is similar to that which we were using over a century ago, which is why we are able to shield ourselves from their sensors."

"It is certainly easier facing these pockets of resistance than their front line troops in the first days of the campaign," Tahl agreed.

"But they are not stupid," Leeoras held up a long, graceful finger. "They are abandoning their guerrilla tactics and relying more on massing their offensive capabilities in centralized locations. Statistically, this is their most likely way of inflicting casualties upon our forces."

"They are proving far more difficult to defeat than anticipated," Tahl agreed. "Yet another in a long line of opponents who view us as a threat to their way of life, rather than a way to improve it."

Leeoras turned her gray eyes to the south and raised a finger to her thin lips. A ripple of laughter from one of Tahl's squads who were servicing their plasma weapons seemed to suddenly break the Mandarin's concentration, causing her to frown momentarily before turning back to Tahl.

"We are a threat to their way of life," she said, her tone almost stern, "but their way of life is outdated and favors an elite minority rather than providing care in equality to all. Regardless, there is a major concentration of Prostock Alliance forces in a settlement which is 8,450 yan from here on a heading of 193. More specifically, an old fortification which they have fitted with defensive weaponry and shielding. It will take time we cannot afford to spare to bombard them out, so we need to close with the enemy. Your company is to neutralize this threat at 1000 tomorrow."

Tahl nodded. His people were showing signs of fatigue, despite the continually achieved objectives and facade of normality in between actions – sloppiness in routines, arguments breaking out of inconsequential disagreements, lapses in concentration – they needed rest. But it was the same across the rest of the regiment. Tahl had already raised his concerns to his chain of command, but had received no feedback.

"Is your company fit to carry out this task?" Leeoras asked.

"Yes, they're fine," Tahl replied after a pause. "I'll take point myself with my command squad."

"I do not think that is a good idea," the NuHu narrowed her eyes ever so slightly, "exposing yourself to a dangerous position which could be carried out by another without any loss in operational capability. You should be directing your forces from a central position, not leading from the front."

Tahl ran a gloved hand through his short, dark hair. He looked around at the men and women of his company. Whilst the average life expectancy of a human was two and half centuries, it was most common for the IMTel to select recruits in their late teens and early twenties for a typical military tour of five years. At 35 years of age, even though physically he looked no older than any of them, Tahl felt himself to be a generation apart from the troopers who looked to him for guidance.

"No, I'll lead from the front," Tahl declared as a soothing tone sounded briefly in his ear to announce a briefing package had arrived in his battlesuit's processor; the details for tomorrow's mission, no doubt.

"I have sent you the file," Leeoras said. "I assume you will be sending it directly to your company now?"

"No," Tahl disagreed again, "let them have their evening. I'll brief them face to face in the morning."

"Why?" Leeoras asked, her head cocked to one side again.

"Because with all of our technological advantages, if you are ordering a person potentially to their death, it does a world of good to take the time to at least look them in the eye as you do so."

Leeoras nodded slowly.

"I am glad of our relationship, Commander," she said with a slight smile. "We... need the human touch in our military leadership which NuHu cannot provide. And you, Ryen, what are you to do with your evening?"

"Forms," Tahl replied. "They are the very essence of my art. Without them, the karampei practitioner grows stale. Given my somewhat high profile entry into the world of competition fighting outside of the Concord, I now take every effort to return to the proper path of the art."

"Of course," the NuHu said, "the wandering warrior. Do you... miss those days?"

"It was over a decade ago, this is who I am now. Goodnight, ma'am, my company won't let you down tomorrow."

***

Glad to have a few moments alone, Strike Leader Katya Rhona sank down on a rubbled wall which stood at a third of her height, a couple of dozen yan away from the rest of the company. She slid a hand from her chin to the crown of her head and took in a breath of fresh air as her face mask followed her palm and retreated into the back of her helmet, before she reached back and removed the headgear entirely. Her jet black hair hung over her eyes as she leaned forward and steadied her breathing.

"Take that rag off your head!" A voice boomed from behind her. "You're a strike leader now, you're supposed to be setting a damn example!"

Rhona looked over her armored shoulder and met the furious gaze of Feon Rall, the soldier who up until yesterday had been her own strike leader. The tall, dark skinned man folded his arms across his broad chest and sneered down at her.

"Go screw yourself, Rall," Rhona flashed a smile, "if I want your opinion, you'll know 'bout it."

The veteran trooper swore and shook his head.

"Two days holding rank and now you know better than me? What the hell is this army coming to, putting the likes of you in command of Concord soldiers..."

"Truth be told, I don't give a damn about you or your army right now," Rhona shrugged, "besides, I knew better than you when I was a new recruit, let alone a strike leader. Now, I've come out here to be on my own, not to talk about all things military with an idiot like you. Run along, honey, you're boring me."

The tall trooper muttered an obscenity and turned to leave. Rhona reached up and took the 'rag' – her sweat soaked purple bandanna – from her head and held it in her hands, remembering her father with a brief, affectionate laugh before replacing it and carefully arranging her hair stylishly over the bandanna again. The campaign was nearly over, and maybe soon she could go home for a few days. Maybe, just maybe, the IMTel would decide that she was not meant for soldiering and discharge her from C3 altogether, to return to her previous life before military service. Still, even with the freedom of thought which a military shard allowed her, she knew that she was where she was supposed to be - the IMTel did not make mistakes.

A few minutes and she would have to return to her squad, back to the overwhelmingly negative environment where she could physically feel their resentment and dissatisfaction with her through the shard, as well as see it in their eyes. That was nothing new. She was used to resentment; it was the curse of being more beautiful than everybody else. And being promoted to strike leader less than a year into her military career – four of five years ahead of the average promotion time – certainly did not help.

None of it mattered, this was just a phase of her life and at twenty-five, she had already seen more change than the average Concord citizen would in two centuries. Better to just word a quick letter to her little brother and then get back to work, even if it would take a good two or three days for her communiqué to reach him. With security and transmission distances to overcome, it was a comparative age corresponding with family from the front line.

"Dear Micha," she began, "hope this finds you doing good, and still trying hard at school. I guess it's the start of batterball season now? You must have been picked for the team, Pa made a damn good striker out of you..."

***

The lead C3T7's generator pulsated faster and a little louder as the transport drone pitched up at the bow and headed uphill. Each of the T7 drones in the shard of five was capable of carrying ten troopers into battle within its armored hold. Rain pattered off the drone's protective energy shields above the hull as the five armored vehicles drifted closer to their target, their suspensors allowing them to hover a good couple of yan from the rocky ground beneath them.

In the lead vehicle, Commander Tahl sat closest to the left hand side cargo door, holding his plasma carbine with its beak shaped muzzle pointing down at the vehicle's floor. Each of the other four T7s carried a single one of his strike squads inside, except for his own vehicle which his command squad shared with the six surviving troopers of Van Noor's team. The other strike squads were at or closer to their full strength of eight troopers. Mandarin Leeoras sat within the second transport drone with Strike Leader Rall's troopers, insistent on joining the attack. In Tahl's drone, Van Noor stood in the center of the troop compartment in between the two facing rows of seats, his legs splayed for balance as the transport drone rocked and bucked in response to the undulating terrain which unrolled beneath it.

Tahl watched the terrain ahead through the transport drone's forward sensors, which fed directly to every member of both squads. At the top of the shallow hill, nestled amidst the icy rocks, stood the gray remains of an ancient castle, a dim memory of a bygone time hailing back to the years before the Fifth Age.

"We're approaching enemy visual range," Van Noor warned his team, "be ready for a quick egress if we get hit. Best cover for route in on foot looks like the ditch to the right, sending you waypoints now."

A spotter drone which had scouted ahead sent across an image of the castle; six crumbling turrets connected by thick walls of stone a good five or six yan high with a solid keep still intact in the center. The two closest turrets flanked an old gateway to form an almost separate gatehouse building, and thick tentacles of spiked vines writhed up every one of the slanted defensive walls. The drone highlighted the almost impermeable, if aging, defensive shields, although the actual generators were hidden somewhere within the castle walls.

"As soon as we're through that gate, get clear and follow me to our objective in the first tower," Van Noor reminded his troopers.

He had always spoke more than was necessary when being transported into battle, Tahl observed. He could feel the nervousness of his strike leaders – all of them – permeating to him through the shard. He recalled for a second what it used to be like to be a freshly qualified strike trooper, with responsibility for nobody but yourself and only the mildest of emotional feedback from your own shard seeping into your mind. Back then, his fear was his own. Now, as a company commander, Tahl had no idea how much of the fear he felt came from his own troopers, or from within.

The drone suddenly rolled violently to the left as a shell slammed into the frozen earth to its right, pushing the passengers forcefully against their seat belts and sending Van Noor sprawling into his troopers. The right hand side shields flared up in their distinctive violet as they safely converted the energy of the incoming fire. Diagnostics reports of the drone's operating systems immediately scrolled across the left hand side of Tahl's visual array - all good, so far.

"X-howitzers," Van Noor reported as he hurriedly strapped himself back into his seat, "Looks like they've got them on top of two of the turrets."

Tahl nodded and took a deep, calming breath. Right now there was nothing he could do. He could not make the transport drones any faster or any better armored; he could not change the plan, and he knew better than to offer some contrived morale boosting speech. He closed his eyes and focused on the sensations he was experiencing – the cool, artificial air which his regulator pumped into the space by his mouth and nostrils, the feel of his battlesuit's firm but comfortable neck and wrist seals, the familiarity of the plasma carbine which lay waiting in his hands...

Another shell impacted the ground close by, lifting the drone higher in the air and tossing it back down on its suspensor field with a loud bang. Defensive shields crackled and fixed as alarm klaxon blared and a trooper yelled out in terror.

"Ten seconds!" Van Noor shouted, as loud as if he was trying to communicate verbally rather than through the shard. Tahl heard the soft clicking of lines of damage report text scrolling along his visual array. They were still moving. Above him the drone's plasma light support opened fire, sending long bursts of explosive energy up toward the militia positions across the ramparts and the turrets. Tahl felt a gut churning crash accompanied with the sound of splintering wood and metal as the transport drone smashed straight through the castle's ancient gates before coming to a halt inside the walls.
Tahl opened his eyes.

"Command, Squad Wen, my lead," he said calmly as he jettisoned his seat belts, sprang to his feet, and opened the cargo door.

A mag bolt slammed into Tahl's midriff even as he jumped from the drone to the ground, his HL shield flaring purple and crackling as he sprinted across to the doorway of the first tower, directly left from the main gate. Concentrated fire poured from the ramparts above him, lighting up the ancient fortifications with the red glow of rapidly heating mag guns.

"Spotter drone, thermal imaging," Tahl commanded through the shard to the squad's buddy drone which hovered nearby, immediately changing his raw view into one of predominantly cold blue, punctuated with crisp, humanoid outlines of red and yellow body heat. There were perhaps two, maybe three hundred enemy combatants lining the castle walls or waiting within the turrets.

Tahl reached the first tower's sturdy door and kicked it down, waiting by the doorway to count his troopers safely inside before following them in. Nine, including himself – no casualties so far. Quickly pushing his way back to the front, Tahl led his men up the stone stairwell and past the first and second floors, eager to reach and neutralize the howitzer on the roof but conscious of the enemy troopers he could see through his thermal imaging on the third floor. Behind the closed door was a semi circular room where six militia men knelt with their mag guns trained on the entrance.

"Room clearance, lance and slings," Tahl ordered.

Squad Wen's plasma lance gunner quickly ran up to drop to one knee by the door before opening fire with his weapon set to automatic, blasting the door down and sending a rapid stream of fire into the militia men on the other side. Simultaneously, Tahl and Van Noor fired micro bombs from their wrist mounted x-slings in through the opening, the explosive effect of their own munitions adding to the deadly fire from the plasma lance. Tahl was the first trooper in through the doorway and amidst the smoking chaos of the semi circular room, his plasma carbine hugged into his shoulder, ready to eliminate any survivors. There were no life signs, only limbs and body parts scattered across the stone room and heat signatures up the walls which told of the violence of their attack.

"Room's clear, next floor," Tahl ordered.

Then the plan started to go awry.

"Command, Transport Lead," a cold, feminine voice issued through the shard from the artificial intelligence of the lead transport drone which waited in the castle courtyard.

"Transport Four has been destroyed."

***

Her vision slowly began to focus again. Rhona staggered to her hands and knees as lines of damage text flickered along her visual array. She could feel terror through the shard, hear screaming, and memories of the impact began to filter through. The damage report told her that her suit's power relay had been severed and she was operating off the battery; that explained the delay in the shot of adrenaline she was expecting to help her focus.

She felt a small pain in her right forearm as her suit injected her with a shot of stimulant. Instantly she remembered – she was at the door of the T7 drone when they suffered a direct hit, and she was thrown clear. Staggering back to her feet, Rhona turned around and saw the transport drone dug into the hillside, its roof and the left hand side of the hull were torn open as flames licked out of the jagged remains. Mag fire continued to pour down from the castle ramparts, impacting with the rocks by her feet and flicking up cuttings of stone and debris. Her HL shield flared up as she felt a push in her back from accurate enemy fire.

Gritting her teeth, Rhona sprinted across to the burning vehicle and back through the open right hand cargo door. The vehicle's interior was unlike anything she had ever seen – Drack, Fenn, and Wilder were all dead already, having been sat directly beneath the shell as it had plunged through the roof. The closest surviving member of her squad was Raltor; the middle aged man of 160 years, celebrated as a poet in his youth, lay screaming in the flames with both of his legs severed at the knee.

Rhona dashed across to him and grabbed him by one of his shoulder plates, dragging him out of the flames and toward the cargo door. Still sat down next to where Rhona had waited to egress the vehicle, Varlton's head lolled groggily from side to side, the only feedback coming through the shard from him was confusion and nausea. Rhona grabbed the central buckle of his seat belts and tore them free before looping an arm around him and guiding him out of the burning T7. She managed to drag both of her squadmates back around to the other side of the blazing wreck to shield them from the continuous stream of enemy fire which clanged against its buckled hull.

Conscious of the risk of explosion, Rhona hauled both of her injured comrades back down the hill and to the relative cover of a cluster of rocks.

"Katya..." Raltor held up both of his shaking hands toward her, his voice weak.

There was no feedback from his suit - he had lost all power and all support. Rhona flipped open her waist panel and quickly uncoiled her auxiliary aid lead, plugging it into Raltor's suit and diverting power from her own battery. She was instantly rewarded with a sensation of relief through the shard as pain suppressors flowed into Raltor's bloodstream, congelag streaming down to his legs to stem the flow of blood.

"Kat, what the hell happened?" Varlton asked as he crawled over.

"Get your aux power into Raltor and get him stabilized," Rhona ordered, "I'm going back."

"They're all dead!" Varlton snapped. "And that thing's plasma core will detonate any second!"

"Jacki's in there and still alive!" Rhona growled as she dashed back around the cover of the rock cluster and sprinted back up the hill to the burning transport drone.

Halfway to the vehicle, a mag bolt penetrated her HL shield and slammed into her hip, twisting her around and knocking her to the ground. Ignoring the pain, Rhona forced her way back to her feet, limped across to the vehicle, and back into its blazing interior. She saw Jacki, her last living trooper, dragging her way toward the open door with her one remaining arm. Rhona hauled the wounded trooper across her shoulders and ran back out, pain flaring up in her hip with every unsteady step she took before finally reaching the cover of the rocks.

She lay Jacki down next to Raltor and Varlton, only then noticing the extensive trauma the trooper had suffered to her torso. The feedback she felt from Jacki through the shard was weakening with every heartbeat. The normally quick witted woman reached up and grabbed Rhona's wrist with her remaining hand.

"Guess… you're not a complete bitch after all," Jacki hissed through gritted teeth before sinking back down to the ground, her shard feedback fading into nothingness.

Behind her, the T7 exploded.

***

Fire poured into the buttresses of the old castle tower from various points to the south and east as squads of militia men targeted the Concord strike troopers from other towers and lines along the ramparts. Chips of rock splintered up into the air and pattered off Tahl's armor with every salvo from the enemy troops, and the air was thick with the smell of burning.

"Command from Mandarin," Leeoras' ethereal voice echoed across the shard, "we are moving to secure tower five."

Accompanying the flow of information, the fifth tower to the south of the castle flashed red in Tahl's visual array and he saw the thermal image of the NuHu and her accompanying squad fighting their way up the stairwell inside. Good – that would cut off one of the enemy's axis of fire and allow another squad to move across the courtyard to support them.

"Boss!" Van Noor dropped to one knee next to where Tahl took cover behind the circular wall atop the castle tower, "there's still over a hundred of them! After losing Squad Jai, there's a real chance they could drive us back out of here! We need to push across to tower three and cut off the fire that's keeping Squad Denne in the gatehouse!"

The company commander looked across to the next tower along to his left where a concentration of fifteen, maybe twenty, militiamen were dividing their fire between the Strike Troopers in the gatehouse below Tahl and the command squad itself.

"Agreed," Tahl replied, focusing his mind on transmitting his plan through the shard to his own squad and Van Noor's strike squad, "Squad Wen; suppressing fire on my waypoint – Command Squad, follow me."

Tahl sprang to his feet and sprinted headlong across the rampart leading to tower three, his plasma carbine tucked in to the hip as he fired a succession of bursts ahead with the sole intention of forcing the militia squads to take cover. Accurate fire pelted across from Squad Wen, their plasma lance blowing a smoldering hole in the rocks at the edge of the tower. Mag fire continued to crisscross the air ahead of them, causing Tahl's HL shields to flare up and crackle with every few paces. Behind him he heard a cry and one of his troops clatter to the ground; the feedback through the command shard informing him that it was Mendez – down but not dead.

Only a few yan from the enemy positions now, Tahl brought up his wrist and fired a pattern of microbombs from his x-sling. At precisely the same time, a similar salvo of microbombs, fired from his adversaries, exploded at his feet and flung him up into the air.

Landing with a crash and screech of alloy armor across rock, Tahl leapt straight back to his feet and, realizing he was now atop tower three and amidst his enemy, dropped his plasma carbine and rushed forward. Twisting his hip as he stepped forward to maximize the force of his blow, he punched a short, bearded militiaman in the gut with enough force to rupture internal organs and send him wheezing to the ground. Immediately following up with a side kick to the next man's knee, he snapped his opponent's leg and sent him down screaming before dispatching him with a second kick to the temple.

Calm, calmer than before, Tahl was now in his element. The IMTel had told him at the age of six that he would be a martial artist, and for nearly two decades his life had been one of training and competition. Surrounded by a dozen men, he felt safer and more at ease than he had with a carbine in his hands and a rock wall to take cover behind.

A tall man with red hair rushed at him with a clumsy right hook. Tahl swept the attack aside and used his momentum to counter with an elbow to the face, the combination of his years of training and the mass of his battlesuit easily breaking the man's neck. Side stepping a stocky militiaman who swung his mag gun at Tahl's neck like a batterball bat, he stepped into a striding stance to deliver an elbow strike to the gut, bending him over double before snapping a backfist into his face and breaking his nose. The dazed man staggered back and was cut down by plasma fire from the strike troopers who advanced behind Tahl.

A volley of mag fire cut across the tower and swept Tahl's legs from beneath him. He felt pain from the impact even before the smooth, wet stones beneath him rushed up to smash him in the face. A diagnostic report scrolled across his visual display and painkillers, coagulants, and steroids were automatically injected into him as his battlesuit fought to keep him in the fight Gritting his teeth, smoke wafting up from a jagged hole in his thigh armor, Tahl forced himself back up to one knee and recovered his plasma carbine as the survivors of his team's assault broke and ran for tower four.

***

His mag gun hissing as rain sizzled on the glowing barrel, Reece risked another salvo of fire as he peered over the buttresses of the tower roof and fired a volley into the Concord strike troopers which hunkered down in the gatehouse across the courtyard. Three of the towers had already fallen to the invaders and Reece had no idea how many of his comrades had been killed by the seemingly unstoppable armored soldiers. He fired three well-aimed shots, his appreciation of the battlefield already a world apart from his first firefight only the day before. A just visible purple flashed over the abdomen of one of the strike troopers as the Hyper Light shield safely dissipated the energy of his shot; his accuracy being rewarded with just a flashing color, momentarily reminding him of the shooting games he used to play as a child.

"Hold it together!" Vorten growled at the dozen militiamen who fired across the castle rooftops at the Concord troopers atop the gatehouse towers, as well as down at those pinned on the other side of the courtyard.

Seemingly from nowhere, a burst of plasma fire cut down Vorten, punching holes across his back and emerging from his gut and chest. Reece span around to face the entrance to the tower stairwell, a sickening fear clawing at his stomach as three green and white armored Concord Strike Troopers advanced onto the tower roof, their carbines spitting out lines of glowing plasma. Either side of Reece, militiamen fell down dead. Others broke and ran.

Then, only just able to walk through the tower doorway without crouching, Reece saw the tall, slim figure of a robed woman with pink tinted hair. The woman's smooth features and pale skin seemed almost alien, and her grey eyes registered little emotion as they locked directly onto Reece's gaze. She was a NuHu. The first he had ever seen in the flesh.

The NuHu raised a plasma pistol and pointed it directly at Reece. Reece found himself frozen to the spot, his eyes focused on the muzzle of the deadly weapon and his hands unable to register the commands sent to them as the battle seemingly raged on around them both in slow motion. The tall woman's lips parted ever so slightly, and the hand holding the pistol began to shake. For a fraction of a second he thought he saw fear, sympathy, or a mixture of both in her eyes. Then his trigger finger finally obeyed his brain's commands and he fired a quartet of mag blasts directly into the woman's abdomen, punching through her armor and painting the cold, grey stone behind her with showers of blood before she crumpled to the ground.

***

Ignoring the sickening emptiness of her shard feedback after suffering so many casualties, Rhona led Varlton out of the cover of the gatehouse and across the courtyard as enemy fire kicked up the earth around them from the ramparts above. Summoning the last of her reserves of strength, Rhona managed to pick up her speed and sprint for the safety of the towers on the far side, her shoulders hunched up and her eyes nearly shut as enemy fire continued to rain down from above.

She clattered through the doorway of the structure which her visual array identified as tower six, pausing to catch her breath as Varlton dived into cover next to her. She quickly plotted a mental route up the stairwell ahead to the roof of the tower and fed her plan back to the command squad.

"Stay there, Katya," she heard Strike Commander Tahl's voice through her headset. "There's only two of you and this thing is nearly over."

Clenching her fists, Rhona opened her mouth to respond but immediately thought better of it.

"I know you can take that tower," Tahl spoke again, "but we've lost enough people today. Stand down, Squad Jai, you've done enough and this firefight is over."

As if in confirmation, the din of battle outside the tower began to fade; the snapping of mag guns dying away to leave only the blast and hiss of the last few plasma carbines up above. Rhona leaned back against the tower wall, tore off her helmet, and sank down to the floor before burying her head in her hands.

"They've surrendered," Varlton said, more to himself rather than Rhona as he removed his helmet and ran one hand through his sweat soaked hair. "We've taken the castle."

Rhona felt relief seeping through every channel of the company's shard as pulse rates began to drop and breathing slowed. She dragged herself wearily up to her feet, magnetically clipped her carbine to her back, and picked up her helmet before walking back out into the pouring rain which fell down into the courtyard.

***

Tahl pushed his way through the small semi circle of strike troopers who had gathered at the top of the castle turret, pain still flaring up from his leg wound. As soon as his eyes confirmed his worst suspicions he let out a long breath and felt his shoulders slump. Leeoras lay propped up against one of the shattered buttresses, a pool of blood surrounding her and diluting away into a puddle of rippling rain water. Strike Leader Rall knelt next to her, an auxiliary coil unraveled from his battlesuit and plugged into the IV port at her neck. The NuHu looked wearily up at Tahl as he approached.

"I've stopped the bleeding and got a transfusion line in, but the type converter is taking a damn age in switching my blood," Rall breathed frantically.

"Give her some room," Tahl ordered his men as he dropped down next to Leeoras and Rall.

The assembled troopers quickly dispersed.

"My first battle... I was always an explorer, not a soldier," Leeoras said weakly. "Came face to face with a soldier, he was... just a boy. I could not shoot. For the first time in my life, reason did not feel right."

"I've got a medi-drone on the way up here," Tahl nodded as he swept back his helmet visor. "We'll get you fixed up."

Through the shard connection, Tahl felt the medi-drone disobey his command and divert to a group of injured troopers who had been assembled near the gatehouse.

"No," Leeoras shook her head slightly, "there are troopers who stand a better chance of survival than I. Rank is irrespective; it is simple logic. Use your assets to save who you can, Ryen. Even with a medi-drone my chance of survival is less than twenty quantum."

Tahl reprocessed his order for the medi-drone to route to his position. Again, his order was overridden.

Leeoras reached up and unplugged the transfusion line connecting her neck to Rall's battlesuit.

"Let me go... on my terms," she whispered. "Let me have that dignity."

Tahl swallowed, certain that the hollow sorrow in his heart was his and his alone, not emotional feedback from the shard. He pulled off one of his armored gloves and held one of Leeoras' cold hands in his own, real physical contact being the only comfort he could think of.

"Leave us, Leader," the dying NuHu said to Rall. "Thank you for all you tried to do."

Tahl carefully lifted the frail woman's torso and lay him across her, holding her head against his shoulder gently.

"I have a clone," Leeoras said.

"Then we have to stabilize you!" Tahl urged. "We can transfer your consciousness as soon as we get you home!"

"Less than five quantum probability of success," Leeoras murmured. "Let her have her own life when she is activated. If you do ever cross paths with her, tell her about this. Tell her that in another life, she tried her best to do the right thing. For the greater cause."

"I will," Tahl forced a smile.

The rain cascaded down on the two figures atop the cold, grey castle tower as the clouds finally began to break up to the east. Leeoras did not speak again. She lay across Tahl for several minutes, holding onto his hand before finally the pressure of her grip faded away.

***

A crude bandage stopped the bleeding on Reece's forehead where he had been smashed with the butt of a plasma carbine during the final stages of the battle. It was late afternoon and he had been marched in a single file along with the other fifty or so survivors to a Concord staging facility, back along the icy hills they had retreated across the previous day. Nobody spoke. Concord strike troopers – ten in total – flanked either side of the weary column of prisoners, their faces hidden behind their intimidating face masks.

Reece thought of his parents and his life back home, only three days' travel to the south. He hoped and prayed that even if he was to be put up against a wall and executed, perhaps some mercy would be extended to his mother and father. One of the strike troopers walked closer and held out a hand to Reece and the prisoners walking with him. In the armored palm were a few white pills. Reece exchanged a glance with a short militia-man ahead of him.

"It's chewing gum," the Concord trooper said, her feminine voice distorted by the mask, "I'm not trying to kill you guys or anything. Look."

The woman removed her helmet, and Reece physically recoiled with surprise to see the most outstandingly beautiful woman he had ever laid eyes on. Her black hair fell over a tatty purple bandanna wrapped around her forehead, which seemed to jar awkwardly with her hi-tech battlesuit. She took one of the pills and began chewing before offering them again. Reece accepted the offer.

"Don't look so down," the Concord trooper said, "it's not so bad. Sure, there's bad stuff about being brought into the Concord, but the good outweighs the bad. Most days, anyway."

"How would you know?" The short militiaman ahead of Reece asked.

"I was in a similar place to you about three or four years ago," the dark haired woman explained. "It wasn't my home planet or anything, I was just in the wrong place at the wrong time. I got forced into the Concord but I'm sorta glad it happened. Some things are better. You'll see."

The woman replaced her helmet and resumed her place in the formation, leaving Reece alone with his thoughts. A strange blend of emotions now replaced the rumination over death that had dominated the last hour of the march. They weren't going to be executed? The troopers they had fought had once been like them? Would something good come out of this?

Perhaps a hundred yan's march later, the prisoner column met up with a Concord outpost, made up of a collection of hastily erected shelters guarded by a company of troopers and a handful of fixed gun emplacements. The militia prisoners were filed into a containment area made up of electrified barrier walls and an electric-shield roof. After being lined up, each prisoner was handed a cream colored datapad by one of a trio of strike troopers who moved up and down the lines of militiamen.

"You are now ECUCCs," a cold, feminine voice played through the datapad speakers to each man, "an Enemy Combatant Under Care of the Concord. Your forces have been defeated and your authoritative body has surrendered. The conflict is at an end."

Further down Reece's line, one prisoner swore and shouted out that this was all lies. There was no reaction from the guards.

"In a few moments, your world will be connected with the IMTel of the Panhuman Concord and you will be one with us, for the greater cause. As a show of our goodwill toward you as new members of our community, you will now be connected to your families and loved ones."

Reece's eyes opened wide as his mother and father appeared on the datapad screen in his hands. They sat together on the plush, old sofa in the familiar front room of his family home. Immediately, both seemed just as surprised to see him.

"Kona?" His mother gasped. "Is it you? Are you hurt? What happened to your head?"

Tears were already streaming down her face.

"Ma?" Reece felt tears in his own eyes, "I'm fine, Ma, I just banged my head. Are you okay? Are the Concord troopers there? Have they hurt you?"

"There's nobody here," Reece's father responded. "We just received a communication prompt a moment ago. What's happening? The newsprompt says we've surrendered – is it all over?"

"I... I think so," Reece swallowed.

His mother burst into tears and cried hysterically. Reece felt tears stream down his own grimy cheeks as he watched his father embrace his mother and whisper reassurance to her, stroking her hair affectionately.

"What happens now?" She wailed. "What will they do to us all?"

"It's okay," her husband said, "we're together, Kona is here with us, he survived. We're all fine. It'll all be fine."

Reece was aware of other men breaking down around him as similar conversations were carried out with mothers, fathers, wives, and children all over the planet. He wiped his tears away and pressed the palm of one hands against the screen.

His mother stopped crying abruptly. His father sat up straight.

"All is fine," his mother said casually, "we are part of the PanHuman Concord and our quality of life will now improve. This is all for the greater cause."

"Ma?" Reece exclaimed.

"Don't worry, Kona," his father smiled calmly, "the Concord will care for us all. We never need to worry about income, healthcare, equality, security, none of it. We are happy now."

The screen faded to black. Reece looked up frantically at the strike troopers who were guarding them.

"The civilian populace of this planet is now fully integrated with the IMTel of the PanHuman Concord," the cold, female voice spoke through the datapad's speaker. "Your families are safe. Each of you is now being assessed by the Combined Concord Command for potential military service. Those of you whose datapad screen lights green will be connected to the IM-Tel and reintegrated into civilian life with your families. Those of you whose datapad screen lights blue will be transported to a Concord Combined Command Behavioral Activation Training Center as the first stage in your conversion to your military service with the C3..."

***

A C3R2 repair and salvage drone rumbled through the air along the main roadway between Settlement Rural 14 and Settlement Urban 5, a large suspensor platform towed behind it with a disabled C3M4 Combat Drone ignobly lashed in place. Rhona stood near the entrance of the Medical Aid Station on the outskirts of the town and watched the unmanned vehicles hum past before turning to walk back up to rejoin her company. Rays of sun cast long shadows from the skeletal remains of the buildings which had once housed families, shops, amenities, and social venues. Strike and drop troopers from a dozen different companies arrived or departed in transport drones as the medical facility quickly turned around those with light to moderate combat injuries.

Up ahead, sat on a crumbling garden wall in front of a collapsed residential block, Rhona recognized Tahl. The tall man had, like all other troopers, removed his helmet and now sat almost serenely on his own, watching the world go by. Rhona watched her commanding officer for a few moments – he possessed a real rugged handsomeness she was drawn to, combined with an almost permanent look of sadness which hinted at some loss or melancholy. For a brief moment, Rhona remembered the men and women she had worked with who had died in the past few days, but the feeling of hollowness and regret quickly faded as her battlesuit's dispenser pumped another salvo of post-engagement anti-depressants into her system. She shrugged and walked over to sit on the wall next to Tahl.

"Sir," she greeted, fishing a chewing gum pill out of her utility belt pouch.

"Hello, Katya," he offered a warm smile without looking at her.

Remembering her father's keepsake, she quickly reached up and tore off her purple bandanna.

"Keep it on," Tahl said, "I figured it's more important to you than just a fashion statement. Besides, it looks good on you."

Rhona smirked as she replaced it around her head, realizing that this was the first conversation she had ever had alone with Tahl. At the start of the week she was one of his many troopers, not one of his squad leaders, so opportunities had been few if any.

"What was it like," she suddenly found herself blurting out, "going from being this famous martial arts champion to suddenly being a soldier?"

"It wasn't so much the job change as the circumstances which surrounded it," he turned and fixed his blue eyes on hers. "It's a long story. But ultimately, one day the IMTel told me that I was better suited to this and then I was in Behavioral Activation Training. It was the BAT which was a real shock to the system, not the change of occupation. Same as all of us. Well, most of us. I guess it was very different for you."

"Yeah, sure was," Rhona leaned back and crossed one armored ankle over the other. "I was free of all this IMTel 'til I was twenty-two. Then I was suddenly a Concord citizen for two years and then soldiering. It was more like waking up from a two year dream and slowly getting back to normal rather than starting life anew."

"Do you miss the way it was?" Tahl asked, genuine curiosity in his voice.

"I miss my brother. And my dad," she admitted, "but I'll see my brother again real soon. We've got thirty days leave now, right?"

"Right," Tahl gave a slight smile. "I'm sorry about your father."

"He was a great dad, but not a good guy," Rhona reflected, "but you reap what you sow, right? He brought it on himself, he upset some dangerous guys."

"What did you do before you were a strike trooper?" Tahl asked, a very obvious attempt to change the subject, which Rhona appreciated.

"I was a dancer. Same as I was before being a Concord

citizen, since I was eighteen."

"Really?" Tahl's face became more animated. "That's fascinating! We probably have a lot in common with our arts, what with timing and precision, footwork, physical conditioning..."

Rhona narrowed her eyes and smiled slyly as she bit her lower lip.

"Not that kind of dancing, sir."

"Oh... oh. This is a little awkward."

"It shouldn't be," Rhona said casually, "I'm not ashamed about anything. I thought it was kind of cool."

She felt an instant sympathy for Tahl as he looked down at his feet.

"Say," her turn to change the subject, "did you ever teach anybody karampei?"

"Only one or two people," Tahl replied. "It's difficult, takes a very long time to even grasp the basics. It needs one-on-one tuition, really, classwork is rarely effective."

"Would you teach me?" Rhona found her mouth engaging before she had properly thought it through, again.

A small, dark blue bird flew and perched on the burnt tree just above the garden wall they sat on and began to sing a merry song in the morning sun.

"Yes," Tahl replied, "yes, alright."

Gateways
By Scott Washburn

"**I** hear she's been killed six times!"

Concordian Cadet Tamika Gatchnall looked at Cadet Marc Nierney as they walked across the Academy campus and rolled her eyes. "Where did you hear that?" She demanded.

"Lundy! He said he looked it up!"

"And how would he do that? Personal files are restricted, you know. Lundy's pulling your leg."

"Well, she's been killed at least once, Tam! She's in a machine body after all!" Insisted Nierney.

"No denying that," admitted Tamika. "Once, I can believe, but six? I'd think that once would be enough."

"Guess she likes the soldiering life. But what about you? Did you tell them to restore you if you get killed?"

"That is none of your business," she said, scowling at him. Nierney smirked at her, but finally shut up. She liked the guy, but his boundless enthusiasm for... just about everything could be irksome at times.

They had been talking about their Cosmology instructor, Captain Krissa, whose class they were on their way to attend for the first time. She seemed to be something of a legend at the Academy. The Concord Combined Command Training Academy on Hadley IV was a large place and had a campus that was as beautifully landscaped as a formal garden. Tall trees—she assumed that was what they were, even though they were unlike any trees she had ever seen before—lined brick walkways, and there were perfectly trimmed hedges and perfectly arranged flower beds in perfectly placed locations between the stately buildings. To Tamika it all seemed ridiculously ostentatious. What was the point of all this? Why even have a campus? Or classrooms for that matter? The cadets could attend class via the Integrated Machine Intelligence, which connected everyone, from anywhere on the planet. Why waste resources on something like this?

Or was that just her envy talking?

Tamika came from the planet Geasey II, which only a few years before had been at war with the mighty Panhuman Concord. The Geasans had lost, of course, as most independent worlds did when faced by the Concord. But Geasey had put up a better fight than most, and much of the planet had been devastated before the last of its defenses had been beaten down and the nanites of the IMTel had absorbed the survivors. Perhaps Geasey II had once had a military academy like this one, but if so, it was long gone now. A few places on Geasey were starting to look like Hadley IV, but most of it was still being rebuilt. Tamika had been living with her mother and younger sister in a refugee camp before she went to Hadley.

Tamika and Nierney reached Vivacqua Hall and joined the crowd of other cadets marching up the steps to the front doors. They walked across the soaring lobby and a grav-tube whisked them up to the fourth floor where the lecture hall was located. The room could hold several hundred and was filling quickly. She and Nierney went about halfway down the steps between the seats and then found a spot in one of the rows. Soon, everyone who belonged there was inside, the doors closed, and the lights dimmed except for the area near the lecture podium. A moment later Captain Krissa emerged from a side door. Tamika—and she was quite certain everyone else in the room—stared at her. She had been a woman once and presumably would be again after they grew her a new body. But right now she was a humanoid machine which looked quite a bit like a suit of combat armor—gleaming white ceramite plates with green trim—except with a head instead of a helmet. The head had a human shape and vaguely feminine features, but no one would mistake it for an actual organic head. She/it stopped next to the podium and ran her unblinking vision pick-ups over the assembled cadets. "Good morning, class," she said in a voice which was entirely human; synthesized no doubt. "I am Captain Natchia Krissa."

"Good morning, Captain!" Came the automatic reply from two hundred flesh and blood mouths.

"Welcome to Cosmology 101. In this course we will examine the nature of our universe with a focus on its effects on military operations. Before we get started, are there any questions?"

There was a stir in the audience and lot of whispers and eventually one cadet stood up. "Did it hurt when you got killed?" Tamika winced. She didn't think that was the sort of question Captain Krissa meant. The machine-woman was utterly still for a few seconds and then replied:

"Cadet Bellatar, if you had studied the briefing materials you were assigned when you arrived here, you would know the answer to that question. Memory backups are done prior to combat and immediately afterwards, but not during combat. Not only do the jamming and EMP effects common on a battlefield endanger the quality of the recording, but study has concluded that allowing a soldier to relive the moment of their death can have... adverse effects on their performance in the future. Now as I was..."

"How many times have you been killed, Captain?" Asked another cadet.

Krissa's robot body didn't need to breathe, so Tamika wasn't sure where the long sigh came from, but it was loud enough to grab everyone's attention. The even longer silence that followed was unnerving. But when the answer finally came, it was plain enough: "Six." Cadet Nierney elbowed Tanika in the ribs and grinned. Another pause and then: "Anything else, people? We may as well get this all out of the way since it seems to be such a distraction to you."

Everyone hesitated for a moment, but then someone asked: "Are you getting a new body or are you going to... to stay where you are?"

"My new body is growing right now. But it takes nearly a year and I saw no point in wasting all of that time, which is why I'm currently in this... thing." She spread her arms. "When the new body is ready I'll shift over to it. In the meantime, I have light duty: instructing the flower of the Concordian youth." The machine tried to smile. "But that's enough of this! We need to proceed with today's lesson: The Strategic Ramifications of the Gates."

A holographic display activated and suddenly a large red sphere appeared at the front of the classroom. It seemed to seethe and throb. Tamika knew instantly what it was.

"As you should all know," said Captain Krissa, "Antares, the red supergiant star, is actually an artificial construction. No one knows who made it—although we often refer to them as 'The Builders'—or how it was made, or even how it works. What is known is that it is a transport device which allows travel between the stars." The red orb seemed to rush toward them. It grew and grew until they were looking at just a tiny part of its enormous face. A few dozen cylindrical tubes stuck up above the flaming surface, like the hairs on a patch of Tamika's arm. "Protruding above the photosphere of the star are the gates. A ship entering a gate will be transported in a short time to the other end of that particular gate, which is invariably on the edge of a star system." The image followed a tiny space ship which entered one of the tubes and then was sucked through a tunnel and emerged in the blackness of space with a dim star in the distance.

"Each gate leads to one star system and one system only. Ships can enter the gates from either end. Entering from the Antares end will deliver the ship to the star system. Entering at the star system will deliver it to Antares." The image reversed the process and the ship was back above the red surface of the supergiant. Captain Krissa folded her arms and said: "While our records don't go back that far, I have to wonder if the first humans to make the trip knew what they were getting themselves into. The Antares end of the gates is, after all, hovering very close to the surface of a star—artificial or not. Without shields, a powerful drive, or anti-gravs, a ship would be destroyed in short order, burned to a crisp or sucked in by the powerful gravity."

"Sir?" Tamika dared to speak. "I've heard that some people think the Builders did that deliberately, to make sure that anyone coming through the gates were advanced enough to use them properly."

"Yes, that is a popular theory, Ms. Gatchnal. Although considering the technology needed to just reach one of the gates from the star system side, I have to wonder. Perhaps the fabled Builders weren't even thinking about other species using their system—or maybe they just didn't give a damn." This produced a small chuckle from the cadets.

"But once we—and a number of other species—did manage to get there and survive, we discovered that we could use the other gates to get to other star systems. While it is technically possible to travel to other star systems through normal space, using slower-than-light ships, the travel times involved make any sort of large, multi-system civilization impractical. With the gates at our disposal, interstellar civilizations became a reality."

The display drew back a bit and showed a larger area of Antares. The gates, too small to see at this scale, were picked out by blue dots. "The surface area of Antares' photosphere is one hundred and sixty million-billion square kiloyans, more or less, and while that is about fifty billion times the area of a typical habitable world, it still means that with an average gate density, the gates are usually less than a hundred thousand kiloyans apart—easy traverse for a modern ship."

Despite having it all in her head for easy reference, Tamika still automatically converted everything to the system of measurement she'd grown up with. Let's see, a yan is about six paces... a kiloyan a little over six thousand paces... a square kiloyan...

"So," Captain Krissa, continued, "a ship entering a gate from its star system of origin can travel to Antares, then move from that gate, above the surface of Antares, to another gate, enter it, and find itself in another star system. The total travel time being measured in days or even hours compared with years for a voyage through normal space.

"It is this ability, to give us a shortcut from star to star, that makes Antares so important. Without it, humanity would have been confined to its planet of origin or at most to a few stars within reach of sub-light starships. With Antares, our distant ancestors spread out from Old Earth to millions of other star systems, creating empires, federations, and Concordias great and small over the millennia." The display now showed a web of golden lines growing out from a single blue dot to hundreds and thousands of other dots.

"Captain Krissa?" A cadet raised his hand.

"Yes, Cadet Rembert?"

"Just now you mentioned 'Old Earth'. I've run across this reference quite a few times, but there is never any information about it. Do you think such a place ever existed, or is it just a legend?"

"My beliefs are immaterial, Cadet. But from what we know of how life arises and evolves, it seems logical that humanity originated on some single planet and expanded out from there. Where that planet might have been, or what has happened to it, is now unknown. Unless, of course, you subscribe to the belief that humanity was deliberately created by some sort of progenitor race. And even then that doesn't answer the question of where the progenitors came from. But this is a course on strategy, not philosophy!" Some of the cadets laughed politely.

"Moving on, there are several other key attributes of the Antarean gates which need to be grasped to fully understand the strategic realities we face. First is the fact that there seems to be no correlation between the positions of the gates on Antares' surface and the star systems that they lead to. Two gates which are close by on Antares may lead to star systems which are a hundred thousand, or even millions, of light years apart in real space. That means there is no way of 'by-passing the shortcut'. If enemy naval forces were blocking the quick route to a nearby gate, the possibility of trying to get to the system that gate leads to through normal space—a desperation move in any case—isn't even an option. For all practical purposes, each gate leads to a cul de sac—a dead end."

Captain Krissa paused and paced across the stage and then back to the podium, as if marshaling her thoughts. It was such a completely normal action that it made the machine seem much more human.

"A second attribute is the fact that whatever is controlling the Antares device apparently does not want us lingering or fighting in its vicinity. There are forces at work in the regions above the photosphere. Ships cannot establish a stable orbit around Antares, nor can they escape from it. Attempts to pull away from Antares into a distant orbit have always failed. A ship which emerges from a gate onto Antares will sooner or later—probably sooner—be forced to enter a gate and return to another star system or face destruction. Powerful ships with large energy reserves can hold their positions for a few dozen days, but a typical ship must get to its destination gate as quickly as possible. It should be noted that such conditions make it impossible to fortify or in any other way lay permanent claim to the Antares end of a gate. Naval squadrons can temporarily interdict the approach to a gate, but even that is difficult. Any attempt at combat in the close vicinity of a gate will provoke an immediate response from the gate, scattering or even destroying the vessels involved.

"Another factor of importance is that from the Antares side, there is no way of knowing where a gate may lead to, except by trying it. Each time we pass through an unexplored gate, we have no idea what might be waiting for us on the other end. There might be rich, uninhabited worlds ripe for colonization, an advanced civilization eager to join us—or a dangerous enemy. On rare occasions there might even be some natural hazard which could destroy a ship before it could report back. Exploration is a very dangerous occupation and even a strong military escort is no guarantee of a safe return. We typically send a robotic probe through a new gate first, but if the probe doesn't return, we are left in ignorance of the reason why. Ultimately, we must send a ship or ships through—or give up.

"The situation on the star system side of a gate is different from the Antares side in some ways, similar in others. The distance a gate lies from the sun is in proportion to the mass of the star and its energy output, but in most cases it is at least a few billion kiloyans away, often much more. Gates almost always appear in star systems with substantial stars and planets. Only a few have been discovered leading to dwarf stars. This means that gates are usually a great distance from any habitable planet in the system. Also, the gate is not in orbit about the star. While it moves with the star, its relative position remains fixed—on a direct line with the star Antares." The display image now shifted to show a graphical representation of a typical star system; star in the center, out-of-scale planets in elliptical orbits, and far off to the side the gate.

"The same 'no fire zone' that exists around the Antares end of the gates exists on the star system end," said Krissa as the display zoomed in on the gate. "The diameter of this zone is several times the range of our most powerful weapons, so again, there is no possibility of fortifying the actual end of the gate. It is, however, possible to build fortresses and other defenses outside the zone, and many worlds have done this, stationing powerful mobile units there as well, to intercept any intruder who might try to move past the first installations. Such defenses are, of course, extremely expensive and few worlds have the resources to construct an absolutely impenetrable barrier. In most cases a determined invader will be able to penetrate these gate defenses and get loose inside a star system. This requires the defender to have additional forces available to protect the inhabited planets and other vital spots in the system. The strategy and tactics involved in system attack and defense will be dealt with in several future classes. And those of you who eventually end up on the naval track will become very familiar with the concepts indeed! For now I will simply say that they are complex. For those who end up with the ground forces, the bottom line is that in the vast majority of cases it will be possible for an attacker to land troops on a planet despite the efforts of the defender. That means ground combat, ladies and gentlemen!"

The change of tone in Krissa's voice was sudden and dramatic. It was proud and almost eager. The machine body took on a pose that was nearly a combat stance, looking ready for instant action. Tamika supposed that Krissa had been in the ground forces. Presumably that was how she got killed—six times! Right now she looked ready to go out and get killed again. But then the moment passed and the machine-woman looked and sounded as she had before and she continued.

"Despite the dangers, the Panhuman Concord expands ever outward. Our goals are benevolent, our methods humane. Not all welcome us, however, and some non-human entities are implacable foes. It is the job of the Concord Combined Command—our job—to safeguard our people against all enemies."

Tamika frowned. Her own people had not welcomed the arrival of the Concord. They had fought them for years, seen their planet devastated rather than submit. And yet in the end they had submitted. And somehow Tamika was now here, learning the skills to force others to submit. The thought was disturbing... but it quickly faded and her attention was drawn back to lecture.

"However," continued Captain Krissa, "there is one other aspect to the Gates of Antares which may make all of our efforts in vain. Who can tell me what that is?" A number of hands went up and Krissa picked one. "Yes, Ms. Nagucchi?"

"Uh, the gates collapse?"

"Yes, the gates collapse. For reasons no one understands and at times no one can predict, the gates collapse, severing our shortcuts from star to star. And this is not just a matter of some gates collapsing at random times. Once a collapse begins, it does not stop until all the gates are gone. Every last one of them. This has happened six times in recorded history and there is evidence that the cycles have been going on for far longer than that. Note that the gates do not all collapse simultaneously; the process can take centuries, but in the end, they are all gone.

"The effects of these interregnums have usually been catastrophic. Multi-system civilizations suddenly found themselves cut off from the other worlds they often depended upon for trade, supplies, and leadership. Many worlds, unable to cope with this sudden isolation, have seen their civilizations collapse, sometimes the planets becoming completely depopulated. Even worlds with advanced cultures have fallen, simply due to the lengths of time involved. These collapses can last for hundreds or thousands of years and it is no more possible to predict when the gates will reappear than it is to predict when they disappear. And the reappearance of the gates also takes place over considerable lengths of time—centuries, usually.

"And finally, the real kicker is that when the gates do reappear, their Antares ends are almost always in different places than where they were before the collapse. Multi-system civilizations, even if their planets survive the collapse, will find their gates scattered all over the surface of Antares and the nearby gates may now lead to new enemies rather than old friends. Trying to reassemble the prior civilization usually proves impossible. Or at least so it has been after the last six collapses."

While the captain had been talking, the display had been changing. The earlier image of a thousand blue dots connected by a golden web returned for a moment. But then the dots began to vanish and the strands of the web broke, reattached themselves, and then broke again, until all the dots and all the strands were gone. After a few moments dots began to reappear, but now only a few of them were blue. Many more were red or green or yellow or other colors. The blue dots tried to send out gold threads to other blue dots, but there were usually clusters of other colored dots in the way and only a few connections were made. Eventually, there was a multi-colored mass with no discernible pattern or order. The entire class stared at the result in silence. Tamika suddenly realized that her hands were trembling.

"Any questions?" Asked Krissa.

Tamika stood up. "Captain?"

"Yes, Cadet Gatchnall?"

"Then you're saying that anything we build is doomed to be destroyed? That the Concord's... efforts are useless? That we're wasting our time?" *That conquering my home was all for nothing?*

"Tam!" Hissed Nierny at her side. Everyone else in the room was gawking at her, but her eyes were fixed on Captain Krissa's vision receptors—which seemed to be fixed on her. There was a long silence, but finally Krissa turned away.

"Who can know? But as I said earlier, this is not a philosophy course. We do our duty, Cadet, and at the moment our duty is to finish this class. So let us continue..."

Krissa returned to her lecture, but Tamika scarcely heard her. The class ended and the cadets filed out. Nierny walked beside her. "Tam, what the hell was that? You trying to get yourself kicked out?"

"I don't know. Look, I don't want to talk about it." She quickened her pace and left him behind. She went through dinner and evening dress parade on automatic pilot, her thoughts as much a scrambled mess as that final display in the class. Once she was dismissed, she avoided the other cadets and headed out the Academy's main gate and down to the little seaside park of the adjoining town. Hadley IV had the most amazing sunsets and Tamika found a bench to watch.

What am I doing here?

That was the question, wasn't it? But what was the answer? Was there an answer? She watched as the sun touched the water, but she found no answer.

A tiny sound from behind made her realize she wasn't alone. And the even fainter sound of servos activating told her just who it was. "Captain Krissa?" She turned her head and yes, there she was. The machine-woman was standing a meter off to her right, staring at the sunset.

"Beautiful evening, isn't it? Mind if I join you, Cadet?"

"N-not at all, sir."

Krissa sat down next to her, the bench creaking slightly under the machine's weight, but didn't look at her. They sat in silence as the sun slipped beneath the sea and then Tamika said: "I'm sorry if I disrupted the class today, sir."

The captain made a noise which sounded like a snort. "Don't be. It'll do 'em good. A new thought now and then never hurt anyone. I'm not worried about them."

"But you're worried about me?" Why else would she be here?

"Not exactly worried. Concerned maybe. You're the one who's worried, am I right?"

Tamika stiffened and frowned. "If you're reading my mind, why do you have to even ask?"

Krissa snorted again. "No one's reading your mind, Ms. Gatchnall."

"But the nanites... the IMTel... It knows exactly what I'm thinking!"

"Yes, the IMTel is reading your mind, and my mind, along with a billion others here on Hadley IV, and trillions more throughout the Panhuman Concord. But when I said 'no one', I mean exactly that: no one is reading your mind. The IMTel isn't someone. It isn't anyone. It just is."

"That's what we were told again and again by the occupation forces back on my home world," said Tamika, bitterness in her voice. "They said the IMTel wasn't mind control, we weren't being absorbed into some big super-consciousness, that we'd still be individuals, we'd still have free will. None of us believed it at first. And then we did start to believe it—and that made it worse. The fact that we did believe it made it seem all the more a lie!"

"The transition into becoming part of the IMTel shard can be confusing. I've witnessed it a few times," said Krissa.

"We fought so hard against the Concord," said Tamika. "My father died, my older brother was terribly wounded. I would have joined the fight if it had gone on much longer. When our defenses collapsed, one of our neighbors killed his entire family and then himself to avoid being assimilated. Everything I'd been taught growing up, everything I saw around me told me to fight the Concord!" Tears were rolling down her cheeks now.

"And yet here you are."

"Yes! What am I doing here?" She sniffed and angrily wiped her eyes. "How can I be siding with the enemy? Why would the Concord even want me? Why did they choose me?"

"No one chose you, Cadet."

"Well someone chose me! I was back on Geasey II, doing my chores at the camp, and then suddenly there were instructions in my in-box telling me to report here! Someone sent that! And when I got here they were expecting me!"

Krissa was silent for a moment, the sunset had turned the white of her machine body into a glowing orange. "That's probably the hardest thing for newcomers to understand—hell, even those of us born to it have a hard time grasping it. The IMTel isn't a person or a group of persons or a ruling council or a government, or an unfeeling tyrant, or a group mind. Or maybe it's all of those things at once—or none of them. It just is. Things happen. Food gets grown, energy produced, transport systems constructed, houses and schools built, fleets and armies dispatched, worlds added to the Concord... and people recruited. But no one orders it. No one decides. No one decided to bring you here." Tamika opened her mouth to make an angry reply, but then Krissa added: "And you could have always refused to come."

"What? I could?"

"Of course. And you could leave right now and go home. No one would stop you. The Concord Combined Command is perhaps unique in human history in that is entirely made of volunteers—perhaps not conscious volunteers, but the IMTel would not have picked them unless they had the right mind-set and a desire to serve. Anyone can quit at any time—although few ever do. Quitting in the middle of combat can be awkward and a bit rude, but I've seen it happen. Damn near got me killed one time as a matter of fact."

"You have been killed..."

"Six times."

"But you keep coming back again. Is that... typical?"

"Not really. Almost every new recruit opts for being backed up and restored when they are inducted. They're young and expect to live forever. I sure did. But less than half return to the ranks after the first restoration. They leave the C3 shard and go back wherever they came from. Only about ten percent come back after a second death. Six times? I'm part of a real elite, Cadet, less than one tenth of a percent go for more than two times."

"They say... Some people say... I've heard that when they restore you... it isn't really you anymore..."

"Yeah, some people say that. But until they find some way to measure a person's soul there's no way to tell, is there? I have all the memories of all six of those Natchia Krissas who came before me. Nothing's missing as far as I can tell. And if my soul did flitter off to some heaven or hell after my first death, what difference does it make? I'm here right now." She turned her vision pickups right at Tamika. There seemed to be a red glow deep inside them—or was that just the last of the sunset? "And so are you, Cadet. What will you do?"

"I don't know!" Cried Tamika, it was almost a wail. "Part of me feels that being here is the right thing to do—and another part tells me that feeling that way is the wrongest thing of all!" She paused and looked up to where the stars were coming out. Hadley was close to a small globular cluster and the fuzzy grouping was right overhead this evening. "I do like being here... the other cadets are nice people and there's something very... appealing about all of this... But then I think of my father and my neighbors. And then today when you were talking about the collapse of the gates and it all seemed like it was pointless in the end anyway. I don't know what I should do, Captain."

"Only you can answer that question, Cadet," said Krissa. "Like I said: you could walk away from the Academy, go down to the starport, and catch a ship that would take you back to your home. No one will stop you. The Concord Combined Command has over a thousand academies like this one spread out through the Concord and I have to believe that every one of them must have cadets with the exact same doubts as you. I could call up the numbers on how many quit and go home, but that doesn't matter. We are individuals, Cadet, and what others might choose doesn't matter a damn. Only your choice does."

"So... so why are you still here, Captain? After dying all those times? What keeps you coming back? Do you believe in the Concord that much?"

"I don't suppose I think about it anymore than the next person, but yes, I do believe in the Concord. Or at least in the idea of a Concord. There needs to be something here to watch over humanity. Because there are other species out there who hate us, or only think of us as food, or just want us gone because we are in their way. As individual worlds we don't have a chance against them. Believe me, I've seen what they can do.

"So the Concord, or something like the Concord, is necessary if humanity is going to survive. We need to allow our civilization to grow and get as strong and as advanced as it possibly can be before the next collapse. That will give us the best chance of recovering quickly when the gates come back and getting ourselves organized before some enemy gets too strong to handle. And who knows? If we get smart enough, maybe we'll figure out how to control the Antares gates and keep another collapse from happening at all."

"Is that possible?"

"Who knows? Presumably the Builders knew how to do it. No reason we can't figure it out eventually. Until we do, C3 will stand watch." Krissa paused for a moment and then went on. "Whatever it was that called you here must believe that you would be a help to us—because as we all know, the IMTel doesn't make mistakes."

"Yeah, right!" Laughed Tamika.

Krissa laughed right back at her. "Yeah. Right." The machine body stood up. "It's getting late." She turned and walked away. Tamika got to her feet and hurried to catch up. In silence they went through the Academy gates. Tamika turned toward her quarters, but Krissa went the other way.

"I'll see you in class, Cadet."

"Yes sir."

I'll see you in class.

Batu Meets the SITAI
By Tim Bancroft

Batu Delhren hung his head as the Vard continued to berate him. He did not hear the words or, at least did not hear the exact words, for he had heard such remonstrations about his inadequacy many times before. His only hope was to sound sincere in his apologies, to offer to try and correct whatever it was he had done or the damage he had caused.

The trouble was, this time he had no idea what it was that had aroused the ire of the Vard. The dives of Moralan Down Port had been his only entertainment for several months – the Vard himself had seen to that with his punishment after Batu's last escapade. Batu could not help but think that being confined to the city was an excessively hard punishment, even when the city was the capital of Delhren III, the jewel in the Delhren clan's planetary possessions. Mind you, he had found a rather attractive Boromite dancer in the Spyker's Rub...

Silence intruded into his imagination. He looked up to see the Vard glaring at him. "Are you listening to me?"

"Of course, sire," said Batu. He put on a look of indignation.

"Then tell me what I have just asked of you."

"Sire, I am hurt you should even imagine I would not hang on every word that comes from your lips." The words came automatically; internally he was querying his Delhren shard interface. "MyShard: summarize what the Vard just said."

"The Vard offered a way to clear your name, leadership of a survey to explore a newly discovered gate."

"I am, sire, at your service and would gladly lead any expedition to a new planet." Batu smiled.

"You are too good at covering your data queries." The Vard sighed volubly. "Frankly, Batu, you are a massive pain in the side of this house. There are many who would wish to get rid of you." He paused to let the words sink in. "Unfortunately, you are family."

"Thank you, Dearest Uncle."

The Vard winced. "I would rather you did not remind me of the closeness of our relationship." He waved at his personal bodyguards. "They will show you to your new command where you will be briefed by the ship's master."

"I hope to acquit myself well, Uncle, and bring another planet into the Delhren fold. Improve our revenue stream."

The Vard scowled. "If you do not, consider whether you should return."

Batu bit back a retort, bowed, and backed away from the Delhren throne. A pair of grinning guards stepped out of the audience chamber with him and the doors irised shut behind them.

Out of earshot of the Vard, Batu relaxed. "What are you smiling at?" He snapped. "Take me to the ship and make sure my vardinari and travel chest are on board within half an hour. Otherwise..."

The grins grew wider. *They know my threats are empty.* "Of course, sire," the guards chorused. One bowed, swept his hand to one side in an extravagant gesture. "After you, sire."

Batu clenched his fists. *No one takes me seriously.* There was little else to do but hold his head high, back straight, and stalk out.

***

The stench made Batu choke. For a moment, he thought the transmat had been given the wrong co-ordinates. He seemed to be in a warehouse from the look of the compression crates and collapsed stacks of supplies around the walls, but it was dark and shallow pools of fetid water puddled on the uneven floor. The only light came from the transmat console.

He covered his nose. "MyShard: where in the seven ages are we?"

"We are in hold 01S-forward, onboard a scoutship. Apparently called *Death is Only the Beginning,* a recommissioned Sixth Age vessel."

"That old? And what a stupid name. What about the stench, the mess?"

"The ship has a poor opinion of its crew."

Batu groaned. Rejects, perhaps, or Mhagris. "Feral Mhagris?"

"Transmissions suggest soma controlled, yes. Not Mhagris, but natives of Tamala-3."

Batu closed his eyes and leaned against the transmit console. "Don't tell me that, please. The Tamalair are useless; even more primitive than the Mhagris. Can you confirm, MyShard?"

"I cannot lie. Prepare yourself: the captain approaches." The Doma-familia grade shard interface followed the warning with a nerve activation, a shivering sensation down his spine. Lights flared on around him to reveal the plain walls of a poorly maintained hold.

A doorway morphed open to reveal a slender NuHu with androgynous features, its robe and cloak in the house colors of the Delhren. Like many NuHu it had a narrow face with otherwise perfectly balanced features. To Batu's surprise, its hair – pulled back in a knot – was gray and the lines around the corner of its intense, amber eyes suggested great age. Its stave was a bizarre mix of technology and primitive symbolism, a shriveled head held in a stasis sphere near its tip. Over its head hovered a pair of nano drones, their surfaces dirty, scuffed, and scarred. Behind the NuHu came robed guards armed with swords, their faces hidden by bronzed helms. The primitive weave of their clothes were a stark contrast to the modern mag repeaters each held across his or her chest.

"Well, well," said the NuHu. It took a breath and wheezed. "A real Delhren from the Delhren domas."

"MyShard? Who in the millennia gates is this?"

A message appeared on Batu's retina. "*NANOSPHERE IN-TERFACE OFFLINE.*"

There was a faint smile on the NuHu's face. "Shall we use speech?" It turned toward the mummified head. "What's that, my love? Oh, yes. It does not know who we are." It glided into the cargo space, robes barely moving. The bodyguards fanned out to either side, splashing through the puddles.

Batu stepped forward. "I am Batu Delhren, nephew to the..." His mouth was clamped shut as if by an invisible hand. "MyShard, block these nanospores!" There was no response.

"Yes, yes," wheezed the NuHu, "we know who you are. But we - we are Rayala and Rayasan, once misled by the IM-

Tel, now pledged to the House Delhren." It paused. "We are the Raya."

Oh, skark. The names of the Raya were infamous. One of the renegade NuHu pair had been killed centuries ago and the survivor had fallen into a complex insanity. No one knew which one had died, so the name had remained: the Raya. *What have you dropped me into, Uncle?*

The transmat hummed, drawing Raya's attention, and the pressure around Batu's jaw eased. In the bright light from the transmat array, hazy shapes materialized, solidified, then the light faded to reveal his bodyguard with hyper-compressor transit crates at their feet. Seeing Batu threatened and surrounded, the sergeant barked a command and the squad acted as one to protect him. Their weapons lowered into readiness.

The Tamalair remained motionless. The Raya cackled. "Put down your weapons. You are guests aboard my ship."

His sergeant, Baray, glanced at Batu before addressing the Raya. "Then re-activate our shard interfaces."

Another cackle. "In time. I am merely reintegrating your interfaces with my ship's... older technology – a personal shard, if you will." The Raya turned and led the way from the cargo hold. "Please, follow me. I will show you to your quarters. Then we can be on our way."

Baray raised her eyebrows querulously. Batu shrugged and signaled for his vardinari to fall in behind. He followed the NuHu from the hold and was not surprised when the Tamalair hung back for his bodyguard to leave. *Are we guests or prisoners?*

***

The door slid shut behind them, audibly clunked as latches engaged. "Who are they kidding?" Said Batu, turning to stare at the locked doors.

"I think, sire, they are just making a point."

A speaker crackled into life. "Guards have been posted at your door, which has been sealed for your own safety and protection during transit. This is an old vessel and you may place yourselves in danger through innocent exploration."

"A loudspeaker?" Asked Batu, incredulous.

Baray shrugged. "Well, our shard interfaces don't work, so how else?"

Batu shook his head. "Physical locks, a leaking hold, stairwells? This ship could fall apart any moment." He snorted. "Death is Only the Beginning indeed!"

The speaker crackled again. "There will be continual, basic surveillance of your luxury suite. Until transit, please feel free to settle in and make yourselves at home." The words were followed by a cackle of laughter that turned into a cough. "Please freshen up and prepare yourselves for a formal dinner in the ship's mess hall at which you are to be our guests. The noble Batu will be a dinner guest in our private cabin." The speaker hissed and then went silent.

"It's mad," said Batu.

"I think they can hear everything you say, sire."

"Okay, I'm sorry." Batu glared round at the walls. "You're insane!" He shouted. He swirled his purple impact cloak round him in frustration and deliberately allowed the gold chains hanging from its brooch to clash. Beneath the cloak, however, he had discarded all adornment in favor of functional, blue reflex armor identical to that of his bodyguard. What set him apart was the intricately decorated plasma pistol in a dark, real leather holster and the single brooch that sat on his left lapel: the badge of the Delhren. He ran his fingers through his hair in exasperation, then pulled them away, conscious the motion would attract attention to the fact he was now thinning and graying. It wasn't like that before Shamasai, he thought. At least my moustache is still full. And, at least, his aquiline nose marked him out as a relative of the Vard. He stroked it, proudly. Stop preening, Batu. The Raya might be watching.

Baray rolled her eyes. "I'm not sure the Raya cares about your opinion, sire." She unclipped her carbine and looked around. "It looks comfortable, at least." Like Batu, Baray was dressed in a purple impact cloak and blue-black reflex armor, though at her belt were as many ammunition and equipment pouches as the rest of his bodyguard. Like all the vardinari, she was muscular and, also like theirs, her skin was darker and bore facial features more in line with the square-faced phenotyping currently commonplace amongst the Delhren.

"It's only comfortable if you like Tamalair nomad chic," muttered Batu. The walls and floor of the suite were covered in abstract-pattern rugs that smelled as if they had been woven from live animals, heavily padded cushions were strewn every-where, and alcoves – presumably bedchambers – were separated from the main chamber by heavy curtains. What little furniture there was seemed shaped from bone, wood, leather, and fur.

Batu strode over to an alcove and pulled back the curtain to reveal a deeply-padded cushion almost half a yan long and just as wide. "No sleep fields? I hope we have decent toilet facil-ities."

"Shared, sire," said Baray, who had followed him over. "With a decent, very modern, food synthesizer and medical fa-cilities. Tamalair chic it may be on the outside, but the Raya did not stint on the basics."

Batu looked around, surprised, and noted the rest of his guard squad were making a thorough search of the central cham-ber and adjoining rooms. He settled on a cushion that seemed more intricately decorated than the rest. "So?"

"One entrance, sire. Places to hang or store weapons and kit – no compressors; food and medical synthesizers; top-of-the-line hygiene facilities. Rather primitive entertainment systems and library access, but essentially that's it."

"So we're to feed, entertain, and wash ourselves. And we're watched?"

"There is an active nanosphere, sire. We're certainly watched."

Batu sighed in exasperation. "Better make the most of it then. I could do with a drink."

***

Sergeant Baray was waiting for Batu when he returned from his meal with the Raya. "Pleasant dinner, sire?"

Batu shivered. "With an insane NuHu who chatters away to a mummified head? That's in stasis? Hardly."

"Any useful intel?"

Batu glanced sharply at Baray, but she appeared to be sincere. "No. Only that our captain's paranoid, the bridge is locked up tighter than a skark's arse, and my shard interface has rebooted but cannot connect anywhere onboard. Apparently its low-level interfaces have been completely corrupted. It acts like it's drunk."

"Droll, sire. Our interfaces are also active but still unable to integrate with the ship's nanosphere. The 'sphere's not Delhren standard. What's more, its security protocols aren't derived from any Freeborn or Concord configuration that we know. We have no access, control, or influence over the ship or its crew whatsoever."

Batu pouted. "So no integration and no hacking. Is there anything we can do?"

"Short of mutiny, no. Even then we'd be outgunned, outnumbered, and legally in a very awkward situation. The Vard regards any mutiny as a very serious crime."

"Your recommendation?"

"We go along with it. That you try and carry out your duty, sire."

"My duty," said Batu, gloomily. "Yes. It seems I have little choice but to do my duty." He headed over to the alcove they had designated as his bedchamber. "Wake me if anything happens."

* * *

Days later the door slid open to reveal a single Tamalair guard. "Bring weapons officer." Though he spoke in the universal tongue, his accent was thick and almost unintelligible.

"Did you understand what he said, Batu?"

"I can understand his accent, thank you MyShard, and I speak Tamalair, as can Baray. Such sarcasm suggests you are better, though. Are you?"

"Am I better? What do you mean, Batu?"

"Are you still drunk?"

"I was never 'drunk', Batu, merely struggling to integrate with what was available."

"And you've found something to connect to?"

"No, Batu. I have merely adapted my user interface to better utilize the Shamasai spore remaining in your body. It has a remarkable ability to adapt."

The guard repeated himself, this time in Tamalair and Batu responded in the same language. "Why do you want me to bring my weapons officer?"

The guard looked relieved and continued, now also speaking in Tamalair. "Thank you, Lord Batu. Lord Raya prefers us speaking our own language. The Raya believes your officer will be more proficient than our own in manning the ship's weapons systems and demands her presence. We expect to exit into the new system in less than an hour."

Batu smiled at the request. "You mean you cannot do it yourself?" He beckoned to Baray. "We're needed on the bridge, Sergeant."

Baray saluted and winked at him under the salute. "Certainly, sire."

They followed the guard. He took them to a surprisingly modern and well-maintained proximity transmat.

Makes sense they'd keep these functioning properly, thought Batu. "Do you maintain these yourselves?"

"No," said the Tamalair, nodding his head from side to side. "They are checked and serviced every time we return to a Delhren fleet."

Interesting. "Don't you have any engineers aboard?"

"We have the chief engineer, but his focus is on the important ship's systems – generators, engines, shields, and such."

"Ah. Does the Raya use intra-ship transmats?"

The Tamalair bobbed his head sideways again and continued to lead them toward a blank bulkhead. Batu risked a glance at Baray, who grimaced in return. *Maybe we ought to avoid the shipboard transmats.* As they approached, the bulkhead phased into permeability to reveal a softly-lit bridge beyond. Raya sat in the command chair, staring at the bridge screen on which could be seen the swirling, actinic glare of the Antares photosphere. To either side, in the navigator and pilot chairs, sat regular vardosi, humans wearing the purple and blue uniforms of flight personnel. The lesser bridge stations were in remote mode, though monitoring each were Tamalair, looking incongruous in bronze armor and display headsets.

How odd. Controlled by the Raya's personal IMTel? "Very, ah, interesting set-up," said Batu. He yawned and deliberately addressed Baray. "Such striking anachronisms, Sergeant. Anyone would think the captain is making a point."

For a few moments the Raya made no reaction. Then the stasis globe in his stave seemed to turn so the eyes of the mummified head faced the newly-arrived pair. "Sergeant Baray can take over weapons command." Batu was not sure from where the voice came: the NuHu or its stave.

"I cannot access the ship's nanosphere, Captain Raya."

"I will grant access to the lower levels of the ship's external command hierarchy. You will be able to command our weaponry. Not that we are expecting an attack, of course." The Raya still faced the bridge screen. "As a precautionary measure, I have released your vardinari and placed them in control of individual weapon systems."

"I'd have liked to have been asked," said Batu. "And what about me?"

"There is no need to open our superior shard to one as infantile as yourself. You are superfluous in all respects other than your title. Stand by me and watch."

"Thanks," muttered Batu. He nodded to Baray. She marched over to the tactical station to relieve the Tamalair on duty. Batu ambled slowly over to the Raya's command chair and leaned on it. He was sure the head followed his movements with a disapproving gaze.

"Transmitting," said the navigator. The pilot made a few deft movements and the bridge display changed to a swirling, multicolored tunnel.

"Inside," said the pilot. "Smooth. System exit in 20 minutes."

"A short gate," said Batu. The Raya made no response but the navigator twitched. They're jumpy.

The exit was anticlimactic, the bright haze of transit suddenly fading to pinpricks of stars in darkness. One star shone larger than the others, dead ahead in the center of the screen.

"Pretty," said Batu. "Who's operating sensors?"

"I am," said Raya, absently. "Just as I am operating every

other station." It pointed to the empty Sensors desk. "You may observe from over there. Remain silent."

Batu frowned at the Raya's back. He sauntered over to the Sensor Station and manually called up readouts from the system scans. There were four rocky planets and two gas giants, one world in the water-life zone. He frowned. "Is there something wrong with the sensors?"

"All the ship sensors are fully operational and performing multi-band scans. I doubt you can see anything I cannot."

"There are only three to five million human-sized life-signs in the system – that's pitifully few. Yet I can see countless orbital habitats, artificial satellites, and bucket loads of transmissions." There was no answer to Batu's comments. "Something's wrong." The Raya remained silent so Batu turned to Baray instead. "Threats?"

"Not that I can see, sire. Three unmanned system craft are heading our way." Baray threw up a tactical display onto the sensor station for Batu. "Drones. Slow, even compared with us. Orders, Captain?"

"Remain on standby," said Raya, its voice distant and distracted. Both it and the head had their eyes closed. "How interesting. Pilot, slow to a rendezvous course with the incoming ships." The ship slowed, the bridge display changed focus and direction until the oncoming ships were directly ahead.

"What's interesting?" Asked Batu. "MyShard: how can I manually call up a comms channel with these ships?"

"You are limited to passive displays only."

Batu seethed. Damned if I'm going to show frustration. "MyShard, get us on-line, build a connection – to anywhere."

"The Raya and Death is Only the Beginning have corrupted our lower-level interface routines. The security hierarchy has prevented further destruction but I will need replacement modules or a complete refresh."

"Just do it, MyShard, however you can." An idea came to mind. "Try and connect to the local sphere when you can. If there is one, that is."

"Acknowledged."

Batu strode across the bridge to the Raya. "I am the authorized representative of the vardos, a Delhren of the Delhren.

I demand you tell me what is going on."

There was an audible intake of breath around the bridge. The Raya opened its eyes and slowly turned to stare at Batu. "Of course you are of the Delhren domas and vardos: that is why you are here, after all. I am establishing a common language with the oncoming intelligent species, the AIs."

"Stop obfuscating. I have the authority to relieve you of command." Not that anyone will take any notice.

The Raya's amused smile remained. "They are the SITAI – Substrate Independent Transcendent AIs. They have downloaded instances of themselves onto their ships to meet us." The Raya looked at his stave and the smile softened. "Did you hear that, my love? Substrate Independent. Perhaps they can show us a way to be together."

Batu looked around the bridge. The crew acted as if they had not heard what the Raya had just said. He cleared his throat. "You mean like Concord drones? Independent AIs?"

The Raya sighed. "You are not listening. Perhaps once the SITAI were Concord, but the crew members of those ships are much more than simple drones. There are sentient, fully sapient beings. Each is independent of a physiological or technological implementation – a pure mind and machine merge." The Raya looked jealous. "It is possible they could transfer their minds into our technology and still survive."

Baray had been listening. "Sire, I've locked the ship's nanosphere defenses against intrusion. Their ships have magrail weapons, drone missiles, and what look like multi-warhead, unguided, nuclear torpedoes. Very primitive."

The Raya inclined its head. "Such simple weapons would be useful against advanced countermeasures. The lack of AI or nanosphere to subvert would be of considerable advantage."

"Well done, Baray." Batu stared at the three alien ships. "No humans? Other life-signs? I wish to deal with their commanders."

Raya glanced sideways at his stave. "Certainly. We are heading for their... inhabited planet. I suggest you make your way to the shuttle."

"Baray, join me." Batu entered the transmat. "Shuttle bay," he snapped. He shut his eyes against the blinding light of the transmat. "I can deal with this," he muttered. "Tricky negotiations... delicate first contact."

I could get my reputation back for this.

* * *

The shuttle was uncomfortable, the interior decor in bad repair though the equipment was functional. A pair of Tamalair sat at the controls, though neither looked as if they knew what to do.

"MyShard: Can we access the shuttle?"

"No."

"Get the Raya on-line."

"I still cannot."

"The old way it is, then." Batu manually requested a connection to the bridge of the old scout ship. "Raya, I need access to the shuttle controls."

The Raya coughed. "I cannot see an overriding need for such access. To ensure we are not compromised, use of the shuttle's control systems has been restricted to myself. We do not know the capabilities of the SITAI, nor how close their own technology is to that of the Pan-Human nanosphere."

"Give me control," snapped Batu.

"Do not disturb me, Batu Delhren. I am managing an orbital insertion in a crowded space." The link was terminated.

Transmat controls lit up, a flare of light came from the hold, and moments later Baray stepped through. She was armored, though much of her equipment was covered by her cloak. She strapped in next to Batu. "The Raya kicked up a stink about me leaving, sire, so I had to hand the weapons console over to one of the seniors. It only let me go when I said my orders to protect you came from the Vard himself."

"Thank you, Baray. I am relieved to see you. No carbine?"

"The Raya insisted it might be seen as an act of aggression, sire. He forbade me or even any of his Tamalair to carry anything other than sidearms."

"Do you have access to the shuttle?"

"I'm connected to the scout ship's commsphere but it's locked down tight. Defense systems only. Definitely no access to the transmat or flight controls."

"And the Tamalair don't know what they're doing." Batu rolled his eyes. "Great. I guess the Raya's our pilot."

One of the Tamalair crew called back over his shoulder. "Launch in five. We've been given authorization to land on an orbital, not on the planet itself. The Raya says there's a reception committee."

The shuttle lurched and eased away from the small hangar. Through the front screen they saw a cylindrical orbital come closer, its two kiloyan length rotating slowly on the axis. Baray pointed. "Look. They've got rotational rather than artificial gravity. My scans found several hundred thousand human-sized life forms on that orbital, the highest concentration in the system."

"Perhaps a headquarters habitat, then?"

Baray shrugged. "Maybe, but I honestly don't know. All transmissions went through the Raya." She nudged Batu. "Looks like we've been queued up."

The shuttle aligned itself with the hub of the orbital behind one of the escort vessels as it cruised closer to a non-rotating docking platform extending from one end. Their escort pivoted, landing neatly on the pad; the shuttle mirrored the maneuver.

A Tamalair checked his display. "Ship gravity is going off. Local gravity is from grav plates on the landing pad."
Lights changed color, a display flickered, and abruptly Batu felt lighter. He stretched. "That's nice. I like the gravity, here."

"Be careful, sire. We have no idea what the real gravity is likely to be."

The deck beneath the shuttle moved, lowering them into a recessed bay beneath the landing area. Lights flared to reveal a clean, clinical, and functional space that lacked any decoration. At one end, a heavy airlock doorway slid open and a troop of soldiers – humans – trotted into the landing bay. Behind them came a number of suspensor drones, some with weapon mounts, others with extensive sensor arrays.

"Wonderful," said Batu with a satisfied smile. "The drones' Sixth Age styling is superb. It's not a perfect replica but a development. This looks as if it is a lost colony after all."

"How do you know that?" Baray looked at her ward in surprise.

"Genuine Sixth Age artifacts and antiques are quite the rage. Good money. All our traders have been tasked with keeping an eye out for sources." Batu could not keep the look of satisfaction off his face. "I may have hit a motherlode."

"Very Boromite, sire."

"Thank you. I thought so."

Another announcement came from the Tamalair. "Atmosphere compatible. Oxy-nitrogen levels within human tolerances. No breathers required. Local nanosphere is dense, but probably harmless to Seventh Age vardos security. You're good to go."

Batu unbuckled himself. "Quick. Before the Raya 'mats through." He strode to the shuttle's exterior hatch, waited, then tutted in exasperation and triggered the manual override. "This shard isolation is a pain in the proverbial."

The ramp slid out and he waited for the honor guard to form up at its base. The drones hovered to either side. He tried to comprehend what he was seeing. The guards were dressed in a uniform gray with functional helmets and no obvious signs of rank insignia. A lone human stood at the foot of the ramp, though dressed in red and gold. The drones were a riot of color, some complementary, others deliberately contrasting.

Batu paused for effect. "Here goes," he murmured to Baray.

He stepped forward and was about to speak when MyShard interrupted. "Local shard security protocol adaption has succeeded. Integration complete as per current orders." Batu stumbled in surprise, fell down to one knee. "We are connected to a local, Sixth Age nanosphere." MyShard's internal voice had a note of pride. "I managed to transmit a signal and the local nanosphere automatically rebuilt my low-level interfaces. Apparently it's an automated emergency response protocol in case one of their own drones becomes corrupt. I adjusted my lower-order interface functions to known Sixth Age specifications and retained higher-order Delhren security protocols to ensure isolation from local absorption." It sounded smug. "Now gathering environmental, security, and trade data."

Baray caught Batu's arm. She looked concerned. "Are you all right, sire?" She whispered.

"Yes, fine. Just..." He paused. "Are you connected to the local nanosphere?"

"To the ship's? Yes, still." She lifted him to his feet. "Your interface is a different spec, sire. Top of the range, I believe, even Doma-grade security. It may have been more badly affected." She inclined her head toward the waiting natives. "Sire? The delegation?"

"Yes, you are quite right," said Batu, thinking furiously. He raised a hand in greeting, addressing the colorful human commander and his accompanying drones. "I am Batu Delhren. I greet you in the name of House Delhren, a trading nation of great repute. We are honored to be the first of a new age to encounter the SITAI."

The human looked unimpressed. There was a flare of light from inside the ship. That will be the Raya, thought Batu, struggling to suppress his facial expression from reflecting his annoyance. He heard limping footsteps, then the Raya appeared at the top of the ramp.

The red and gold clad human glanced at the drone beside it and nodded. "Felicitations," said a voice.

Batu jumped: the human had not opened his lips to speak. "Who said that?" Asked Batu. He gathered himself quickly. "I am sorry, I did not realize you spoke our language."

"The SITAI spoke," said the Raya. "We decided it would be easier for us all to download our language data to their own databanks."

"You are the superior intellect?" This time Batu noticed a light pulse on the underside of the drone as it spoke to the Raya. "Can you confirm you are the partially-transcended in command of the alien vessel?"

"Yes." The Raya held up the stave, the stasis field now opaque so the grisly contents could not be seen. "We are the Raya."

"Then communication can proceed. Follow." The drone backed toward the exit of the hangar. The human at the foot of the ramp pirouetted on his heel and followed. Batu turned to Baray but she shrugged, clearly mystified. Batu strode down the ramp and across the bay floor, the SITAI guards falling in behind.

Are they rude on purpose? He sent an instruction to his reconnected MyShard. "Give me research on the SITAI humans' mores, will you? Find out why they're so rude. And find out something about their language – we can't have the Raya having private conversations. And tell me whatever you can find out about this local IMTel, MyShard, I am concerned."

"Is that all?"

"For now, yes. And stop being cheeky."

* * *

"This is more like it," said Batu. They entered a large, circular assembly hall and stepped up to a high platform attached to one edge. The walls and domed roof of the hall were richly decorated with banners and a slowly changing spectrum of colored light. Armed humans and guard drones stood or hovered around the circumference in niches whilst the space in the middle of the spacious hall was filled with a colorful array of drones and humans.

Baray spoke quietly in Tamalair. "Have you noticed that every human is accompanied by a drone?"

Batu responded in the same language. "No. I was thinking there were many more drones than people." He sniffed. "Have you noticed there is almost no smell?"

"Makes a change from the Tamalair and the ship."

"There's not even any body odor from the humans."

"They must shower regularly, sire."

MyShard pinged for attention. "Batu, you asked for information on the local IMTel."

"Thanks, MyShard. What do you have?"

"It does not exist."

"What? But..."

"I mean, it does not exist as we know it. It is a broker, not a sharded intelligence. It seems to respond to requests and dispatches them to individual service units, each of which appears to be a separate, discrete intelligence in its own right."

"What about data access?"

"Access to library data and information is simple, readily available, but their search and service intelligences are narrow, highly specialized, very responsive but limited."

"A data transport nanosphere? Not an IMTel?"

"Correct. But still a highly effective storage and communication medium."

"How strange. Keep looking, MyShard."

Baray muttered to Batu again. "Perhaps the drones have as much authority and independence as the C3's IMTel drones."

"Maybe. There isn't a communal IMTel beneath everything, though. I wonder what they mean by 'transcendent' or 'substrate independent'?"

"I have a bad feeling, boss." Baray looked at him oddly. "How do you know about their nanosphere?"

A group of drones and humans approached the Freeborn trio. Batu could not help but notice the humans' costumes: each was dressed in the same combination of colors as the drone they accompanied. He bowed and was pleased to see Baray and the Raya emulate his action. "The Delhren are pleased to rediscover a lost civilization."

"We, too, are interested in such contact. How did you travel through the gate?" A light on a red and gold drone at the front pulsed in time with the speech.

"From Antares. The red giant. I'm Batu, Merchant Lord of the Delhren."

"We know who you are. Do you mean you come from the Antares system?"

"No. We came through from the giant's photosphere itself. Um... who are you?"

"I am currently the First of the SITAI. Beside me are the Second and Defender." A bright green and purple drone bobbed, then a deep blue and orange.

Batu turned to the humans. "You are?"

The Raya held up a hand to Batu to stop him talking further. "May I suggest I talk to the drones, sire, whilst you talk to the humans? I am, perhaps, closer to their minds."

Since when does he call me sire? Batu was suspicious but could see no reason to object. "Sure. I mean certainly. Good idea."

First hesitated a moment, then bobbed in the air. "That might be highly efficient."

"MyShard: what's going on?"

"There was a communication burst between the Raya and First, just prior to the drone's acquiescence."

"Okay, see if you can monitor any further communication between them."

"Above your other requests? In this ancient nanosphere, I am limited in functionality."

"Can't you use Baray's shard interface?"

"I am still locked out from the ship's shard. And her access routines are locked into the Raya's security protocols. Likewise, now the SITAI's protocols have merged with my own interfaces, I am immune to the Raya's access."

"That's good to know."

The humans gestured for Batu to follow them and then led the way through the assembled SITAI to a conference room to one side. The room was bare, but as they entered, chairs and a table morphed into existence. Human guards followed in and stood at ease against the walls.

"I am for First," said the red-gold garbed human. He gestured to the two beside him. "These are for Second and Defender. Sit."

They sat. The chairs were solid, uncomfortable, and failed to adjust to Batu's physique. "I am Batu, this is Baray. What shall we call you?"

The speaker frowned slightly as if puzzled by the question. "For-First, For-Second and For-Defender." He stared at Baray. "You are a warrior?"

"I am Batu's bodyguard, yes."

For-First glanced at For-Second and For-Defender. Only after they each acknowledged his gaze did For-First speak directly to Batu. "Are you truly her transcendent? Not For-Raya?"

"Transcendent? If by that you mean her master, then no, just her employer. And no, I am not a For-Raya – he is merely the captain of the vessel who brought us here, one of my own." Batu felt that, right now, explaining the complexities of Freeborn house politics and structure might be too difficult.

"MyShard, what the hell does he mean by transcendent? And what are these people?"

"Evaluating. Searching cultural databases."

Baray picked up on the discussion. "Are you saying you are owned by First?"

For-First muttered to the other two at the table. They all looked troubled. It was For-Defender who finally spoke. "We are owned and controlled by our SITAI masters, our transcendents. We struggle with the idea you suggest that a purely organic intelligence is allowed freedom or can even be a master to a partially transcendent."

"Batu, the transcendent are the intelligences who occupy the drones. It seems they move drone bodies at will."

"And these people?"

"They are Janissaries, slave-soldiers. Searching for more data. The servitor programs here are very eager to please."

"If you are not SITAI," continued Baray, "are you controlled by them? Dominated by the SITAI? Forced to obey?"

For-First parted his hair. Underneath, embedded into his skull, was a metallic circle half a centiyan in circumference. "It is right that all error-prone organics have governance implants. It prevents us being fearful or irrational. Do you not have such an independent intelligence, such implants?"

"No," said Batu. He looked away and swallowed hard to restrain his horror. "Well, yes. We have shard interfaces, and some of our cultures have the IMTel, but not your.... governance implants. They are not considered ethical." He thought of the soma grafts used on the Mhagris, of the similar implants used on the Tamalair by the Raya. "Generally, anyway. And those that do, have them voluntarily. And still have free will."

"Mostly," muttered Baray.

"Batu, local library data suggests the Janissaries are not from this system. They were brought here hundreds of years ago by interstellar slow-boat."

"To serve the SITAI."

"For tasks which they realized they needed 'meat bodies'."

"Thanks for that."

Baray leaned forward. "You are obviously useful to the SITAI, which means you have some commercial value."

"We could provide services, technology," said Batu. Good thinking, Baray. "Dumb servitors. You could reduce your dependence on the SITAI." He paused nervously, but decided to ask anyway. "Why don't you free yourselves? Or bargain for better conditions?"

The guards who heard the questions froze. For-First, For-Second, and For-Defender became rigid. Batu waved his hand across the face of For-Defender but saw no reaction. A trio of drones swept into the chamber. Two were undecorated, metal and polished ceramic reflecting the light, but were armed with weapons resembling mag repeaters. Baray jumped to her feet, placed herself between the drones and Batu, and put her hand on her holster. Lights flickered on the surface of the third drone, bright yellow stripes over its shell. "What were you doing?" It asked.

"Talking to these fellows, here," said Batu, peering round Baray. "Private business."

"We have been monitoring your conversation."

Batu frowned. "That's intrusive."

"These Janissaries are our property, under our control and management."

Batu held up a hand. "Hold on a minute. You can't control..."

"I am security. Do not correct us."

Batu overheard the squeal of a compressed transmission. Small gun drones swept in from the main hall. The facial expressions of the Janissaries around the walls turned stoney and they raised their weapons. "MyShard: what's happening?"

"You are being arrested."

"Some help you are."

The red-gold drone, First, appeared in the doorway with the Raya close behind. The Raya glowered at Batu. "What is going on?"

First spoke. "Your underling has been inciting rebellion amongst the Janissaries."

"Hold on," said Batu. He stood and leaned on the table as he spoke. "I was just talking about freedom, reduced dependence on drones. All I said was that we could provide personal servitors."

"Condemned from his own mouth," said First. "Arrest them." It backed away leaving the guard and gun drones aiming their weapons at the three Delhren. "Drop your weapons and your interface-stave."

Defender slid into the chamber. "They are irrational organics, as I warned the Consensuality."

The Raya turned a look of fury onto Batu. "What have you done?"

"Nothing!" Protested Batu. "I just thought the Janissaries could do with some help, some independence."

MyShard flashed a warning. "Another secure transmission. Beware." Batu got to his feet.

The Raya turned to First. "There has been a misunderstanding. From organic ignorance. I was not aware."

"You are the superior, so are responsible," said Defender. A large, gunmetal combat drone slid in behind Defender, heavy railguns on pylons to either side of its body. An ominous click echoed round the chamber.

The Raya glared at Batu. "You fool." It placed the stave on the table. "I will come for you," it whispered. Baray placed her own pistol alongside it.

"This way," said the security drone and led the way from the chamber. The combat drone turned so its weapons remained aimed at the Delhren and backed outside. Janissaries closed around the trio and shepherded them from the chamber. All trace of the Raya's limp was gone and he displayed aloof dignity and grace in every step.

The look of fury the Raya directed at Batu was plain. "First, I do not wish to be imprisoned in the same cell as this meat," it said. "I would be contaminated by this mindless organic."

"We understand," said First. "Defender will co-operate."

* * *

"Well," said Baray, looking around the cell. "It could be worse."

"How?" Grumbled Batu.

"I've slept in worse quarters than this." She pointed to the bunks and the sanitary facilities. "At least they're clean and its warm."

"And we're imprisoned. By a bunch of drones worse than the Concord." Batu waved a hand at the walls. "And there's no door. It's got door-morph walls."

Baray shrugged. "If I may say so, sire, you could have handled that a bit more diplomatically."

"I what?" Sputtered Batu.

"Going head on to challenge a new society's mores and integral culture is never going to get you any friends. Sire."

Batu stared at Baray. He reddened and sputtered, unable to think of anything to say. Baray looked at him steadily. "I'm here to watch your back, sire, and that means telling you when you've made gross mistake."Batu recovered and stared at her in disbelief. "And please stop moping, sire." She tilted her head to one side. "Transmissions are being blocked from the ship, by the way."

Batu swallowed his pride and self-pity, remembering that she'd saved him on Shamasai; that when the Ghar had attacked and destroyed their temporary shelters, she had been the only one of his bodyguards to survive; that she had dragged him through the maze of tunnels under the ancient, deadly surface; that she had protected him with her life. He felt ashamed. "Sorry," he muttered, then raised his head and took a deep breath. "I apologize, Baray."

"Don't be sorry, think of something to get us out of here."

"Like what?"

"You still haven't told me how you knew about their nanosphere." Baray watched him closely.

The observation caught Batu off guard and he slumped onto a bunk. He sucked his teeth thoughtfully. *She's smarter than she looks. I should have seen that ages ago.*

"Well?"

"Well, the Raya corrupted my shard interface's lower functions, something to do with Sixth Age protocols, I'd imagine. As soon as we landed, MyShard managed to rebuild its connectivity protocols and interface with the local nanosphere."

Baray raised her eyebrows in surprise. "Safely, so don't worry. Our Freeborn security is way better than what they have here." Baray smiled. "Now that is something that might help us get out of here. Can it tell the local nanosphere to release us?"

"I don't know."

"Fine, so what can it do?"

"MyShard, how are things going?"

"I have been processing your previous requests. I have links to surveillance spores in which the Raya is involved. I have historical information on the SITAI and their Janissaries."

"Give it to me. No, wait. What's happening with the Raya?" An image slowly formed on his lens implant: the Raya sat in a small conference room facing Defender and Second. Two warrior drones hovered in the background.

"Can you get sound, MyShard? Or sharpen up the image?"

"What are you doing?" Asked Baray.

"Hush, I'm trying to listen in on the Raya. He's negotiating something." The image solidified and the sound faded in from his binaural implants.

The Raya was speaking, his voice still cracked with age but now much more firm that it had been earlier. "...relatively common practice amongst some houses. It only makes sense. The ferals are primitive, need restraining."

"You possess enlightened thought processes. We have few Janissaries, have had to transport them many light-years. Not all survive the journey in hibernation. They not only need replenishment but also greater genetic diversity. How many can you supply?"

"As many as you need. Millions. They are only biological-substrate dependent organics, after all. I have some similar on my ship."

"Those will be useful. What about access through the gate?"

"I can give you keys to systems that have no advanced organic life but which you can make your own." The Raya smiled emptily. "You are already capable of building the shielding to withstand the photosphere of Antares."

"And in return?"

"I use your technology to transcend my meld-partner and I."

"Two minds in symbiosis? Our experience shows such a situation to be highly unstable."

"Two advanced minds in a symbiotic, technological meld. NuHu are highly advanced, as dissimilar to humans as you are." Defender interrupted. "We must test our governance implants on your cattle before negotiations can continue."

"You can use some of my Tamalair and the two you have captured."

Batu gasped. "What is it?" Asked Baray.

"He's betraying us. Wait."

"...the captured pair superior specimens? One claimed to be of high status."

"He is a human, of no consequence. A renegade. She is a soldier, a good test for advanced Janissary functioning."

"Very well." Defender backed away, leaving Second to finish the conversation.

"We shall put it to the Consensuality. However, expect agreement." It bobbed and a Janissary entered with the Raya's stave. "I have decided to return your property as a gesture of goodwill." The NuHu snatched his stave from the Janissary's hands.

The doors closed behind the drones and the Raya were left on their own.

The image faded and Batu slumped down on a bunk. He rested his head against the wall and rubbed his face. "We are in deep, deep trouble."

"Don't keep me in the dark, Batu." Baray's expression turned grim as he explained what he had heard and seen. She waited until he had finished before speaking. "Never trust a renegade NuHu," she growled. "Batu, what else can you influence?"

"I can't access their military layers, yet. They're too secure."

"So you can't get us out, yet?"

"MyShard, anything key about their technology? Summary, please, major points."

74 Beyond the Gates of Antares

"They do not have stasis nor transmat technology. Their nanosphere is an open medium, the first planet in the system already mined to produce the components. Their own planet is being replanted with food for the Janissaries but is mostly abandoned. Most of their life is on orbitals like this."

"No transmat or stasis."

"Of course not. What use would AIs have for either technology? They can transmit themselves across systems at light speed and stasis would give no advantage over storage matrices." She thought for a moment. "But why do they need Janissaries at all? They transcend, become SITAI, but promptly bring back humans – us organics – when they encounter them in another star system. At sub-light speeds, too. What aren't we seeing?"

"What's wrong with humans?"

"We're resource-heavy. Think of this orbital: without humans, the SITAI could turn it into a huge research or recreational space, get rid of most of the life support and use hot and cold, shadow and sunlight differentials better. Instead they induce simulated gravity and turn it into a home for their slaves. It's a long-term investment, incredibly costly. There must be something more."

"Where is the money?" Murmured Batu.

"They don't need it, I guess. They don't yet deal with anyone from Antarean space."

"I meant, where is the advantage? Is it trade, politics, reputation, resources?"

Baray snapped her fingers. "Long-term. Of course. These guys knew about the gate, just couldn't get through it. I mean, they must be almost immortal – unless something happens to their backups, they're like millions of individual IMTels – they last forever." She paced up and down the cell. "They knew someone would come through sooner or later."

"Yes." Batu was confused. "But what's that got to do with the Janissaries? These guys can do anything – pure IMTel, you've just said."

Baray smiled. "What's the worst thing you can do to C3 forces?"

"Everyone knows that. Subverter attacks. Ruins the..." Batu stopped and sighed. "Of course."

"Yeah. Totally befuddles the drones. So they need support that's immune to subverters."

"Hence the Janissaries." Batu whistled softly. "Once through the gates, though, they'll be unstoppable. They're resource-constrained at the moment – hardware and organic. They've already had to take apart a couple of planets and they must be worrying about disrupting the system balance. With more resources, there is nothing to stop them copying themselves into millions more drone bodies."

"And with the ferals and Tamalair the Raya's promised them..." Baray fell silent.

Batu nodded and tried to sound brighter than he felt. "All the support they need. Yeah, that's the money."

* * *

Batu was dozing when Baray shook him awake. "The Raya is nearby!" She whispered. "Find out where."

Batu sat up. "How do you know?"

Baray tapped her head. "I've picked up his attempts to communicate with the ship. He's as isolated as I am. The local nanosphere doesn't respond to him."

Batu rubbed his eyes. "They don't trust him yet, then." He switched modes. "MyShard, find out, will you?"

"How do you...?" Began Baray. She caught herself. "Right. If they did they'd have allowed him access."

"Whilst I cannot open the doors due to military grade protocols, I can access the surveillance grid. He is accompanied by the two Tamalair from the shuttle. Unfortunately, he also has some Janissaries and a SITAI drone. One of the Janissaries is For-Defender."

A door morphed into existence. For-Defender stepped into the cell. "Please, come with us. We have been asked to perform some... contamination tests on your physiology." Over the Janissary's shoulder, Batu was sure he could see a smirk from the Raya.

"That's nice, isn't it, Baray? And after the tests you'll let us go?"

"Then you will be released from detention, yes."

Crafty little snikes, thought Batu. "Come along, then." He swept out with Baray in tow, gratified to see that the combat drone and the Raya's escort had to catch up with him. "This way?" He headed down a corridor toward a grav-shaft MyShard highlighted on his enhanced reality. Along the corridor sat the blue and orange Defender with a pair of gun drones as escort.

Batu increased his pace and waved. "Defender! Good to see you. We're being released – after some infectious body tests, I believe." He fixed his expression into a smile. "MyShard, I hope you have called us a space in the grav-shaft."

"I am at full, anticipatory functioning, Batu. The doors will open in moments to a large gap in the traffic."

"You should probably have done such tests when we first landed," said Baray.

"What are those doors?" Said Batu. He turned toward Baray and inclined his head toward the grav-shaft access.

Baray frowned briefly, but then caught on. "I have no idea." She turned to the Tamalair. "Do you know?" She asked in Tamalair, then Batu caught a slight defocus in her eyes as she transmitted a private message.

The Raya opened his mouth; Baray kicked the stave from his hands, caught it before it hit the floor, and whirled, knocking the Raya and the two guards to the floor. The doors opened. Batu grabbed the startled Tamalair by the shoulders and threw himself into the grav-shaft, pulling them with him by sheer momentum. Baray jumped in behind as flechettes hammered into the closing doors.

They floated up the shaft. Above and below them were startled Janissaries and taciturn drones. Any shots would cause considerable damage. Except. "We'll have to get out as soon as possible. They'll open the doors and shoot."

Baray looked grim. "I know. They can just restore their own kind and they don't care about the Janissaries."

"Quite."… "MyShard?"

An exit became rimmed in pseudo-color. "These doors lead into a Janissary warren which eventually exits onto the landing dock."

"What's happening?" Stammered a Tamalair, breaking free of Batu's hold.

"We're saving your life," said Baray. "They were going to replace your Delhren interfaces with their own governance implants - you'd become zombies."

"We did not give such permission," said the Tamalair. "That is dishonorable. And you?"

"Us too," said Baray. She put her hand on Batu's shoulder. "I hope you have a plan, sire."

"MyShard does." The doors opened. Gravity shifted and they were ejected smoothly from the shaft into a corridor that noticeably curved up to either side. He felt lighter. "We must be close to the spine," said Batu. "This way."

He led the way, following the twisting track MyShard displayed on his enhanced reality. "Batu, I have calculated a path that should expose us to minimum lines of fire."

"Thanks. I'll take your word for it, MyShard." He glanced at Baray who jogged beside him, the Raya's bizarre stave still in her hand: the stasis shielding had become transparent to reveal the shrunken head. It swiveled and, though its mummified eyelids were closed, it seemed to be taking in the corridors as they passed.

"It's still alive," he gasped, then had to back track a couple of steps as MyShard flashed up a translucent wall before him. "Oops. Back this way."

Baray followed his gaze, gasped, and almost dropped the stave. Her eyes defocused a moment. "I can't communicate with it, but there is something there, in the stave." She frowned at the globe in puzzlement. "It's just not responding."

"We're probably too primitive," said Batu. He turned down a narrow corridor.

Janissaries stepped out from doors ahead of them and looked surprised to see the four of them. Batu pushed through, closely followed by the others. "Excuse us." The Janissaries offered no resistance as they passed. They rushed on, turned a corner.

"All initiative's been taken from them," said Baray. They heard shouting from behind them. "That sounds like orders being given. I think they know where we're going," she said. Running footsteps could be heard from around the corner.

"MyShard?"

"I have readied a landing area alignment bay."

"Prep two. We don't want them to guess where we're going."

"Very well."

"Close whatever doors and bulkheads you can behind us." Even as he gave the order, he heard clangs and crashes from behind, yelps of pain. He slowed; despite his exercise regime, he felt out of breath from the constant running.

"Comms indicate armed squads are heading toward the loading bay. Mostly drones, not Janissaries."

"They're anticipating a blow-out," gasped Batu to Baray. The arrow abruptly changed direction and the Tamalair crashed into him. "Other way."

"Beware," cautioned MyShard. A wall blew out ahead of them and the lights turned out in the corridor. A squad of Janissaries charged through, shooting randomly. Batu dived into a side corridor and rolled back to his feet. He could see nothing in the dark, and his ears were ringing. Unable to see or hear the others, he had to trust MyShard's projected directions.

"This way!" He called and scrambled forward. A door became highlighted in green and opened into a large lift. He turned as the doors closed: Baray and the Tamalair were nowhere to be seen.

"Artificial gravity," warned MyShard and the floor lurched.

The opposite door opened to show his shuttle; the ramp was still lowered. Batu poked his head out warily: the hangar was empty. "I have sealed all entrances," said MyShard. Batu trotted across to the shuttle, his footsteps echoing around the empty bay. Once in, he hit the manual seal on the lock and leaned back against a bulkhead to gather his breath.

"Where's Baray?"

"She is stuck in a firefight. She and the Tamalair disarmed the Janissaries and now have their weapons."

"Why is no one here?"

MyShard picked up his meaning. "I have hidden your presence from the surveillance circuits, set up numerous sub-routines to muddy nanosphere transmission around you."

"You can do that?"

"In a relatively unsecured nanosphere anyone can. IMTel and the C3 Special Forces do it all the time."

"Good man... er, thing, MyShard."

"Thank you. I suggest you go to the bridge. My priority is now to get you off this orbital."

"Without Baray and the others?"

"Correct. Your safety overrides all my other functions. I am a Doma shard interface, after all."

"Baray won't like it."

"She will understand."

"What about the transmat?"

"I still have no access to the Raya's nanosphere and he has locked out even manual operation."

Great. Batu made his way forward and strapped himself into the pilot's chair. "Okay, MyShard, launch. Or is this manual, too?"

"Manual only."

"Do you know how long it's been since pilot school?" Batu flicked the manual override and projected controls appeared above the console. They were archaic, unfamiliar to him. He fumbled his way through the activation sequence – power, engines, shielding, life support.

An explosion and a booming clang erupted from the exterior microphones.

"What was that?" He scooted over to the sensor console and tried to operate the unfamiliar interface. Instead, an image formed on his ER overlay: Baray, the Tamalair, and a frightened Janissary in front of a fire-blackened launch bay door. Shots ricocheted off the walls to either side. Baray and the Tamalair whirled and shot back down the corridor with SITAI weapons.

"They're here, MyShard?"

"Outside, yes."

"I think we'd better let them in."

"There is a risk the SITAI..."

"Not half as bad a risk if Baray found out I was going

without her. Open it a crack."

"Very well." The second bay door slid open a body's width. Shouts came from outside and a Janissary was pushed through. Then came the Tamalair, one with the Raya's stave, and finally Baray. The heavy door boomed shut.

Baray glared at Batu through the cockpit's transparency. He could sense her accusation but shook his head and reactivated the ramp. They four of them ran on board, the Tamalair threw the Raya's stave to the deck.

Baray thrust their captive into a couch. "Strap him in, securely." The Tamalair obeyed and Baray swung into the co-pilot's station. "You weren't going without us, were you?"

"No," said Batu, innocently. "I was just warming it up. I can't remotely fly this thing."

Baray was unconvinced. "Still no connection to the Death?" He shook his head. "Give me control." He swiped the controls over to her console.

The console projection morphed into a pair of NuHu standing beside each other. Each resembled younger versions of the Raya and were surrounded by a halo of sparkling particles streaming from IMTel staves.

"Are you doing that, sir?"

"No." Batu glanced at the Raya's stave. The stasis field was a swirling, multicolored pool, hiding the disembodied head within. The image above the console altered, faded to a single Raya, this one aged, the one they knew. The image shifted again, this time to a stave, then back to the Raya.

"MyShard, is our 'sphere breached?"

"Not yet."

"It's not the SITAI," said Batu. "It's internal."

Baray stared at the images as they cycled through again. She released the seat constraints, picked up the stave. "I think it's this."

"But it's not making sense."

"It wants the Raya."

"We can't pick him up. Without a lock for the transmat we'd need to go after him physically." Batu pushed back in his seat as the images over the console abruptly changed: a transmat ring, the stave, the Raya, then the original three images.

"It's just displaying things we mention," said Batu.

Baray watched the cycle through one more time. "It's picking the images up from my interface. Wait." She dashed back through to the hold.

"Where are you going?" Batu glanced outside. The door to the bay was red-hot, air shimmering before it. "We can't hang around," he called. "They'll be through any moment." There was no answer. He cursed, undid his belt, and barked an order at the closest Tamalair. "Sit here, for goodness sake." He ran through after Baray.

The stave was on the transmat console, a physical cable winding from its manual interface port to the transmat controls. "I think it knows where the Raya is. There's a homing link between them."

"We ought to send the stave to the Raya. Dump it."

"And leave the pair of them to educate the SITAI in Concord technology? Not a good idea."

"Good point."

"We just need to know his general location."

"MyShard, where is the Raya? Give me relative co-ordinates for a transmat." MyShard reeled off a three-dimensional locator stream; Batu pushed Baray aside and punched in the co-ordinates.

"Got him," said Batu. Intense light flared from the transmat pad and then faded to reveal a bewildered Raya.

Baray jerked the Raya's stave away from the interface lead and jumped down onto the pad. The Raya looked at her, raised a hand, and then the heavy end of the stave caught it on the temple. Raya slumped to the floor, unconscious, and the stave's stasis field opaqued.

Batu smiled at Baray. "Nicely done. Now, can you just get us the heck out of here?"

* * *

"So why were you not destroyed?" The Vard's own Foreign Affairs Secretary seemed suspicious. That she was Batu's cousin, elderly and close to the Vard, had made the debriefing difficult.

"Other than through Sergeant Baray's combat skills? My shard interface had made us – me – almost invisible to their sensor sphere, cousin. The routines it created propagated through their communications 'sphere, infected most of the Orbital's sensors."

"And they are hardware based." His cousin narrowed her eyes. "So you are immune to infiltration by their nanosphere. Are you sure we cannot trade your new protocols?"

"Not without sending recipients to the SITAI after their own interfaces have been completely corrupted. I'm having a subset of shard interfaces grafted onto my existing interface to give me access to the Delhren nanospheres."

"A tricky operation."

"Dangerous. It may not work." *But I'll be helpless in Delhren space without it. What choice do I have?*

MyShard intruded. "I agree. We can hardly return to the SITAI."

"Stop listening in to my thoughts all the time!"

"That is something I now cannot avoid. It is the SITAI connections." Batu scowled, then quickly made his face expressionless to avoid sending the wrong impression.

"At least we can sell the information we have about the SITAI. That should get us something," said the secretary. She stroked an immaculate eyebrow as if to smooth the perfect lines into place. "We could, of course, sell your services as a military advisor – an observer, perhaps."

"I think the SITAI will be on the lookout for me, cousin, and may even have cleansed their sensor routines of MyShard's interference." *I doubt it, but I'd better change the subject.* "What of the Raya?"

"The Raya claims it was offering the SITAI a legitimate trade deal. Unfortunately, we cannot access your own recordings to contradict the claim."

And long may that remain so, despite the occasional frustration. "Not on the terms the Raya was offering. If the Tamalair found out, they'd revolt and every feral would be against us. What's more, Raya's negotiation was personal, not of benefit to the Delhren. Voice analysis can show I'm telling the truth. The Raya should be punished."

"So you say." His cousin sat back. "We will... isolate the pairing, make sure it has proper medical care."

"That is a start, though not ideal. I still remain the best person to deal with the SITAI on this side of Antares."

"Perhaps. So?"

"I suggest a permanent consultancy retainer in your department, cousin." Let's push. "As a floating diplomat advisor my yacht would need to be returned, of course."

The Foreign Affairs Secretary grimaced. "We'll see about the yacht, in time. However, despite my objections, it seems you have partially returned to favor. The Vard has already recommended your services to both me and Intelligence."

Strongly recommended, I think is the term. My uncle almost freaked when he discovered what the SITAI could do. Batu bowed. "Thank you, cousin. I await your suggestions as to future assignments." He turned smartly and marched out the audience chamber, all the while feeling her eyes on his back. Batu hummed to himself as he stepped into the transmat.

"Now where, MyShard?"

"May I suggest somewhere less dangerous?"

Batu smiled. "Fine. The Spyker's Rub, it is."

Light flared, and he was gone.

Aggressive Negotiations
By Tim Maguire

The scented oils were a nice touch. Their fragrance was barely noticeable, but it perfectly erased all other scents. Here, in a room just recently dug out of void-exposed rock, the change was palpable. It could have been a saloon from back home, but the effect wasn't for him. His guest had probably never been anywhere other than the depths of a mine or the bowels of a liveship. The change could only push her even further off balance.

Matriarch Melith of the Under-Fallen took a single breath and sneezed. The volcanic explosion wracked her mountainous frame, shockwaves rippling through her gnarled hide like an earthquake. Shaking her head, she glanced up at him with a cold smile.

"I have no idea why, but this room stinks." Her voice was just as gravely as the rest of her, as though she was talking through a mouthful of rock. Of course, she was a Boromite, so no doubt some of the rocks were on the inside. It would have explained a lot. "Is this what you Freeborn consider a pleasant environment? No wonder you don't want to stay."

"Guildess, thank you for coming. Hopefully we'll be able to reach an equitable arrangement." That was a lie of course. The entire point of a negotiation was to get as much for themselves as possible. This situation was no different.

"Translation: I'm going to take the dumb rock-monkeys for everything they've got." The titanic woman huffed and leaned forward on the table. It was made from Italican mistwood, which was even more expensive than the oils that scented the air, so of course she 'accidentally' scored a line across it with the nodules growing from her arm. "Well, let's get on with it then."

"While we'll leave the exact details to our shards," Janus took his seat opposite her, "the basics are very simple. We will rent this facility's C-Reactor to the guild of the Under-Fallen in return for half the materials mined here."

"I'm impressed how you utterly failed to mention that you just found that C-Reactor." That was true if irrelevant to the matter at hand. The asteroid they were sitting in had been some sort of science facility, back in the Sixth Age. That alone wasn't particularly unusual, but the facility's C-Reactor still working was. Normally an asteroid mine would be powered by a solar collector, but the Under-Fallen no longer had any, courtesy of the Ghar that had kicked them out of their mines.

Of course, they wouldn't be getting the reactor cheap. Half their production meant they'd barely be breaking even, but that didn't matter. What did matter was that the K'zana vardos was going to profit tremendously.

"Allow me to advance a different proposal," the guildess said, leaning back in her seat with a smile. "You evacuate your people and turn this facility over to me and mine. We'll pay the costs of your exploration and a nominal finder's fee, but that's all."

"And why would we do that?" Clearly the stress was getting to her. She hadn't even offered a compromise, merely demands. It was the panicky move of a novice, unworthy of a proper negotiation. "We control this facility. What do you have to give us in trade?"

"Oh, that's very easy," she said, touching a button on her belt. "Your lives."

***

"This is the worst plan ever." Reann tried not to shiver as the Delved Too Deep's cargo bay opened. They'd already depressurized, so the air bubble didn't even ripple, but that really didn't reassure him much. It was hard to shake the knowledge that all there was between them and the void was an almost invisible layer of transparent plastic. The tiny membrane shivered slightly as the gas motors pushed them out of the ship and toward the asteroid beyond.

In any sensible situation they'd have used a nanite-suspensor field to sustain the air bubble and that only as a last resort, but battle made for strange choices. The Freeborn shard would instantly pick up on that kind of power usage, so they had to go low-tech. They couldn't even carry any compression tech for worry the Freeborn would detect it, which sorely restricted their choices, but Reann was used to it.

It was the Boromite way, no matter how much they'd have liked to change. They never had access to the technology or knowledge of the planet-bound PanHuman shards, especially not the resources the Concord or the Isorians could throw around. No doubt a NuHu could throw together a stealth lander in a few hours, but the Under-Fallen couldn't, so they had to take risks instead.

"You all know why we're here!" Rock Father Lorenn bellowed over the hiss of the thrusters. "You all know what's at stake, but I want to remind you: you can't help us if you're dead, so don't!"

The whole kludged-together affair rotated slowly until its base was pointing toward the asteroid. Reann and the rest of the assault party were strapped in, reduced to helpless passengers. They couldn't even move as they drifted through the void, in case they'd destabilize the bubble's path. Their shard did all the work, cold-gas thrusters flaring to adjust course. This far from both the Dug Too Deep and the asteroid, there was no artificial gravity, so they'd just drift if they had nothing to direct them.

They touched down with only the slightest bump, bouncing slightly as the thrusters compensated. Anchors drove themselves into the rock with a soft 'thunk' and a gel seal foamed into place in the join. Within seconds, they were at least technically docked. Telltales turned green as their shard checked and then pressurized the seal.

"Reann, Dornn," Lorenn said as he began to unbuckle himself, "you're up."

"Working." The commands were simple enough that their shard was awaiting permission, which he gave the moment they'd arrived. Unlike the rest of the force, his charges had remained completely still during the transit, hibernating as they waited for orders. Orders he'd just sent. The moment the airlock opened, they scuttled through and got to work.

Reann found himself waiting impatiently for the battle to come. Compared to the void mere atoms away, the Freeborn's ire was much more attractive.

***

Long ago, Anicia had come to the conclusion that she was the only person in the K'Zana's entire domari who actually liked guard duty. Sure, sitting in the docking bay waiting for nothing to happen was only slightly more boring than the Vard's speeches, but that was kind of the point. It was the only part of the job that didn't involve either being shot at or being run ragged by a shouting vardanari, so, in a weird way, it was almost like being on vacation.

The best part of it was that there was nothing to guard against. The sole reason they weren't back in their barracks right now was the Boromites' envoy, and she wasn't going to do anything. Her ship was orbiting the asteroid and there was no way the Boromites could cross the void without being noticed. Their squad was an honor guard and nothing more.

Beyond even that, taking the base was impossible anyway. The prospectors who'd found the C-Reactor had dug straight down toward it, and the facility was little more than some rooms extending off that tunnel. Even if the Boromites did somehow manage to find a way in, they'd have to fight their way past all the defenses. It would be little more than suicide.

"What the hell is that?" Jacques asked in shock, pointing across the docking bay. The rock wall was beginning to glow, cracking and hissing as it turned a rosy red. Their shard was already analyzing it, posting black-body radiation graphs and chem-snifter reports to Anicia's monovisor, but it was well behind her memory. She'd seen this before.

"Lavamites!" The squad dove for cover a moment behind her, shouts and orders filling the once quiet air as they took up position behind their prepared barricade. Her hands moved with a life of their own, bringing up her reflex shield at the same time as booting up her rifle. As usual, she suddenly needed to pee, but that was normal, the Anicia-version of combat stress. Automated orders and positional highlights danced across her monovisor, clearing a wide space for the incoming Boromite attack.

The stone wall melted into orange-yellow magma and gnashing sword-teeth. Gnarled hides of jagged stone burst through molten rock like whales broaching the sea's surface, stabbing legs digging into the tacky stone around them and scuttling out in every direction. In moments, a tidal wave of hound-sized insects was flooding toward her.

"Open fire!" Denell yelled, firing his mag rifle into the oncoming horde. The rest of the squad joined him in a ragged chorus, training their fire to controlled bursts that shattered the first line of oncoming lavamites into clouds of bloody meat. Anicia held back, raising her compression carbine to her shoulder as she swept the battlefield.

Her carbine was easily worth more than the rest of the squad's gear put together, but it was worth it. Vastly more lethal than any mag weapon she could lift, the true beauty of any compression weapon was how much more one could do with it. The field it projected excised chunks of the battlefield as easily as it did flesh, and for one as good a shot as Anicia, that opened up a world of possibilities.

Their shard knew her proclivities, so the moment she raised her rifle to her shoulder, it filled her vision with highlights picking out appropriate targets. None of the lavamites' handlers had emerged from the quickly cooling tunnel, and shooting at the giant insects would only slow them down, not stop them. No, she needed a better target, one that would tear a hole in their charge.

Like always, their shard provided. The docking bay also doubled as the facility's stores, so it was littered with all the equipment they'd needed to build it in the first place, like, for example, a powerful frag borer capable of cutting a man-sized hole without any real fuss. More importantly, it was sitting right next to the lavamites' tunnel.

The moment she focused on it, their shard overlaid the borer's schematic, highlighting the compression field generator at its center. Losing that would cripple the machine, but it would be an explosive crippling. The shot was child's play, and she smiled as she pulled the trigger, clean through the compression field's main bus.

The borer's compression field began to collapse, forcing the contents back into normal reality through the hole she'd just made. Capacitors bent and shattered as they were squeezed out, the trapped energy exploding free. Lightning flared out in every direction with angry cracks, earthing itself in everything nearby. A dozen lavamites died instantly as the escaped forces crashed through them, those close to them staggering backward as stone shrapnel tore through their ranks. The lavamites reeled, leaving them open to her squadmates' fire.

"That should make things a little easier."

***

The tunnel was hot enough to bake a PanHuman alive, its atmosphere thick and metallic-tasting. It felt like home. Reann stood in the center, letting the 'mite reserves race past him as they abandoned the air bubble. The Freeborn's trap had blown a hole in their assault, but it wasn't going to stop them. After all, they didn't have any choice. The Under-Fallen had to win this battle.

"Reann!" Lorenn stood at the far end of the tunnel, clearly uncomfortable with the lavamites swarming around him. His hand kept reaching for the tractor maul hanging from his belt, starting and stopping every time another lavamite brushed past him. Apparently he didn't know that a 'mite was as much a threat as an unloaded plugger. "You need to clear that frag borer!"

Nice of you to make it my problem. Apparently Lorenn was some kind of tactical genius and the guildess clearly had confidence in him, but he always seemed to expect Reann to solve his problems for him. Still, that was what happened when you were one of the guild's best 'mite handlers. If there was anyone to ask, it was him.

The borer's eruption was still continuing as the last remnants of the compression field collapsed. The capacitors had almost fully discharged, just a few sparks leaping between the ruined components, but the rest of the machine was still expanding at unpleasant speed. The volatile components of the fractal generator were being vomited out of the hole, forcing out gouts of gas and shrapnel that triggered every warning their shard knew. Going anywhere near it was a death sentence, even for a Boromite.

That was what lavamites were for though. The huge rock-insects only looked like dumb beasts. In reality, they were riddled with cybernetics, far more than any PanHuman other than a NuHu. They were little more than organic drones, just as malleable and expendable as any mechanical unit.

He flicked through the perspective of a dozen 'mites in a few moments. The Freeborn squad holding the docking bay was exchanging fire with the 'mites' front rank. They were winning the duel, courtesy of them actually having cover, but their victory was a slow one. They could safely be ignored for a while.

More interesting was the frag borer itself. It looked like the same design as their own, a spherical body with a nipple-like projector. The hole had cored it directly in the projector and the collapsing compression field was forcing it slowly apart like a steel flower slowly blooming. Despite that, it was still predominantly spherical, which was all that mattered.

Make your problem their problem. It only took a moment to issue the necessary orders on his wrist-comp, their shard quickly comprehending what he wanted the 'mites to do. Images of mud and dung collecting insect-analogues flashed across his screen as the 'mites washed up against the great bulk of the frag borer, their shard reprogramming them on the fly. They stacked up behind it, climbing over each other as if using it for cover. Two simply disappeared as the compression field swallowed them whole, leaving legs sliced so fine they didn't bleed. The rest leaned up against it, pushing it off balance. For a moment it teetered, then fell.

The frag borer rolled end for end like a steel boulder as the 'mites flowed behind it, pushing it forward whenever it slowed. The compression field continued to spray random contents in every direction as it went, a 'mite disappearing in a ball of flame as a gout of hypergolic oil splashed over it, while a maintenance sled sagged as acid devoured it. More 'mites fell away as the Freeborn realized what was coming and began to hammer the madly wheeling machine, but it was too late.

A fresh gout of lightning and metal filled the air as the frag borer crashed into the Freeborn's makeshift barricade. Most of them fell back, but one went down when a steel rod smashed clean through his reflex-armor. Still, it had done its job. The malfunctioning frag borer was well clear of the tunnel entrance and the Freeborn were in disarray.

"Rock Father?" He ducked into the hanger as the Freeborn tried to rally, their fire slackened to almost nothing. "The way is clear."

***

"What is this?" Janus demanded, pointing at the battlefield imagery his shard was projecting. His training told him to remain calm, but this was well beyond what was even slightly acceptable. She had turned the negotiations into a battle.

"I am simply changing the state of the negotiations," the guildess said calmly, leaning back in her chair. "Because you hold the C-Reactor, you can set the limits of our agreement. Now, that control is in doubt. So, shall we reconsider our terms?" She produced a small flask from her belt. Opening it, she poured a small measure into the lid. "Tea?"

"Do you really think we're going to reduce the terms just because you're attacking us?" She'd clearly lost the plot. No wonder the Under-Fallen were in such a mess. "Do you really think you can brush our domari aside that easily?"

"I never said it was going to be easy," she said calmly, taking another sip of her drink. "But we are going to take control of this facility. We don't have a lot of choice really. Tell me, do you know why we agreed to your initial terms?"

"I heard a few details." The information had flown between the Freeborn shards in mere moments after it had happened. If the Under-Fallen couldn't make some money soon, they'd be forced to merge with another guild. In other words, they were desperate enough to agree to almost anything, just what any negotiator wanted to hear. "What does that have to do with you attacking us?"

"If we accept the terms you offer, we will be unable to maintain our current operations." She spoke as if it was the difference in choosing between two types of flowers, not the end of her entire guild. "So we need to change the terms." She glanced over at the screens, where her kin were spilling into the docking bay, their mag weapons firing in every direction. "So the question for you and yours is simple: do you really think you can stop us from taking that C-Reactor or not? I'll give you a little something to take home because this really isn't your fault. Twenty five percent of production plus incurred expenses."

"You're seriously going to negotiate at a time like this?" Janus shook his head. "Tell me why I shouldn't just lock you up for this." It would only take a moment to summon his guards, but he stayed his hand for the moment. There was something he wasn't getting and her confidence was only part of it.

"Because you're not certain that your men are going to win," she said with that same placid calm. "And you want to make sure that you've got someone to negotiate with in case it all goes wrong."

A retort died on his lips. She was right. The domari garrison was only a token force, nowhere near the size of the enemy that had already spilled into the docking bay. They would be overrun the moment anything went wrong. If that happened, the Under-Fallen could capture the facility entirely.

"Is this how the Under-Fallen work? Spending lives for a better negotiating position?"

"You sound like some Concord civilian," she said with a smirk. "We don't have any choice. They all know that. If we lose here, we lose everything. My people are willing to die for each other. Are yours?" She asked, taking another sip of her drink. "You sure you don't want some tea?"

***

The docking bay was lost. It was that simple. Anicia ducked behind a battered crate, a hole in its side weeping ration packs, as she searched for a shot. There were simply too many Boromites forcing their way in for them to stop. The sheer volume of fire, both from the mess of different mag guns they were carrying and the huge mass compactors their largest members were packing, was simply eroding their cover, when it wasn't just smashing people flat. Reinforcements had arrived with a light mag, but it was like trying to fight a fire with sweat alone.

That didn't mean they couldn't fight back. Three Boromites were babying their own light mag into position, and in doing so, they'd exposed themselves. A quick shot destroyed the main power bus, turning the heavy weapon into nothing more than an expensive paperweight. The three operators gaped at each other for a moment before turning toward the firefight with plug pistols in hand. Their kin didn't seem to notice, breaking out into a ragged cheer as they pushed forward.

"Sir?" Anicia turned to Denell, who was using the other side of the crate for cover as he fired into the oncoming horde. His mag pistol barely wavered as he worked it across the Boromites, barking angrily as it spat shot after shot into them. They barely seemed to notice, the only one to go down replaced almost instantly by another of his fellows. "Now would be a really good time for the back up!"

"Give it a moment longer." Denell might as well have been on a firing range for all the stress he seemed to be under. Stepping out of cover for a moment, he flicked a grenade underhand at the remaining lavamites that were scuttling toward them. The explosion was enough to drown out all the mag fire for a moment, shaking the entire docking bay as its shrapnel tore through the aliens like they were paper. "They need to be closer."

A burst of fire from behind signaled the arrival of their remaining reserves, their fellow domari racing into the room with batter drones at their side. Unfortunately, it merely turned the battle from absurdly one-sided to mostly one-sided. There were simply far more Boromites than they had in their limited garrison. No one had seriously expected an attack after all.

Anicia caught one of the lavamite handlers in her sights and that was it for the Boromite. He simply collapsed like a marionette with its strings cut and the lavamites he'd been marshaling froze as their orders simply stopped. One of his fellows took over almost immediately, but that moment's hesitation was enough to slow their advance just a little bit more. She couldn't stop them, but every moment she bought was another one where the tide could turn.

"How about now?" Denell said something extremely rude, but he nodded in agreement.

"All units, detonating the back up."

***

"We're almost there!" Lorenn's yell filled Reann's comms and it was hard not to agree with him. There just weren't enough Freeborn to stop them and they clearly didn't have any more. They'd managed to set up a light support mag in the doorway, but even that wasn't enough. Even with their prepared position, the Freeborn were being whittled away. Soon they'd either have to run or die where they stood. Either way, they couldn't win.

Admittedly, they'd paid for it. Barely one in ten of his 'mites were still functional and, from the looks of the shard, their PanHuman casualties weren't much better. Still, a victory was a victory.

And then it all went wrong.

Strobing light and sound erupted all around him. His reflex shield crashed, telltales highlighting a half dozen scrambler emitters all over the docking bay. The remaining 'mites collapsed in piles of thrashing limbs, screeching in agony. Even at this distance he could feel the stomach-twisting vibrations of the scoot mine beneath them. More scoot mines forced the Under-Fallen ranks back, driving them out of cover and into the open.

The Freeborn didn't waste the opportunity. Their fire seemed to double and without the protection of their shields and cover, it quickly found Under-Fallen flesh. Dozens of his kin went down in the first moments, the injured and untouched forced back against their will. Within moments they'd lost all the ground they'd gained.

"Form up! Form up!" Lorenn did everything short of lashing out with his tractor maul as he tried to stop them from collapsing entirely. He fired a chattering burst from his plugger, driving at least one of the Freebon back behind cover. They responded with a barrage of fire that splashed against his reflex shield in an actinic flash. He weathered the attack, waving his tractor maul wildly. "Get in there! This rock is ours!"

The Rock Father's impromptu display of courage was just what they needed. The guild's lines seemed to reassemble themselves without any obvious decision, the front line almost surprised to find themselves facing the Freeborn yet again. Reann found himself among their lines, as they all opened fire at some unspoken signal.

Assignments and directions flashed across their shard, mapping routes around the worst of the Freeborn's disruption. Reann's lead him back toward the crippled 'mites with an injunction to regain control and send them forward. That wouldn't be difficult, not between the Freeborn fire and the scoot mines and remnants of the frag borer. No, it wouldn't be difficult. Not at all.

***

"You were saying?" Janus could feel the tension draining out of him as the Boromites fell back, collapsing around their entrance tunnel. They rallied eventually, but they'd finally lost most of their horrible momentum. They were forced to advance slowly, threading a long route between the mines. While they did so, they'd have no chance to capture the facility. If it took them too long, there was a good chance the domari would be able to dispatch them entirely. "I believe we were discussing our share of the proceeds? Sixty percent was it?"

"My congratulations to your security team, they put up a much better fight than I expected." The guildess was still obnoxiously calm, even as her tea had finally run out. She merely studied the screens for a moment before shaking her head. "Allow me to revise our offer: twenty-five percent of total output."

"I think after your display, I'm going to have to raise our expectations. If nothing else, you're going to compensate our casualties' families. Say sixty-five percent of the total output." A slight scowl flitted across the guildess' face and Janus had to hide a smile. He'd finally shaken her, even slightly.

"Are you sure you're not being overconfident?" She asked, her mien of amused calm returning as quickly as it had left. "Are you that absolutely certain your men will win?"

"Maybe I'm just that certain your forces will lose." She nodded her head as though acknowledging a hit. She glanced at one of the screens and her smile tightened.

"Well, how about we see if one more gamble will do the trick then?" A tap on her belt brought up a screen between the two of them. "It is amazing how distracting a pack of 'mites can be, don't you think?"

***

"What the Vorl is that?" Jacques screamed as the entire docking bay shook like a bell. Anicia had to grab hold of her remaining cover as it tried to shake itself to pieces. There was the crunch of alloys compressing against their will and a siren wailed in the corridor. How they hadn't already set it off was a mystery, what with the firefight and everything, but she quickly pulled up her rebreather. Some idiot was trying to force the docking hatch.

The Boromites, who were clearly insane, didn't pay any attention, advancing as if they weren't about to be exposed to the void. The rest of her squad was understandably more interested in their masks than the combat. If someone was about to vent the facility, mag fire was the least of their problems.

Anicia swung out of cover for another shot, but a warning from their shard pulled her up short. The hangar door was being cut through, sections of the metal vanishing as someone attacked it with a mass compactor. She quickly snapped off a shot at their shard's estimate of the cutter's location, but nothing happened. Whoever was on the other end clearly knew better than to be standing out in the open.

Before her rifle could cycle up for another shot, a huge claw punched through the hatch and tore it out the way. A misshapen mass of rocky and riveted armor pushed its way through the docking hatch, forcing the gap wide enough for it to enter as it bellowed. The entire docking bay seemed to shake with its rage, its maw gaping to reveal an infinite abyss of hooked teeth.

The Boromite advance stalled as they all ducked for cover, clearly planning to leave the rest of the battle to the broodmother. For its part, it forced its way into the bay and crunched forward, a living avalanche of grey stone-like flesh that looked impossible to stop. It was tall enough that its shoulders brushed the roof, sparks spraying as its armor shrieked against the rough stone ceiling.

Even though it was futile, Anicia took aim. Her interface whirled for a moment, trying to pick a suitable target on the mammoth creature. Its brain was buried beneath both its stony hide and the metal infused bone beneath, far beyond the reach of her rifle. It was also the only target she had. Lining it up only took a heartbeat and the shot was perfect, linking the two of them for the briefest instant. The broodmother didn't seem to notice the impact of the shot, continuing its inexorable advance without slowing. The rest of the squad's fire didn't fare much better, sparking off its tough hide like molten metal on stone.

"Fall back!" Denell was completely calm, even as stray mag rounds sparked from his impact-cloak. He squeezed off a few shots at the more opportunistic Boromites, keeping them honest if nothing else. The surviving members of the squad obeyed with understandable alacrity, sprinting for the entrance tunnel with mag fire chasing them. "You too, Anicia!"

"Going." She snapped off one last shot at a Boromite, taking out an inopportunely exposed knee so that he fell flat on his face. It was a petty act, but that didn't stop her from smiling at it. They weren't taking this rock that easily.

They'd only partially fortified the reactor access corridor, but it would be more than enough. It was, after all, too small for the Boromite's tame monster. They'd have to try and rush them, which would result in horrendous casualties. They'd still win, but they'd pay for every step with blood.

Unfortunately, their tame monster didn't seem to notice that the hole was too small for it. It slammed into the door frame with an asteroid shaking thud and immediately thrust its cavernous maw through as though questing for grubs. For a moment, it paused and then it reared back, arm-sized claws tearing into the rock like it was wet clay.

Oh yeah, she thought as she moved further back, it can dig.

***

"Rosie! Rosie!" The assault team had become little more than a scrumball crowd now, cheering as Rosie pushed the Freeborn back all by herself. The huge broodmother was an ornery cuss at the best of times, but she was so much worse for their enemies. Mag rounds glanced off her like rain. Even the characteristic crack of a compression carbine did absolutely nothing to her, purple blood leaking from the wound to run like treacle. "Rosie! Rosie!"

Reann tried to ignore them as he fought to get the 'mites functional again. The Freeborn had ignored them once they'd stopped moving, but the double blow of scoot and scrambler had totally thrown them for a loop. Their control implants were locked into a feedback loop, sending the same commands over and over again. It was as if they were constantly shocking the 'mites' muscles and with much the same effect.

The obvious answer was to reset the operating system, but that was impossible. The same lock-outs that kept enemy IMTel from seizing command of them the minute they came into contact also stopped any other modification of their code once they'd switched to combat operations. Instead, he'd have to switch them back to a rest state, which thankfully only took a few moments of physical access.

Unfortunately, they still lay in the middle of a scoot field, which made getting to them impossible. He'd have to wait until the battle was over and they could get a disarming drone into the area. It wasn't ideal, but he couldn't change it either. All he could do was sit back and enjoy the show.

Rosie hit the exit corridor like the juggernaut she was. It was too small for her, and her roar of frustration made it clear how much she disapproved of that. Her spade-like claws dug into the wall, gouging great lines in it with a single stroke. She began to dig, thrusting herself into the gap as though fishing for the PanHumans inside. Occasional bursts of mag fire escaped from the gaps around her shoulders, spattering against the ceiling like metal rain.

There was an explosive crack and Rosie tore a whole chunk of the wall away, discarding it like a food wrapper. She forced herself deeper, her hide and armor grinding unpleasantly against the stone as she pushed her way in. A plate sheared off, Rosie's sheer fury ripping it off the moment it caught. Worming her way deeper, Rosie roared again, shaking the entire docking bay. She'd be at the C-Reactor before long.

"Everyone stand down." The guildess came across their shard with perfect clarity, her gravelly voice sounding as if she was standing right beside him. "The mission is a success. I repeat, everyone stand down."

"Guildess, this is Lorenn." Orders cascaded through their shard as Lorenn spoke, directing everyone to hold for the moment. "My apologies, but can you provide the pass phrase? I need to ensure that you're not being held hostage."

"Lorenn, if you don't stop messing around this instant, I'll break you down to spill sorter before you can blink."

"That's you alright," Lorenn said, and Reann could hear the smile in his voice. "All units stand down. We've won." Rosie simply stopped, pausing as if frozen. After a brief moment, she stepped back, now as placid as an ox. Her operator raised his head slightly from his cupola and made an all-clear sign. "Medics! Stabilize the wounded and get ready for evac. Take them in via Rosie's new door. Someone fix that would you? I get the feeling the guildess would like to undock sometime this century."

A ragged cheer filled the air, everyone too tired to do more to celebrate. Reann's legs went out from under him in relief, exhaustion finally making its way past the adrenaline. The battle had lasted for a scant few minutes, but it had felt like hours. He could see others doing the same, collapsing where they stood to slump against what cover had survived the battle.

Still, despite their exhaustion, he could see smiles spreading between them. One was growing on his lips. They'd done it. Tired laughter and smug boasts rose from the more closely-knit squads. After months of gnawing worry, they'd finally secured the Under-Fallen's future.

Their children had a home again.

***

"Guildess?" A part of Janus' mind was worrying over how he was going to explain this whole mess to the Vard. Not only had he gotten truly terrible terms from the Under-Fallen, far below even the most conservative projections, he'd also gotten a sizable chunk of his security team injured or killed. Their shard had already pulled together the casualty count. There was only one true death, thank the spirits, but there was still going to be a lot of costly regenerations. "A moment please?"

"I'm not going to change my terms," she said, turning her chair back to face him. Her placid calm hadn't even cracked when he'd agreed to her original terms as he'd watched her pet monster tear its way toward the C-Reactor, and it certainly didn't now. "I trust you're not going to try something stupid, are you?"

"I doubt it would work." That summoned a brief smile from her. "No, it's just, you took a huge risk. How did you know that it would pay off?"

"I didn't." The guildess turned fully away from the doorway. "Do you know why it is that I won this battle and you didn't?"

"I'm going to go with you had a giant monster and we didn't." That got another thin smile.

"True, but not what I was thinking." She pulled out her canteen and tried to empty out a little more of her tea, but there was nothing left. "You lack conviction, simple as that. Your domari fought well, but they weren't willing to risk their lives for victory. Neither were you. I was. I have lost family, loved ones, and even children today, but I know that every single one of them went willingly. I will mourn them, I will scatter their ashes, and I will do that with my head held high, because I know my guild will survive for one more day as a result."

"I understand." He actually did. The Under-Fallen had gambled everything on the battle, purely because they'd had no choice but to gamble it all. It must have been an incredibly difficult decision to make, but in the end it had been no decision at all. After all, who willingly waited to die?

In a way, it was kind of impressive. At the moment they were enemies, but what kind of allies would they make? The K'Zana had many other enemies and they needed all the allies they could get. Perhaps this battle had not been lost at all. Now that the K'Zana and the Under-Fallen were bound together, what could they achieve combined? Far more than they could apart, that was for sure.

Janus smiled to himself as the guildess turned and glided away. It was time for the true negotiations to begin.

Blind
By Craig Gallant

"**W**ho fired that shot? Dammit, who fired that shot?"

The fighting bridge of the Loyal Courser was quiet, separated from the horror and violence of battle by holographic repeaters and tactical displays. Captain Rollen Stihl's roar echoed off the softly-curving bulkheads.

"We need to minimize damage to her hull, damn you!" He tried to control his anger, fingers digging deep into the arms of his command chair. A lifetime's designs were coming to a head, dependent upon taking this prize with minimal damage.

"Rho battery fired with double shot, Captain." Alyce Aymes, his quartermaster, kept her voice light despite the stress of battle.

Stihl cursed. The batteries on the lower gun decks were nearly all mag weapons, large mass drivers firing heavy slugs. Occasionally, the ammunition feeder system of one of the older weapons would stutter, resulting in an empty barrel, often missed in the tumult of battle, followed by a double shot that, although far more damaging, was usually wildly inaccurate and damaging to the gun.

Dagor Puk, his Mhagris master gunner, checked all weapons before battle. But a standard system diagnostic might not catch the problem.

Stihl felt his lips twist in frustration.

"I want each mag battery manually checked before the next salvo." The words grated in his throat as he forced his grip to ease on the arms of his chair.

"Sir." Aymes replied, turning to mutter to the battery commanders.

Within the forward view field, the massive colony ship was beginning to list. His prey was much larger than his own ship, and far stronger. But their initial ruse had allowed them to close to within five thousand yan before firing. It was his ship's only chance against such a large foe.

Most of the damage on the other ship, dealt with plasma blooms from his few advanced batteries, was centered around the drive nodes at the vessel's stern. That accounted for much of the strange cargo jammed into the Loyal Courser's small hold. No matter how far his infamy spread, history would only rate him as a pirate captain, his realm relegated to the deck of his small cruiser and the cold, desolate base he called home. If he wished to accomplish more, he needed to think on a grander scale.

And so here he found himself, facing down the powerful guns of another vardosi colony ship; putting his life, his reputation, and the safety of his crew on the line.

A flash of plasma erupted across the target's flank, well forward of the drives, and he felt his shoulders tense again.

"Watch the fall of those shots! If we damage the doors, or her transfer equipment, we might as well not even be here!"

"Sorry, sir." It was hard to tell when a Mhagris was angry or chastened, but Dagor seemed contrite.

Stihl forced himself to take several slow, steadying breaths. He rarely envied the witless tools of the PanHuman Concord, but he imagined that, swimming through the nanosphere soup of a Concord warship's Integrated Machine Intelligence, a commander would never have to spend so much of his time explaining himself, plagued by constant miscommunication and confusion.

Of course, the trade-off for such clear communication was the loss of your humanity. Better to suffer frustration now than lose yourself in the bland, impersonal fog of the IMTel forever.

He spun his chair around to glare at the volume of glittering mist trapped within a suspensor field behind him. The vardosi were far less freehanded with their machine servants than the Concord or Isorians, but even his Freeborn cousins would have been shocked at the state in which he kept the cloud of nanites that comprised the Loyal Courser's machine intelligence shard.

"Dog, status on target." He had been calling the thing Dog for so long, he had forgotten its chosen designation long ago.

The shard's voice appeared to float out of the air as it responded. "Return fire has dropped by 73% since the beginning of the engagement. Analysis of the data captured through the target's hull temperature and signal traffic would indicate decompression through 36% of the interior spaces with a commensurate loss of life among the crew."

Stihl turned back to look into the viewing screen. The loss of life was inconsequential at this point, but the damage to the ship was regrettable.

"Aymes." His eyes remained on the dying starship. "I think it's time the boarding parties were sent across."

"Yes, sir." She nodded and turned to leave the fighting bridge. He stopped her with one raised finger.

"Spare those you can, but time is of the essence." Even as he spoke, a barrage from the dying ship shivered through the Loyal Courser's bones and he gritted his teeth. "And try to do it before they take my ship apart, will you?"

She nodded again and was gone.

"Sir," Dog's voice was bland as he demanded. "Hull integrity along the dorsal mainline is down to 87%. Another strike such as that last and we risk a massive breach."

He forced himself to settle back in his chair. "Well, then Alyce better hurry up."

The deck beneath them shook again, incongruous in the humming near-silence of the fighting bridge.

"Each such impact endangers our cargo, Captain Stihl." The hissing voice was like a shriek in the relative calm, and several crew members threw disconcerted looks over their shoulders at the red-headed stranger standing beside the captain, one long-fingered hand caressing the strange equipment that had been recently installed by the captain's chair. The ghostly blue-white glow emanating from containment vessels running throughout the pedestal bathed the creature's long, gaunt face in otherworldly light.

Trust for any NuHu was hard to come by on a Freeborn crew. Most of the freakishly tall mutants were willing servants of the Concord or the Isorians, and they used their incredible powers to hunt and destroy the Freeborn, not to serve them. But Mei-Hana was a renegade. Something had driven her from the comfort of the Concord, and drove her now toward a terrible revenge of her own.

Stihl nodded, not deigning to cast a glance at the towering, hooded woman. "I am aware, Mei-Hana."

"Any damage to either of my systems will render all of our efforts useless. Neither of us will secure what we wish from this arrangement then."

He snarled, but nodded again. "I said I was aware."

A violent tremor swept beneath their feet as the prey continued to fight back.

One more blow like that and the Loyal Courser could well shiver apart around them.

***

The Golden Venture was the crown jewel of the far flung Pharaxi trade empire. Although not nearly so powerful as the Oszoni or the other Great Houses, the Pharaxi were definitely on the rise, having taken full advantage of a recent fall in fortune of their chief rivals.

The Golden Venture was the latest, and most powerful, sign of that rise.

As much space station as starship, the Golden Venture had been constructed in secret so as not to attract the unwanted attention of the more powerful vardos. Only the most powerful houses could field such enormous world ships, and that status was guarded most jealously. They were trading centers, military installations, and defenders of a clan's most secret assets.

The Golden Venture was the first such ship the Pharaxi had been able to construct in living memory. When deployed, it would stand guard over a newly-discovered system's riches; standing sentinel over the rise of the house to the very heights of vardosi society.

The Pharaxi had spirited nearly all of their material wealth into this backwater system. The gate leading here was locked within a series of solar storms that had not abated for generations. It was a barren system, useless save for modest iron deposits discovered by a Pharaxi drone during a routine survey mission.

It was a system perfect for housing this particular secret project.

The fleets of the Pharaxi had been repositioned to avoid

arousing suspicion, their main strength rotating through the system to guard the Venture throughout its construction.

But now it was nearly finished. The fleets had been dispatched to prepare for the flagship's arrival, and the Pharaxi were poised to take their rightful place among the Great Houses.

Admiral Bha ko-Rhan settled back in the massive command throne of the Golden Venture, surveying his domain with a contented smile. If he was allowed to retrain command of the vessel once it arrived on station, it would be an enormous boost to the prestige of his own doma.

The smile faltered. He had commanded some of the most important Pharaxi warships during his career, but his rise lacked any one great accomplishment that would single him out above the other candidates. Without that, securing command of the Golden Venture would be a harrowing, political struggle.

Still, his doma was well-versed in vardosi politics. Which was just as well; the chances of a great victory falling into his lap in this backwater system were slim.

Almost as if on cue, a soft, atonal alarm washed over the general murmur of the command deck.

"Admiral, we have an unsanctioned gate transition." The communication tech spoke in a calm voice.

Ko-Rhan leaned forward, resting a forearm on his knee as he peered into the swimming chaos of holographic vector lines and symbols at the heart of the command center. With the rest of the Venture's fleet gone ahead, the ship was more vulnerable than usual, but he was unconcerned. The Pharaxi had never launched a more formidable vessel. It could deal with anything that might have stumbled through the gate, no matter their intentions.

"Have they identified themselves?" He grunted the words, his hands twitching. The Venture had not yet fired her weapons in anger, and he found the sudden temptation nearly overwhelming.

"No, sir." Another watch officer snapped, turning to face him, her shaven head gleaming in the gentle light. "They've made no report at all, sir."

"We're receiving a signal, Admiral." The voice of the communications tech faded away into disbelief, causing most of the other members of the command crew to crane around to stare at him.

After a moment of heavy silence, ko-Rhan slapped the arm of his command throne, the sharp report sending the crew members near him jumping. "What is it, damn you?"

The man turned slowly, as if in a dream, his eyes wide. "She says she's the Loyal Courser, sir."

Ko-Rhan stared incredulously at the man. There was no way the Loyal Courser had just gated into his system. The flagship of the most notorious unsanctioned pirate in known vardosi space could not have just fallen into his lap.

"The ship is venting atmosphere." One of the gunnery officers muttered. "There's extensive damage."

The watch officer broke the stunned silence. "She's requesting permission to dock."

The Golden Venture, as all ships of her class, had a docking bay that could accept all but the largest colony ships. Captain Stihl's Loyal Courser was little more than a light cruiser, and should easily fit within the massive facility.

"What in the name of the Builders could Stihl be thinking?" Ko-Rhan muttered under his breath, but the sensor chief heard and responded.

"It's hard to be certain, sir. The sensors are having a hard time penetrating the debris cloud coming off the ship. There might be a reactor breach, as well, that could account for some of the interference. From what life signs we can pick up through the mess, it would appear that there are very few survivors."

"Probably bit off more than they could chew." A gunner said with a tight smile.

Captain Stihl was a figure of myth to most of the vardosi, having been cast from his clan when he was still a young man. He had plagued the star lanes and Antarean gates ever since, just as likely to prey upon vardosi vessels as Concord, Algoryn, or Isorian. The officers and sailors of the vardosi hated the man both for the danger he posed, and the complication he represented in their interactions with the other polities of the Determinate.

"She's coming into range of the outer defenses." Captain Jhessik, his second in command, seemed more subdued than most of the other crew members. "There's extensive hull damage. It looks pretty ugly, sir."

Ko-Rhan felt the grin stretching across his face and made no effort to hide it. With Captain Rollen Stihl in his containment hold, continued command of the Golden Venture would be all-but assured.

"Give them permission to approach." He settled back in his throne, drawing one knuckle back and forth over his chin. "Have the outer defenses stand down. Prepare the main docking bay."

Tyder Jhessik coughed, leaning down to speak in muttered tones. "Sir, do you think that's wise? If we allow her within the defenses, she could strike."

A hundred possibilities ran through ko-Rhan's mind, and the smile began to fade.

"Admiral, she's on auxiliary power, her reactors are nearly cold." The weapons officer reported. "There can't be more than five souls aboard. I would say the threat she poses is minimal."

"If that ship rams us, even at her current speed, the damage would be catastrophic." Jhessik's voice was hard as he glared at the other officer.

But the admiral was not about to lose this opportunity. Ko-Rhan nodded. "Tell them to make the entire approach at docking speed or we will blow her back through the gate. Have all weapons systems trained on her the entire time."

He saw his own grin, now returned full force, mirrored on the faces of his loyal crew. They, too, sensed the momentous events unfolding around them. There wasn't a man or woman aboard the Golden Venture whose career would not be enhanced by having been aboard this day.

But Commander Jhessik was still not satisfied. "Admiral, do you think we should let her into the bay? Perhaps you should send a squad of vardanari to inspect her first."

His grin soured and turned to glare at his subordinate. "Cowardice does not become you, Commander. Sensors would have picked up any danger Stihl or his scow could represent."

Jhessik looked away with a sharp nod. "As you say, sir." Ko-Rhan allowed his smile to return. He was feeling magnanimous. "Don't worry, Tyder. They pose no danger at their present speed, no matter Stihl's trickery." He turned to look at the blinking signal in the center of the viewing field. "But I'll tell you this, my friend: I don't feel like this is a trick. Stihl met his match, and a higher power is now dropping him into our grasp." Jhessik nodded again, but would not meet his gaze.

Oh, well. There would be plenty of time for the man to come around. Or, if he didn't, there were plenty of candidates eager to replace him.

"You have the watch, Commander." Ko-Rhan stood, straightening his tunic so the honors were aligned. "I will be in my cabin, preparing."

Jhessik looked at him in confusion. "Sir?"

"I will be in the main boarding lounge to greet Captain Stihl and to accept his surrender. Notify me when they enter the docking bay."

He smiled at the thought of the recorder drones hovering overhead, imagining himself in his dress uniform, accepting Stihl's sword.

***

The navigation bridge of the Concord Combined Command battlecruiser Lumen was quiet as they approached the gate. It was always quiet, but there was a heavy weight to this silence that seemed more ominous than tranquil.

Commander Pehn Kowroon sat at his station in the command center of the Lumen and closed his eyes to focus on his communion with the mighty ship's IMTel shard. Conveyed through the combined efforts of billions of nanites pervading the atmosphere of the vessel through the implants and interfaces of her crew, the shard collated emotions, thoughts, and impulses into a calm, reasoned joint intelligence superior to anything an unenhanced crew would have been capable of achieving alone.

All visual contact with the universe beyond the armored hull had been severed when the ship began its descent into the photosphere of the Antarean nexus. All imaging apparatus had been withdrawn, all observation bays closed, and all vision plates sealed against the fury of the celestial engine. They sailed blind through a sea of numbers, now, wholly dependent upon their shard to find the ancient gate suspended deep within the convection zone of the enormous artificial star.

Pehn found these moments, when the shard took full control of the ship, to be the most peaceful of any tour. Without that shared consciousness, the interminable period between the initial descent and translation through the gate would be an agony. But the unique bond between the Integrated Machine Intelligences of Concordian naval vessels and their crews gave a great deal of comfort, even on the eve of battle.

He thought about the current assignment. It seemed simple enough. The feckless Freeborn that controlled commerce and the bulk of transportation among the local gates had requested the Concord Combined Command's assistance in dealing with one of their own. A Freeborn pirate had been raiding the local space lanes from a hidden lair in a barren system. The gate to that system had only recently been discovered, and the Freeborn had sent out their request. In their infinite wisdom, the unified shard of the C3 had decided to dispatch the Lumen to eliminate the threat and pave the way for a more lucrative partnership with the Freeborn House rising to prominence in the region.

They were to report to the system, where a local Freeborn starship, the Even Hand, would guide them in, and then eliminate the threat.

Pirates were a scourge on the Determinate, and Pehn, in so far as he thought about it at all, could fully understand the benefits of destroying this particular nest of vipers, regardless of local politics.

But the beauty of the IMTel, of course, was that he didn't have to think about it. The nanosphere contained within the Lumen, infused and informed by the greater shard of the C3 before their departure, would ensure that their actions were in the best interests of the Panhuman Concord.

His eyes twitched as he felt the approaching gate. He saw it, in his mind, as a huge glowing halo, opening darkly as they approached.

Opening his eyes, Pehn watched as the command crew of the Lumen prepared to translate through the gate and into the pirate system. Each station snapped into readiness, sensors coming on-line, weapon systems powering up; all the preparations necessary for entering unknown, potentially hostile territory.

"It is unfortunate that we require the assistance of barbarians to complete this task." He jumped. Pehn had forgotten that Va'Rana, NuHu Mandarin and personal envoy of the C3 shard, was standing behind him.

Even after several tours with the being, Pehn did not feel entirely comfortable in his presence.

Pehn coughed gently, turning to nod at the towering form. Va'Rana stood head and shoulders above any of the Lumen's crew. Even Pehn, as tall as he was, had to crane his neck to meet the creature's strange, glittering eyes.

As close as Pehn felt to the Lumen's shard, and the other, even more powerful sanctioned shards, he found the presence of a NuHu daunting. The mutants interacted directly with a nanosphere, without the interface units, implants, or personal boosters humans required. Va'Rana was typical of the breed; slight of frame but enormously tall. And they had a tendency, at least in Pehn's experience, to hold the rest of humanity, even their fellow Concordians, in a type of vaguely benign contempt.

Their opinions of other humans, especially the nanosphere-enslaving Freeborn, was considerably lower, and considerably less benign.

"Well, we could hardly be expected to find the pirates on our own." He tried to smile, but as was often the case in the presence of a NuHu Mandarin, Pehn was distracted and out of sorts. "We've an entire system to search. Even focusing the entire shard to the task, it would take too long."

Va'Rana snorted, but he made no further argument. The glittering eyes closed, his gaunt face losing its tension as he communed directly with the warship's IMTel.

Pehn turned back to ponder the repeater's static with a sigh. He was no more excited to deal with a Freeborn captain than the Mandarin. Too many things could go wrong when you tried to coordinate military action between the smooth, single-minded intention of a C3 warship and the chaotic mess of an unintegrated Freeborn vessel.

The Freeborn, as they had been called, valued individual freedom, whatever that meant, over the peace, prosperity, and happiness that an IMTel society could offer the vast majority of its citizens. In his mind, that was not just criminal, it was insane.

He looked up again as the ship's shard notified him that they were about to translate through the gate. His mind supplied the visuals from memory. He imagined the flash of bright light as countless photons escaped the convection zone to stab through the gate into the system beyond. He could see again the streamers of burning gas and heat that a ship left behind as it streaked through, silent and majestic.

Visual systems snapped back on-line as he shook himself out of the daydream. Scanners swept the entire system in a moment, and a holographic representation swirled into being in the middle of the command center: six lifeless planetoids spun endlessly around a dim, red-hued star. There were no signals detected; no sign of habitation on any of the surfaces currently facing the Lumen.

"Typical." Va'Rana ground between clenched teeth.

"They'll be here." Pehn stood and gave a slight stretch.

The Lumen, of course, had arrived at exactly the moment the C3 had intended. Under the guidance of the IMTel, there was never any question of early or late.

The Freeborn, on the other hand, were notorious for their tardiness.

"Nevertheless, we should move deeper into the system. The lair won't be this far out." The ship was underway, through the guidance and surety of the IMTel, before he finished saying the words.

They had not yet reached the orbit of the outermost planet when Pehn became aware of another ship coming through the gate behind them. A woman on sensor watch turned to look at him with a slight nod. The central hologram shifted, shunting the image of the system aside to show an expanded view of the massive gate and the ship sailing through it, ribbons of fire trailing back into the darkness.

"You see, Va'Rana?" He forced himself to smile up at the man. "Hardly late at all."

"By the standards of their own debased race, perhaps." The NuHu growled, glaring down at the holographic image like a giant menacing a tiny ship.

The Freeborn vessel looked like a warship, but then most of their starships did. As a starborn race, they had an understandable paranoia when it came to defending their homes. But this looked even more martial than others he had seen. It was nearly of a size with the Lumen, with weapon blisters studded back along its length.

There was scoring on the ship's flanks; dark gauges clawed from her armor, centered around her propulsion systems. It seemed the Even Hand had good reason to be late.

A face appeared, floating in the midst of the other images.

The man's hair was completely shorn, revealing several ports and embedded interface units that would allow him to plug into systems that a Concord captain would have been able to access remotely through the ubiquitous nanosphere. He suppressed a shudder, not wanting to alienate the man in the first moments of contact. The shard identified the Freeborn captain as Nickai Feraut, but he knew no more about him than that.

And that was another problem with this affair. Had the other ship been a C3 vessel, the two IMTel shards would have interfaced immediately; he would have had free and open access to any piece of information about the other ship or her captain that he wished. Instead, he was left to stumble his way through ancient, archaic social rituals.

"Commander, welcome to Pharaxi space." Mentioning that this operation was taking place in a system claimed by his people was both unnecessary and annoying.

He smiled and nodded as he returned the greeting, but Pehn felt a growing sense of unease. He knew it almost certainly emanated through the shard from his crew, rather than himself.

It would have been customary to allow the local vessel to take the lead as they moved deeper into the system, but Pehn could not bring himself to trust the man, or his crew, that far.

"Thank you, Captain." He hesitated, and then smiled. "It looks as if you've taken some damage. Do you need assistance?" The man's face twisted with annoyance. "No, thank you, Commander. Merely a skirmish. With the inestimable Captain Stihl, in fact. But the Even Hand was too much for him, and he fled. I do not believe we will find the good captain at home today, which should make our work here considerably easier."

Pehn leaned down toward the image and looked more closely at the damage on the other ship. Despite the strikes around her drive elements, it was moving easily enough. They must have repaired the worst of the damage.

But still, there was no denying the ship was damaged ...

"Would you like us to take the lead as we move in, Captain? You can send us the coordinates of the pirate's lair; we will shield you from any automatic defenses as we make our approach."

A bitter look crossed the man's face, but he nodded. "That would probably be best." He chewed out the words. "Thank you."

Pehn nodded, maintaining his pleasant, professional facade. "Very well, then."

The relief he felt through his connection with the IMTel was almost embarrassing, but the visual connection had faded, and he no longer needed to hide his emotions from the Freeborn captain. He sighed, then turned to Va'Rana. "Well, that should keep them out of the way. We will neutralize the pirate base before they even come within range."

The Mandarin grunted, his glittering eyes distant. "The sooner we finish with these barbarians, the better for us all."

They sailed deeper into the system, altering course to follow the directions of the Freeborn Captain, for the cold, dark rock of the fourth planetoid, and the lair of Captain Rollen Stihl.

***

The corridors of the Golden Venture echoed with the hard crack of his boot heels as Admiral ko-Rhan rushed to meet his destiny. Behind him, several vardanari hurried to keep up. They carried rare plasma carbines, power distribution matrices tied to the soldiers' minds through hardwire links rather than the technology's usual dependence upon a saturated nanosphere.

The halls were nearly empty, work crews were off-shift, and there would be no civilians aboard until they reached their final station. Currently, only members of the Pharaxi vardanari and domari were aboard, a skeletal, military crew overseeing the final shakedown of the vessel and its preparation to take its place in history.

Ko-Rhan found himself wishing for a larger audience, but the workers and warriors would have to suffice. Several recording drones buzzed along behind him, capturing the moment for posterity. The name of Bha ko-Rhan would go down in the annals of the Pharaxi for all the Ages. When he marched Stihl and his surviving minions off the shattered wreck of their stolen ship, the images would be broadcast to every Freeborn fleet throughout the Determinate.

No one could deny him command of the Golden Venture now.

The battered form of the Loyal Courser was settling into the central berth when ko-Rhan and his escort came into the primary boarding lounge. Ominous creaks, bangs, and squeals rolled through the empty corridors as the ship settled on the docking buffers behind the massive blast doors. Ko-Rhan watched with a growing smile as the vacuum in the enormous chamber beyond the armored glass was expelled.

The once-sleek ship had taken a pounding. Massive rents in its flanks oozed a dark smoke that swirled in the clear atmosphere of the bay. Dark scorch marks slashed the hull, criss-crossing each other in bubbling furrows across the armor.

"Admiral, the repair remotes have begun to report their initial findings." Commander Jhessik's voice was harsh, buzzing at them from a comm panel beside the big doors. "There are four lifeforms inside. The reactors are cold; there's not enough power to pose a credible threat."

Ko-Rhan's smile widened. He had known it. He had felt it. Somewhere out amidst the countless gates of the Determinate, Rollen Stihl had met his match. The admiral didn't know how the pirate ship had found itself limping into his system, and he could not have cared less. The ship was here now, and it was his.

Four crewmen would have been barely sufficient to sail the Courser; they posed no threat to his beloved ship. This was fate.

He imagined the decks of the Loyal Courser littered with dead from their final battle. He could almost see her operations deck awash with blood, life support systems struggling to wash the stench of burned flesh from the air.

Someone out there had defeated Rollen Stihl, but it would be Admiral Bha ko-Rhan who would claim the glory.

The umbilicus shuddered slightly as it extended through the space between the boarding gate and the ship. The material of the bridge pressed against the skin of the dying ship and lights along the tunnel's pristine white length flashed green to indicate a solid seal.

The span shook slightly as the airlock on the Courser opened, the atmosphere within the tube equalizing. The bridge's walls were opaque, revealing only vague shadows within. Four figures began to cross with a slow, halting pace. One, more wounded than the others, leaned against a comrade for support.

A series of moans and whistles could be heard through the thick bone-colored blast doors as the systems cycled, ensuring that no contaminants -- biological, mechanical, or nanospore - reached the Golden Venture.

An eerie stillness settled upon the receiving area as the systems lapsed into silence. Ko-Rhan rubbed his hands in anticipation. He had never met Stihl in person, but the man was infamous throughout the Determinate.

His grin turned cruel as he imagined the rush of satisfaction he would experience upon seeing the man, bloody and bowed, for the first time.

***

Pehn Kowroon rose out of his gentle reverie knowing that the Lumen and her Freeborn escort were approaching the dead rock of the fourth planetoid. He looked up into the holographic return and watched as the cold, airless spheroid tumbled through space ahead of them.

His eyes flickered as he checked the log of the last several minutes, assuring himself that there had been no further energy readings coming off the object. If this was the lair of the infamous pirate, it would appear that he was, indeed, away.

"It would not surprise me if the barbarians had led us to the wrong system entirely." Va'Rana's voice broke into the calm peace of the chamber.

Pehn looked sideways at the NuHu, schooling his features to a serene stillness he did not feel. Va'Rana was sitting with his legs crossed beneath him, floating above the deck plates at waist-height.

There were countless marvels possible in a nanite-enhanced culture, and the NuHu were far more capable than most. But he would never grow accustomed to seeing someone float in mid-air.

"We need to have a little faith, I think." Pehn turned back to look into the visual field. All around him, his command crew went about their tasks with quiet precision. Many rested against the high backs of their station chairs, eyes closed, processing information and analyses being passed along the ship's shard. Dipping his own mind into the steady stream of communication, he saw that the symbiotic consciousness had only slightly more faith in the Freeborn than the NuHu Mandarin.

"If it truly is a pirate enclave, they would hardly hang out a sign." He tried to make light of their situation, but the farther they got from the global shard of the Concord Combined Command, the more the individual experiences of the Lumen and her crew would color the shard. Sailing through a strange, dead system, followed by a large barbarian warship restrained by only the most tentative web of alliances, searching for the lair of a notorious killer of ships and men, was bound to have an effect eventually; even on a crew as seasoned and disciplined as the Lumen's.

The soft lighting of the command center dipped as an amber hue temporarily washed through the peaceful blue. A gentle tone sounded, and Pehn felt himself relax, the slight tension of his doubt easing, replaced with his usual confidence.

"Commander, systems have detected energy spikes across the planet as we crossed the terminator." The voice was calm, as was the Lumen's shard.

In the holographic field, three crimson icons appeared on the featureless expanse of the dead world below them.

"We are being scanned. Ten more energy returns have registered."

The image of the planet changed again as a scattering of icons joined the first three.

"It would appear our allies have not steered us wrong after all." He smiled slightly, enjoying the sour look on Va'Rana's long, sallow face.

"Someone please order our consort to widen the distance between us to ten thousand yan. We will approach first, assess the situation, and prepare a response."

When the fighting started, the last thing he wanted was a crude Freeborn vessel without the slightest sense of military discipline lobbing shots at a target standing on the far side of his own ship. There was no way the ancient technology and chaotic indiscipline of the Freeborn ship, no matter how well-meaning her crew, could match the ability of the Lumen. They were locked into glacial, human reaction speeds, their AI shard shackled to physical control interfaces and the whims of its masters.

The nanosphere of the Lumen was charged with purpose as the ship dove for the planet's surface. The soul of the vessel was bent to a single purpose; the eradication of the pirate stronghold coming alive below.

As they swooped down on their prey, Pehn was glad to hear the Freeborn ship acknowledge his order. They slowed their progress, widening the gulf between them.

The Lumen would handle Stihl and his stronghold. The Even Hand could watch, and then return to their people with the news that the PanHuman Concord had fulfilled its obligations.

The Lumen's engines pulsed, pushing it forward, as her plasma batteries began to glow with accumulated energy, ready to unleash the fury of a sun on the rock below.

***

Ko-Rhan was nearly fidgeting with anticipation. The armored doors remained shut, the mechanical sounds of their inner workings seeming to go on and on without hope of ever opening.

His future awaited him on the other side of this moment, and it could not resolve itself fast enough for his peace of mind. He found his formal dress boot tapping impatiently on the decking and forced himself to stop. The guards standing behind him, plasma carbines at the ready, were as still as statues, their discipline apparent, and he refused to show any sign, to them or to the recorder drones hovering behind, that he was any less controlled.

At last, after what seemed like an eternity, the deck beneath his feet started to vibrate, and a crack of blinding light flashed through the thick doors as they began to part.

Ko-Rhan refused to shield his eyes from the glare, and so squinted into the brightness, imagining the brave visual he presented to the recorders, standing tall, silhouetted by the lights of the boarding terminal. He smiled, imagining that picture splashed across every news feed in the Pharaxi fleet.

As the doors opened, four shadowy, backlit figures emerged from the wash of light. Behind him, ko-Rhan could feel his guards tense, their weapons firm.

The grumbling of the mechanisms faded, and a stretch of silence scratched across the admiral's nerves. Before he could say anything, however, the injured pirate slumped against the figure supporting it. They both went down with a muffled grunt.

The honor guard moved out to either side, their weapons steady, and the two pirates who had remained standing raised their hands. Ko-Rhan scanned their faces quickly, but didn't recognize either of them. He moved toward the two figures on the floor, aware of his guards' nervous tension. But he needed to play the part, especially with the drones recording every moment. He could not be seen to hang back.

As he approached the pair on the floor, he saw that the injured man wore a dull, brown coat with an uninspired cut; just the kind of gear the fashion-blind corsair captain was known to favor. The hair on the bowed head was white, shaven along one side to reveal implanted ducts and ports that most civilized vardosi hid behind masks and plates.

It was Rollen Stihl. It had to be. The man was famous for flaunting his cranial augmentations like some uncouth Mhagris barbarian.

Ko-Rhan schooled his features into a mask of calm contempt as one of the drones hummed around to catch his profile. He opened his mouth to declare the notorious pirate a captive of the Pharixi, then stopped.

Something was wrong with the man's profile. It lacked the aquiline nose and proud forehead of the famous pirate. His skull was freshly shaven; the ports too basic and too few.

The crewman who had collapsed with the supposed captain looked up with a savage grin on her long face.

A face he recognized from countless security reports.

Alyce Aymes, Stihl's quartermaster and second in command of the Loyal Courser, rose before him. She was tall, towering over the admiral, and there was no sense of surrender in her stance now.

The man he had taken to be Captain Stihl rose as well. He was a stranger, his face no more recognizable than the nameless pirates behind him, their downcast faces rising with grins of their own.

But the worst expression was on the hard face of Aymes, as she looked around, noting the guards, the drones, and finally the admiral.

She barked a laugh that caused him to jump despite himself.

***

Pehn felt the launch of the defensive drones from the base below through the Lumen's IMTel shard. A gently-rising cloud of sensor contacts drifted upwards, through the thin atmosphere of the dead planet, targeting the two ships in orbit.

"Engage defensive systems?" The soft voice of the weapons officer was tentative, and Pehn looked at her with one raised eyebrow as he realized that the warm sense of consensus and certainty of the IMTel shard was colored with a vague confusion.

There was something wrong with the situation below, and enough of his people were aware of it that it was affecting the usually-placid aura of the shard.

"Are there more weapons down there? Any other sign of activity?" He turned to look at the flickering holographic display, running and changing like ink spilled on glass in response to his thoughts, bringing the surface into close relief.

The cold stone of the planetoid's crust was riven with buckles and fissures. Hidden within the cracks, folds, and creases were several armored entrances, at least one large enough to accept a medium-sized starship.

As he watched, he saw four flashes of light spill out onto the pock-marked plains as hatches lifted open, the nose cones of missiles sliding into launch position.

"Fire on the drones!" He heard the rising concern in his voice and cursed, but the data streaming into his mind identified the missiles as capital-class weapons, nearly as large as those carried by the Lumen. If they were as advanced as they appeared to be, they posed a very real threat.

How had a filthy Freeborn pirate managed to acquire such weapons? The Freeborn were as capable of fielding advanced tech as anyone else in the Determinate, but he had never heard of a pirate acquiring even a single such ship killer.

The weapons officer released control of the ship's systems without comment. Sprays of plasma and graceful arcs of solid slugs fell down through the gravity well toward the rising drones, tearing the first flight into burning shreds before it could even pull free of the atmosphere. However, several more waves swept up behind the clouds of destruction. On the surface, the four launchers were venting gas in preparation for launch.

"You need to punch a hole through the drones. Take out the missiles before they clear their tubes."

Va'Rana's inhuman voice rasped against Pehn's nerves as he sat rigidly in his chair. The drones were firing now, but it was a dispersed spray of harmless light, the range too great to pose any real threat.

Although the attacks were blinding his sensors to the launch sites below.

"Concentrate all fire on the center of the drone mass." He leaned forward, trying to ignore the looming NuHu at his side. If those missiles launched, they would reach cruising speed in moments, crashing through the masking cloud of drones without any warning at all.

He watched as his plasma batteries and defensive cannons narrowed their focus, burning a glittering hole in the center of the drone screen.

He felt a jolt in his back; feedback from the ship's IMTel shard. The Even Hand had fired its weapons, despite his orders. They must have panicked in the face of the rising drone cloud, or perhaps their sensors were strong enough to have shown them a glimpse of the missiles below.

Still, the Freeborn ship firing into the Lumen's well-planned solutions could confuse his systems just when he needed his ship to be performing at peak efficiency. In their desperate attempt to save themselves, the Freeborn could doom them all.

"Tell those damned barbarians to keep their - "

The lights within the command center shifted to amber again, with the additional reddish tinge of damage alerts.

"Sir, we've been hit."

"What? Where?" The drones could never have closed the distance to the Lumen so quickly. A glance at the display showed him the armada of drones burning away beneath his ship's continued barrage, nearly 100,000 yan below. There was no apparent damage to the forward sections.

But even as he focused on the distant battle, he felt a strange, cold emptiness behind him. It was as if some dire threat loomed there, just out of sight.

Just out of sight.

He knew what had happened before the sensor officer began his report. "Commander, the control node for the aft sensor arrays has taken a direct hit."

He felt the blind spot shifting and closing as the IMTel shard brought other arrays on-line, sending information flowing around the damaged node.

Whatever their reasons, it had been a bold move. But a C3 warship like the Lumen could not be permanently damaged with such a strike. The nanosphere within the ship facilitated adaptation and repair, and even as he growled, turning toward the weapon sections to order the Even Hand's destruction, the image floating before him was shifting to show the traitor floating serenely off the Lumen's stern.

He had no idea what kind of trick the Even Hand was attempting, but there was little to be gained in trying to puzzle out the motivations of the Freeborn.

The Lumen's forward weapons arrays continued to bore through the dwindling cloud of drones, but there was more than enough power remaining to brush the Even Hand into oblivion.

"Bring aft batteries to full power." His snarl was vicious, but he didn't care. The Freeborn had begged for his help. For them to turn on him now indicated some greater gambit at play, and if there was anything he hated more than betrayal, it was the petty political games of the lesser clans and tribes of the Determinate.

He became aware of the forward batteries, having cleared away the drones, pounding the launch sites on the surface into glowing slag. There would be no danger from that quarter. He directed the weapons to scorch the entire complex, just to make sure.

He would destroy the Even Hand and return to Concordian space; to the rational world of the C3, leaving the untidy chaos of the Freeborn far behind.

***

The Even Hand was not a purpose-built warship, but rather one of the countless colony ships of the vardosi. It carried far more weaponry than any civilian ship of the Panhuman Concord, the Isorian Senatex, or the Algoryn Prosperate, but it had never been designed to go toe to toe with a Concordian battlecruiser.

Unfortunately for Commander Pehn Kowroon and the crew of the Lumen, the current captain of the Even Hand had spent years preparing for this encounter. Her forward batteries, with hours to refine their targeting solutions, had been more than capable of knocking their prey's aft sensor node off-line.

Under the guidance of their IMTel's auto-repair functions, the damage would be repaired shortly, but it would last long enough.

As soon as the sensors aboard the Lumen were blinded by the damage, a pair of large cargo doors amidships on the Even Hand opened and an enormous bullet shape was pushed out into the cold light of the void.

Crewmen swarmed around the object, making last minute adjustments to the drive systems at the rear of the weapon, while others took readings from the heavy containment pods that had replaced the massive warhead. An intense, blue-white light bathed the crewmen and the flank of the ship in stark relief, casting long, menacing shadows across the hull.

They worked with exacting precision, each movement planned and refined, rendered as minimal as could be. Each knew exactly how much time they had, and the stakes should any one of them fail.

They made no mistakes, withdrawing smoothly back through the cargo doors.

As those doors closed, the weapon's drives lit up, and the menacing shape began to slide toward the Lumen.

***

Pehn eased himself back into his chair and tilted his head toward Va'Rana, giving the NuHu a grudging nod.

"I stand corrected, Mandarin. I should have been more discerning about our companions. We'll eliminate them and be on our way." The blind region in his sensor net was nearly closed, and in a moment the full might of the Lumen would be unleashed upon the other ship.

Va'Rana nodded, folding his long, spidery hands over his chest.

"Sir, there's something detaching from the Freeborn vessel. The return is inconclusive, but—"

"Hostile launch detected!" The words were spoken as the shard vibrated with the knowledge, the two sensations crashing together in his mind.

"Launch? What kind of launch?"

Freeborn ships followed no formal build plan, but he had seen no indications that the Even Hand mounted any type of launching system.

But it was too late. Something flashed within the holographic imager, and he felt a sharp, jarring sensation through his link to the shard.

For a moment, there was nothing but cold deadness as he forced his awareness of the link down, bringing the command center back into focus.

"Damage report!" He spun in place, pushing past the tall NuHu, standing as if stunned. Pehn stalked to the status terminals. "What's wrong?"

The woman bent over the display was flustered and confused. The disquiet of the crew was infecting the shard. "Sir, there's been a hull breach on deck C, just aft of section 12. Violent decompression, seven crew-members were lost, but no secondary detonations." She looked up at him, a pathetic gleam of hope in her eyes. "No damage beyond the impact, sir!"

He stared down at her, then back over his shoulder at the imager. It now showed a line-schematic of the Lumen, a small patch of red flashing along her aft quadrant.

"That's it?" He wanted to laugh. He felt the shared consciousness of the IMTel smoothing out around him. The Even Hand had taken her shot, and it had not been enough. Their weapon had malfunctioned, and with that reprieve, he would finish this unseemly farce.

All he needed to do -

"Sir, the imager!" His eyes snapped back to the diagram of his ship.

The red smear of damage was gone. Could the IMTel shard have affected repairs so soon? But then he saw that the schematic of the area had not been restored, but was blotted out entirely.

"What—"

Va'Rana screamed, wrapping his long fingers around his misshapen head, collapsing to his knees.

Pehn looked down to the Mandarin writhing on the ground and back to the imager.

The dark stain was spreading, like a veil being pulled across the map of the Lumen, hiding it from view.

Va'Rana's scream rose again, hopeless terror and agony echoing off the low ceiling of the command center.

"Commander, I have no connection with the dark portions of the ship." The disembodied voice of the ship's IMTel shard, seldom heard over the ship's comm system, echoed dully. Despite the level tones, he detected a note of panic there that terrified him.

Pehn realized what was happening then, but his mind refused to accept it. Even when the darkness on the imager swept forward, around the command center, isolating it from the rest of the ship, he denied the reality unraveling around him.

"Sir, I have no contact with systems in the dark zone!" One of the security officers mumbled the words through clenched teeth.

"Defensive systems are off-line."

"No contact with sensors or weapons!"

And now the danger of a fully integrated nanosphere became apparent as the panic began to spread.

Dull thuds could be felt through the deck. Distant, popping detonations announced the use of mag weapons.

And then the crew of the command center began to shake violently as a sense of pain and surprise swept through each of them.

The IMTel shard was being shredded beyond the blast door. The sense of purpose the shard had always imparted to the crew had been replaced with a dreadful, existential terror.

"Commander." The shard's voice was unsteady, warbling arrhythmatically up and down the register. "Commander Phen, I have no ... Commander you must ... Comman ... Comman ... Com—Com—Com—C-C-C-C-C-C-C-c-c-c-c-c-c-c..."

Va'Rana screamed again, and this time he was joined by several other crew-members as they clamped white-fingered hands to their heads.

Phen drew the sleek, reassuring weight of his plasma pistol and checked the indicator light. It glowed with a warm green reassurance.

And then it flickered.

With a grinding moan, the blast doors to the command center, buried deep within the Lumen's armored hull, opened.

It was as if a chill wind blew through the chamber. An acrid taste burned the back of his throat, and the tiny indicator light on his nanosphere-dependent weapon went dark.

And Va'Rana howled in soul-wrenching agony.

Pehn was torn, desperate to keep his eyes on the gaping door, but horribly fascinated with what was happening to the Mandarin.

As the nanosphere of the Lumen was burned away around them, Va'Rana's long, thin frame crumpled in upon itself. Without the tiny machines to support his mutated physiology, his body was failing.

The grand being, so aloof and powerful, had, in an instant, been reduced to a mewling pile of wretchedness.

Movement at the door caught Pehn's attention, and he found himself raising his weapon despite the cold knowledge of its uselessness.

Several hulking, bestial creatures swept into the room; stocky, brutish looking weapons sweeping the command center.

Mag guns.

Primitive ones, not dependent on a nanosphere.

The guns went off with violent cracks; solid plugs of dull metal smashed several of his crewmen out of their chairs.

One brave security officer rushed at the snarling beasts and took three slugs in the chest. More enemy warriors swept in, another wave of gunfire filled the room, and Pehn was alone with the enemy, the Mandarin, and his dead.

"Who are you?" There was no comforting sense of community in his mind, now. The nanosphere was gone, the shard was as dead as his command crew, and Commander Pehn Kowroon was all alone.

Alone as he had never been in his life.

He straightened his shoulders, rising to his full height. He had no idea who these beasts were, or who they served, but he would be damned before he gave them the satisfaction of seeing a glimmer of fear in his eyes.

The invaders ignored him, moving about the room, checking that the crew was dead. Finally, they took up stations around the perimeter of the chamber, their eyes cold.

On the floor, Va'Rana was barely breathing, the wheezing hiss of each effort the only sound in the room.

The next figure to move through the door gave him a start. It was not a Freeborn pirate captain, as he had expected, but rather the tall, lithe form of a NuHu woman, a cloud of red hair flowing out around her head as if she was underwater.

The woman bent her head to ease beneath the doorframe, and then rose to her full, impressive height once inside. She surveyed the room with glittering eyes that passed over him as if he wasn't there. They found the still form of Va'Rana, and the cool regard was replaced with the unmistakable heat of hatred.

"Mei-Hana." The voice was almost unrecognizable; it took Pehn a moment to realize who had spoken. He had thought Va'Rana beyond speech. But the hatred he had seen in the woman's eyes was matched in the whisper-thin name, spat out like an epithet.

"Hello, Va'Rana. I'm flattered you remember me. The Conservatory was so long ago."

The woman's voice was low and rich, but dripped with acid.

A drone had floated into the chamber behind her; a nano drone, providing the enemy NuHu with the nanosphere she needed to avoid Va'Rana's fate.

She reached out with a long, elegant stave she held in one hand and caressed Va'Rana's face with the weapon's blade-like vanes. A glittering trail of nanites floated around the fallen Mandarin's head, but he waved them weakly away with one hand, as if brushing away flies.

"Keep your filthy creatures off me, renegade." There was no strength in the voice, but a ghost of the old Va'Rana could be detected somewhere beneath the dry, rasping sounds.

"Leave him alone." Pehn moved forward before he realized what he was doing. He still held his useless pistol.

The towering woman turned her cowled head to stare at him and raised a single spidery hand in his direction.

Pehn forced himself to stand strong. He had seen what an angered NuHu was capable of, and the nano drone hovering behind the woman would provide more than enough nanites to power whatever she intended.

But echoes of the temperate serenity of his fallen IMTel shard gave him the strength to stand before certain, agonizing death.

"Enough." A man swept into the command center who would have seemed tall, had he not come to stand beside the imposing NuHu renegade. In dull browns and blacks, he looked nothing like the stereotypical Freeborn leader. But the man's head, half-shaven and half covered in wavy white hair, was enough to identify him.

"Stihl."

The features resembled those of the image the Even Hand had provided of its captain; close enough that Pehn knew, too late, how he had been fooled. It had been an artificially-generated image laid over the pirate captain's infamous face.

The man smiled and shrugged. "I think you probably expected me, by now." He turned to look up at the renegade. "I thought you were going to make this quick? We move on a schedule."

The woman scowled as she turned back to crouch beside Va'Rana.

"In my dreams this lasted far longer, my brother." She reached out and caressed one, flinching cheek. "Your brothers and sisters of the Aan ask that you remember." She stood. "As for me, I don't think you'll remember anything where you're going."

With a dramatic gesture of her free hand the woman drew a glittering stream of light from Va'Rana's mouth and eyes. With a strength Pehn would not have thought he had left, the once-majestic Mandarin thrashed, his back arcing, his scream reverberating around the smoke-filled, blood-stained room.

The stream of light swirled through the air, drawn into the glowing sphere atop the renegade's stave. As the last shimmering motes were drawn from him, Va'Rana collapsed into a limp pool of fine cloth, armored plates, and white, empty flesh.

Pehn looked up as Stihl stepped over the body, heavy heels cracking on the floor, to the center of the command deck. The inhuman warriors stood along the walls, some watching the captain, some staring balefully at Pehn. Stihl's face was twisted in distaste as his dark blue eyes scanned the damage.

"You still think you can reshard this ship in time?" He didn't look back, but the renegade lowered her hands and moved to join him.

"I should be able to connect Dog to most of the systems. Standard vardosi tech should suffice for the rest." She looked down at the pirate captain, who was still lost in thought, his eyes vague and tight. "The ship will be resharded before you reach your destination."

Stihl nodded and then turned back to Pehn.

He felt the heavy weight of the plasma pistol dragging at his hand and looked down at it. With a sigh he tossed it to the floor.

"Thank you for delivering your ship and her payload, Commander." There was no anger or joy on the pirate captain's face. He might have been conducting a mundane business transaction in some savage bazaar. "My quartermaster will be delighted."

Pehn never even noticed the captain raising the small plasma pistol, a thin cord attaching the weapon to one of the ports on the shaven side of his skull. There was a flash of light, a moment of heat, and the commander of the Concord Combined Command Battlecruiser Lumen knew no more.

***

"What is the meaning of this!?!" Admiral Bha ko-Rhan screamed, his voice shrill and shaking. "Where is Stihl?"

The vardanari honor guard moved forward, plasma carbines at the ready.

The four pirates stood before him with impudent smiles stretched across their pale, gaunt faces.

Ko-Rhan began to shake. The drones continued to hover, shifting around to catch as many angles of his embarrassment as they could.

It wouldn't matter. Their memories could easily be wiped. This moment, as mortifying as it felt now, would fade. Even the honor guard would understand, given time. This heartsick pain wasn't the end, merely disappointment at the death of this day's glorious dream. It would have been so perfect, to take Rollen Stihl on the very dawn of the Golden Venture's maiden voyage. He shook his head, his face hardening. There would still be plenty of opportunity for him to cement his command of the ship. The politics would be galling, but his family was sufficiently well-placed, it shouldn't be a problem, in the end.

"Admiral." Commander Jhessik's voice seemed strained over the general comms. Ko-Rhan realized his report was overdue.

"It's alright, Commander." He wanted to spit, but kept his voice calm. "We have four guests in the central boarding lounge. We'll—"

"Admiral, we have a translation through the gate." The strain was more pronounced. "Sir, it's something large."

There was a jumble of nervous voices in the background of the open channel.

"Two contacts, sir. The second is broadcasting vardosi codes, but they're not up to date."

Ko-Rhan shook his head. "Just bring up the defense grid. Not even another world ship could—"

"I believe that's my cue." The pirate woman, Aymes, raised one hand. A small, sleek remote was revealed there, its bronze finish gleaming dully in the pale overhead light.

She pressed a button.

Ko-Rhan reached toward her with a yell, and the vardanari raised their weapons to fire, faces twisted into fierce, threatening scowls.

There was a dull sound from behind the blast doors. A blue-white light seemed to flare for a moment, and the umbilicus, still attached to the Loyal Courser, shook slightly.

And then everything was still.

The admiral straightened and smiled evilly at her. "Well, whatever that was, it appears to have failed."

Ko-Rhan gestured for the vardanari to seize the remote and restrain the prisoners. There would be plenty of time to deal with them when he had finished with this new strangeness.

"Commander, what is the status of the new arrivals?" He turned to move back toward the command center. His mouth tightened into an annoyed frown; he would have to deal with this new crisis in his dress uniform. Then he brightened, waving for the drones to follow. Perhaps the newcomers would provide a suitably impressive conclusion to the day's drama. Images of him leading a battle in his formal gear wouldn't hurt.

"Commander! There's something wrong!" The fear in Jhessik's voice was unmistakable. Beyond the tone, the audio itself seemed to waver, as if the signal was passing in and out of reception.

That should have been impossible on the internal systems.

"There's something wrong with the system! The shard is ... it's dying, sir!"

That brought ko-Rhan up short. "Jhessik? Jhessik, report! What's happening?"

"Sir! I do-do-do-d-d-d-d-d-d-d..." The sound melted into a senseless hiss and then faded away.

Before ko-Rhan could respond, the lights all along the softly curving corridor flickered in a chaotic jumble of dancing shadows, and then died. All around him sounds of battle erupted. Several flashes of plasma scorched pale afterimages across his vision.

It was over in a moment, and silence washed through the blackness. Emergency auxiliary lamps glowed to life. All the vardanari were down. Some lay still on the deck, others nursed various injuries, backs against the walls of the corridor as the pirates held them at bay with long knives of a dull, matte material.

"Golden Venture, this is Captain Rollen Stihl, currently of the C3 vessel Lumen." The voice echoed down the corridor, setting the walls themselves vibrating. "I expect by now you have realized that your shard is dead, rendering your defensive systems useless. Please have my quartermaster escorted to your command center where she will take command of your vessel and prepare for my arrival, and none of your people will be harmed."

The voice paused, and ko-Rhan looked around feverishly, but there was no escape. His entire world was ending, each vibrating rattle of the pirate captain's voice shaking the dust of his dreams down around him. His fevered eyes fell upon the woman, staring at him from behind her long blade. He took a step toward her, heedless of the warning in her gleaming eyes.

"Of course, if you have mistreated Aymes in any way, we will be somewhat less sympathetic to your cause. I will be forced to kill you all out of hand, and then take possession of the Venture."

Admiral Bha ko-Rhan stopped, helpless rage roaring in his ears, as he stared into the woman's cold eyes.

She smiled. "You could still try." She gave him an almost apologetic shrug.

And with that shrug, the last embers of his future spun away into the darkness.

A Fair Trade
By Riley O'Connor

The Attisan Trans-Planetesimal Commerce Hub was an immense structure built into the very foundation of the largest asteroid in the system, a behemoth nearly two hundred thousand yan across. The trading hub was unique in that it was constructed using suspensor fields and deep tungsten-alloy anchors to support a series of long, protruding nanostructures that jutted from the gutted asteroid. The spindly, metallic tendrils could hold well over one hundred vessels at any given time. The dozens of nanite tendrils made the station resemble a monstrous, glimmering hermit crab emerging from its rocky shell, and thus the nickname of 'the Crab' grew into ubiquity.

In contrast, the ship approaching the Crab was little more than a parasite. A large cargo hold was integrated into the sleek vessel to allow for a deceptive amount of storage. The crimson exterior of the ship was cracked and faded from countless years of gate travel.

Not that they were uncountable. Detailed logs were encoded on the ship's system that cataloged every transaction and gate transfer the Carmine Canotila had ever made in its colorful history in serving the Byzantia vardos. Nacen, however, simply had no desire to learn the details of his father's history with the ship. He saw the Carmine not as a craft with which to ply the effectively endless horizons of Antarean space, but as a cage. Its hull was a consignment to mediocrity in the vardos. Nacen placated himself with the fact that if he performed his role as captain well, it might not be his cage for long.

The bridge of the Carmine Canotila was certainly small, but fit its three occupants comfortably enough. Nacen Byzantia stood hunched over a control panel not currently in use by the ship's pilot sitting beside him. He was tall, even for a vardosi. A wave of gossamer auburn hair swept over his pale forehead, styled neatly back over thin ears. He wore a form-fitting suit of lustrous black reflex armor, from which hung a deep crimson cloak.

The pilot was a PanHuman woman with short, pale

blonde hair. She sat back at the main control panel in her gray flight suit, intently focused on the Carmine's path through the crowded tendrils of the Crab. There were no windows in the bridge, but several large displays danced against the forward wall at her whim. They laid out various views from the hull and an incalculable number of flight diagnostics that Nacen rarely acknowledged. Behind the pair stood one of Nacen's vardanari, a distant cousin of his named Camlo. He wore the same iridescent black armor as Nacen, though his own deep red impact cloak hung much shorter around his shoulders. His meager attention was currently being used to inspect the plasma carbine he held as he stood at the entrance of the bridge.

Nacen ran a nervous hand through his auburn hair. At first glance the pilot appeared intensely focused as she weaved the Carmine around the tendrils protruding from the station where the ships docked. However, the longer Nacen watched her languid strokes at the control panel and indifferent glances toward the ship's flight diagnostics, the more he got the feeling she was simply bored. He figured the pilot would be no less stoic if they were gate traveling directly into a supernova. He did not like interfering with Linasette while she was performing these tight maneuvers, but felt he should say something as they approached their destination without slowing.

"We should be docking at bay delta-three on the seventh anterior docking tendril. You're about to pass it," Nacen said, keeping his voice neutral. No sense getting worked up just yet.

"Sorry, Captain, no we're not," Linasette countered.

"What are you talking about? Of course we are." Nacen had to bite back to conceal a twinge of annoyance. He had only been the captain of the Carmine for a few short weeks and had assumed there would be a warming up period, but this bordered on insubordination.

"It's on our predesignated offloading plan. It was provided as soon as we entered the Attisan system."

Nacen brought up the itinerary on the front display screen of the Carmine's small bridge more to emphasize his point than to provide any actual evidence.

"Well it'll be tough to dock in delta-three when there's a C3 frigate blocking the way," Linasette mused with mild trepidation.

"What?" Nacen exclaimed, too shocked to muster much else.

He studied the view of the docking legs more deliberately now, his eyes focused in slits as they flitted across the deceptively thin tendrils of nanostructure. At last he found the appropriate docking tendril, and the point on which the Carmine Canotila was meant to latch. It was currently being blocked by a large commercial freighter.

"You scared me there, Lina. That's just an agriculture freighter," Nacen said.

"I don't think so, Captain. I can't access their ship's IM-Tel."

"Imagine that. It's as if they almost don't want you playing with their temperature control, reading their financial records, or venting their cargo into space."

"Well naturally I wouldn't do anything if I had access. Anyway, if it's good enough to keep us out, it isn't civilian. That suggests military. Second, who needs plants on a space station?"

"Merchants with too much money and a penchant for unnecessary aesthetics?" Nacen suggested.

"Well you would know, Captain."

Nacen ignored the pilot's attempt at humor.

"But why a Concord Combined Command ship in particular?" Nacen asked.

"I used to fly refueling missions for C3 cruisers on Fomalhaut, before I signed on with House Byzantia. Didn't have access to their IMTel, either, obviously. But getting locked out isn't like hitting a wall like you get if you try to hack into a low-level system like an agriculture ship. It's like passing over it and never realizing the wall is even there."

Nacen grunted. Understanding the nuances of Integrated Machine Intelligence was not his strength. It served its purpose and that was all he cared about.

"Why'd you do it?"

"Try to hack into their IMTel? I'm just curious why they're in our docking bay," Linasette replied.

"No, leave the Concord."

The pilot gave a dismissive shrug in her thick, acceleration-resistant flight suit.

"Short answer is you guys paid more. Long answer is you guys pay more and a bunch of other stuff I won't bore you with. Not today at least."

Nacen nodded silently and turned to Camlo. He preferred the company of Beskin. The older, solemn vardanari had much more experience as a bodyguard than Nacen's distant cousin standing nervously at attention before him. Camlo was short, with a shock of auburn hair similar to Nacen's own. Though cropped short, its thick curls waved around his large ears like a mane. Camlo was nearly as new at his role of vardanari as Nacen was at being a captain.

"We'll keep our unload quick and clean. Get Beskin up here, too. I want my vardanari by me when the station sends their welcoming committee. Linasette will monitor station intelligence for anything that looks like military activity."

Camlo gave an eager nod and began walking briskly away.

"It still doesn't make any sense," Linasette said. "If there was a change in our flight plan, which there isn't, the station should have alerted us."

"There are such things as false truths and honest lies," Nacen said.

"Your father used to say that," Linasette replied.

"Don't remind me."

The front display flashed blue as a new message arrived, and an angular orange crab on a brown octagon appeared on the screen.

"Is that the symbol for the Attisan Trading Hub?" Camlo asked.

Nacen turned around to see that Camlo had not seemed to make it off the bridge. He wasn't sure if the question was meant to be rhetorical or not. Knowing Camlo, he was simply seeking validation.

"That, or we're being invited for a seafood dinner," Nacen said dryly. "Go get Beskin."

Camlo nodded enthusiastically again and disappeared around the corner. The message on screen rapidly unfurled in a colossal wall of text and schematics.

"We've been flagged by several anonymous sources. The message doesn't say why," Linasette explained.

"Well, that's something I would like to know more about," Nacen replied.

"I'll see what I can do," Linasette said dutifully.

She made a few hundred taps on the control panel, and Nacen could only guess at how much communication passed between his ship's shard and the station's.

"Updated docking protocols have been uploaded to the Carmine," Linasette said, her gaze not drifting a hair's breadth from the navigation display. "They want us to land in ventral bay two. Apparently we're unloading our cargo into temporary storage."

"Fine, do it," Nacen said dryly, hiding the fact that he had never heard of this ventral bay.

As they swept underneath the station, a much smaller bay revealed itself in the asteroid. A metallic circle, large enough to accommodate a vessel three times the size of the Carmine, hung just inside the surface of the asteroid. Nacen heard footsteps behind him. Camlo and Beskin entered, crimson impact cloaks sweeping behind them. Beskin stood a head taller than Camlo, with close-cropped jet black hair and significantly broader features.

"Well this answers my questions about the gastrointestinal tract of the station," Beskin said.

"How so?" Nacen asked.

"Well, this has to be the anus of the Crab."

There was a moment of tension on the bridge as they approached the ventral bay from below. Linasette pushed gently on the forward maneuvering thrusters and the ship passed through a thin film of nanites as if the surface were no more than water.

"Alright, let's go make an impression," Nacen said, straightening his cloak. "Lina, stay here and keep scouting the station's shard. See what you can find out about that agriculture ship, and keep your eyes out for any sort of military presence on board."

"Will do, Captain."

Nacen strode out of the bridge and withdrew the plasma pistol from its magnetic holster on his thigh. Seeing that it was fully charged, he clamped it back on his armor's thigh plate. He rounded the tight corner past the empty crew cabins and into the cargo hold. Dozens of hyper-compressor crates filled the large room. Scattered around them lounged six domari, the permanent crew of the Carmine Canotila.

All of the vardosi hailed from the Byzantia fleet in one way or another. Jeta, Merripen, and Alifair had worked with Nacen's father while he commanded the Carmine. They refused the offer to serve the homefleet when he transferred, preferring the independence of working on the trade ship. The remaining three domari had been taken from other areas of the homefleet. Ruslo and Tobar had been foot troops and had seen quite a bit of fighting around the Determinate, though none recently from what Nacen had read in their logs. Shukernak was originally a heavy weapons specialist, but was demoted to domari for disobeying orders on a mission planetside that resulted in a few casualties. It wasn't his ideal crew, but then again they were essentially glorified transportation drones.

"Alright, we're about to have some company. No need to suspect any trouble, but keep your mag guns loaded just in case." Nacen glanced around the cargo bay and noticed none of them actually had their mag guns equipped, though they did wear their more compact version of his own reflex armor. "What are you doing? Station security is going to be here any minute."

The six domari looked at each other, their postures a mix of crossed arms and relaxed shoulders leaning against the hold's many crates.

"And you're expecting them to what, shoot at us?" Alifair asked. "Trust me, these guys will go through pains to make sure their shiny little asteroid doesn't get dirtied up."

"We need to be prepared. We've been flagged for hazardous materials," Nacen said.

"With all due respect, Captain," Shukernak said, "this isn't a combat drop. I think you've mistaken the Crab for some automated high-security trade post. The reason this place competes with Cybele and Pessinos in terms of volume of trade isn't a matter of economics, it's the independence."

"It's far more economical than paying the tariffs, gravitational assist fees, and all of the other nanospheric taxes the Concord sticks us with if we were to visit those planets," Nacen said.

"Sure," Shukernak nodded, "but the real draw is the entertainment. The Crab is the best place for a solid drink on this end of the Determinate."

"Or anything else you might want for that matter," Alifair added. "I'm partial to the neural hacking programs. They clean out of your system a lot faster than that Boromite sludge you drink, Nak."

"Fine. Take all the time you want on the Crab. But first we jump through their hoops, and we're doing it armed."

Two minutes later, Nacen stood in the marble chamber of ventral bay two, flanked by Beskin and Camlo. His domari took up relaxed positions around the Carmine's delivery of six of their hyper-compressor crates, which had been withdrawn from the ship through the chamber's transporter pads.

Nacen wasn't sure what he had pictured station security to look like, but it certainly wasn't the eight hulking Boromites standing before him. Immaculate navy-blue attire was stretched over their rugged, craggy gray skin. Rather than hulking mining equipment Nacen normally associated with the genetically-modified race of humans, they carried simple mag pistols at their sides. Their appearance would have been comical to Nacen if they didn't tower over his own tall frame.

One of the navy clad Boromites approached him and extended a massive hand. Nacen placed his own hand in the Boromite's grip, trusting the man would not crush his entire forearm in the welcoming gesture.

"Welcome to the Crab, Captain Byzantia," the Boromite rumbled, his gritty voice carrying a surprising amount of warmth. "My name is Raul Omgar, I am the manager of the station and head of the Boromite trading guild here."

"Captain Byzantia, as you have already pointed out," said Nacen, relieved his hand was still intact.

"I am terribly sorry for the inconvenience," Raul explained. "It is standard station protocol to search ships and cargo that have been flagged by a confirmed source. Standard practice, you understand."

"I don't understand," Nacen shook his head. "Confirmed source? Sounds like someone trying to inconvenience me."

"I assure you, our security algorithms are highly sophisticated. It's possible they simply picked up weaponry on your ship."

"Look, I don't mean to be curt, but do you know how long this search will take? I have a tight schedule to keep," Nacen asserted as he crossed his arms in annoyance.

The Boromite's eyes glazed over, and Nacen assumed he was accessing the station's shard.

"I see your cargo is mostly precious metals, the usual shipment. The search shouldn't take long, a couple of hours at the most. We will unload it for you in the Crab's temporary holding bay nearby. In the meantime, feel free to partake in all the entertainment the Crab has to offer."

"A couple of hours?!" Nacen exclaimed. He assumed the station's shard could do the check in a matter of minutes.

"It must be a manual search of your cargo and the ship's contents. Standard search protocol," he repeated.

"Your standard protocol can go-"

"Listen to me captain," Raul interrupted. "We maintain a contract with House Byzantia based on your continued reliable service. But there are many others who seek to do business with our station. You would do well to remember that."

"Like C3?" Nacen asked, thrusting the question forward like a dagger.

The crags of Raul's brow lowered as the Boromite took on a more menacing tone.

"No elements of Concord Combined Command are permitted on this station. We are a neutral trading entity in the Attisan system, and tight restrictions are placed on military access. Such actions would have severe repercussions for the governing authorities of both Cybele and Pessinos."

Nacen decided it wouldn't do him any good to push the issue any further.

"Then tell us what an agriculture ship is doing at our bay and why we're under this lockdown," Nacen said, feeling a little of his temper loosen.

"I do not concern myself with every ship coming and leaving this station, Captain," Raul grumbled. "Station intelligence handles specific flight plans and transactions."

"Yes, and a great job it's been doing." Nacen raised his eyebrows, his voice laden with sarcasm.

Another furrowing of the brow.

"If you will excuse me," Raul said in a tone that implied he would do as he pleased regardless, "I have other matters to attend to."

The Boromite turned and began walking toward the nearest marble opening, two of the seven guards following in his wake.

"I stand corrected. That man is the anus of the Crab," Beskin said as soon as they were out of earshot.

"I don't trust him," Camlo said.

"He isn't of the vardos, of course he can't be trusted," Nacen said, turning to face his crew. "Camlo, make sure Linasette keeps trying to figure out why that agriculture ship is docked in our space. You stay here with Shukernak and make sure security keeps a brisk pace and doesn't damage anything."

"What? Why me?" Shukernak said petulantly.

"Because I know you want to go have a good time more than anyone else here. The faster you can get these station goons moving, the faster you can do that."

Shukernak nodded obediently, but Nacen could tell he was clenching his teeth awfully hard.

"Sure thing, Nace. You can count on us," Camlo said. He took one hand off of his plasma carbine and placed it on his right breast, extending his forefinger and little finger while tucking the others in at the middle joint in the Byzantian sign of dedication. "Without wood, the fire dies."

Nacen returned the gesture.

"Where the vardos goes, wealth shall rise."

Lowering his hand, Nacen faced the rest of his crew.

"Beskin, you're with me," he said. "Everyone else, go enjoy yourselves. But stay on alert. I don't want Raul or his friends giving us any more surprises."

The five remaining domari nodded in understanding, slung their mag weapons back, and began walking toward the polished door that led to the main interior of the station. Nacen headed in that direction with Beskin at his side. When they approached, the marble door parted.

"Beskin," Nacen said, turning to face the vardanari. "I want you to follow our crew. Make sure they stay out of trouble, and get them ready to go when I give the signal."

"Very well," Beskin nodded. The vardanari turned and set off at an even pace to the door where the five domari had exited, his own plasma carbine kept low at his side.

Nacen heard Camlo's voice chirp in his ear over the squad shard as he disappeared into the hallway on the right.

"So what are you going to do, Nace?"
Nacen recalled another reason why he liked Beskin so much. He didn't ask so many questions.

"Lina sees best through shard interfaces. I see best through my own eyes."

"Oh," Camlo acknowledged.

The marble pattern the nanite composites formed continued throughout the rest of the Crab's interior, giving the halls a regal air. The bays were even more magnificent, the ersatz marble forming huge, vaulted chambers, while the interior of the station had hallways that led to a multitude of businesses. Nacen saw shops with fine clothing, bars with dazzling displays of drinks on display, and establishments with decadent functions he could only guess at, each of them packed with clientele.

To his right, the marble facade disappeared into an enormous, curving surface as clear as glass. The view into space was dominated by the nearest docking tendril, which extended from an opening in the wall far into the void beyond. They appeared immense at first, wide hallways allowing room for ships to dock on either side, before shrinking into the darkness of space.

Nacen passed through six of the bays, taking one transporter pad up to an entirely new level, before reaching bay delta-three. The tendril nearest him was marked as the seventh in the delta bay row, and the area the Carmine was meant to dock in the first place.

He found a restaurant across from the tendril's opening and forced his way to an empty table with a decent view of the bay. The establishment was crowded with the chatter of traders, merchants, and all manner of other PanHuman professions. He had even spotted a pair of Boromite guards in their navy blue attire laughing raucously at the bar. Every nanite surface in the place pulsed with a low electronic beat, and a woman sang from them with an oddly angelic pitch in an abrasive melody that Nacen presumed was supposed to pass for music.

An alert pinged in Nacen's ear as he tapped open a menu on the table's obsidian surface. He heard Linasette's calming voice as if she were speaking into his ear.

"I have some... What is that blasted sound? Are you being tortured with a mining drill?" The pilot asked.

"I wish. It's the music in this bar," Nacen replied, projecting his thoughts through the shard to his pilot.

"I thought you were scouting out that anterior docking tendril."

"I am, I'm just... Just forget it. What do you have for me?"

"Well, accessing the agriculture ship's IMTel is not going to happen. I think someone figured out what I was up to, but they shouldn't have been able to trace my signal. If we're lucky."

"I don't like depending on luck," Nacen responded hesitantly.

"Well you can depend on me," Linasette said, her voice almost sounding excited. "I managed to get into some lower-level access of the Crab's shard. Docking logs mostly."

"Anything useful?"

"Nothing definitive, but I can tell you that agriculture freighter latched on about two hours ago, only minutes after we entered the system."

"Interesting timing, but nothing inherently suspicious about that."

"Well, I also have delivery data. The crew of the ship is comprised of ten PanHumans."

"Seems like a lot for delivering plants."

"Right. I still suspect military. If not C3, possibly independent contractors."

"Well keep looking. Video surveillance records would be extremely useful."

"I agree."

"Anything else?" Nacen asked.

"The crew of the agriculture ship made a delivery shortly after it docked, but not to the cargo transporter pad in delta bay three."

"Is that unusual?"

"Very. According to standard security protocol..."

"Kaha, Lina, now you're reciting that garbage?"

"I read through it a few times. It actual has some interesting points."

"Forget I asked. Where did they deliver their cargo to?"

"The same place ours is going to. Temporary holding in the ventral bay," Linasette answered.

"Seems like a long way to deliver... Wait, what are they delivering?"

"That's where things get really weird. Their delivery is the same as ours: six hyper-compressor crates."

"Do you know what's in them?" Nacen asked.

"Nope, that's all I know from the docking logs."

"Nice work, Lina. Keep on it. Try to get me those video feeds."

"That's going to be a lot tougher, if not impossible. But I'll try."

Nacen reconnected to the squad's shard, opening up a private link with Camlo.

"Hey, Nacen," Camlo said cheerily. "These Boromites are working pretty fast. A bunch of them went into our ship, they wanted to check our cargo hold too. I said that was probably fine."

Nacen gritted his teeth. This was anything but fine.

"Listen, Cam, I need you and Shukernak to get Lina out of the Carmine."

"Why?"

"Because it's filled with Boromites, Cam. Heavily armed Boromites. I need Shukernak to get her to Beskin and the crew wherever they are in this kaha of a station."

"Got it, Nacen. It'll be done."

"Good. Next, I need you to follow security into the temporary holding bay."

"They already finished loading our crates."

"Well, then tell them you need to inspect one of them for damage and that your captain will be very angry if something is wrong with it."

"Alright, will do. What do you want me to do in that bay?"

"The temporary holding bay," Nacen stated carefully. "I need you to give me the live video feed from your helmet. Keep on the lookout for uniformed men and six crates very similar to ours."

"Will do, Nace."

Nacen cut the link. He then used the squad shard to access the visual feeds on the Carmine. He saw them imprinted on his own vision as if they were projected directly onto his retinas. Station security was indeed pouring over every inch of his ship. He saw Camlo appear in the cargo hold and make his way toward the bridge. In the corner, he watched as several Boromite guards used some sort of device to scan the contents of the hyper-compressor crates in the Carmine's hold. One guard in the corner, he saw, was clumsily using a drone to stack one of Nacen's crates on top of his skyraider, an airbike he kept in pristine condition.

"No you idiot, don't set that there!" Nacen exclaimed.

"Excuse me," said a gravelly voice. "We will set these wherever we please."

Nacen quickly closed out of the video feed and was confronted with the sight of two Boromite security guards standing over his table. Their dark blue uniforms stretched awkwardly over their jagged flesh and stood out plainly in the sea of ostentatious fashion of the bar. To his dismay, one had set his mag pistol on the table, pointed at Nacen.

The vardosi captain forced himself to laugh once. It did not come off as carefree as he would've liked.

"No, I was talking to my ship," he said, gesturing across the table where the guards currently towered over. "Please, sit."

They did so, and Nacen thought the nanite composite chairs would break under the Boromite's enormous weight. On the video feed of the ship in the corner of his eye, Nacen watched Camlo and Shukernak escort a defiant Linasette off of the Carmine Canotila.

"So why is a Freeborn commander wasting away at a place like this?" The guard on the right said. "Pretty rare to see you vagrants off your ships."

"Well, I thought I'd try out this air people are always going on about," Nacen said jovially.

"Impressed?" The guard on the left asked. He was a touch more handsome than the Boromite on the right, considering their resemblance to walking boulders. Perhaps it was the chiseled jaw, Nacen thought.

"Well, the increased oxygen levels are certainly helping my mood, but I can't stand the bitter aroma that seems to linger on every breath I take," Nacen explained.

"That's supposed to simulate plant life. From what I hear, the vegetation stimulants are spot on," the left rock explained to the right rock.

"All the more reason to stay star-side then, I suppose," Nacen replied. He blanched in the silence that followed and tried not to look at the mag pistol on the table in front of him.

"Can I get you hard-working gentlemen a drink?"

"We've had plenty."

Nacen offered a weak smile and accessed his squad's shard. He was not receiving video from Camlo yet. From the keel-side cameras of the Carmine, he watched Shukernak escorting Lina through the leftmost door where Beskin and the domari had exited.

"Alright, I'll go ahead and order myself a hard rye drink," Nacen said, tapping on the table once again. The obsidian surface rippled and a black digital surface appeared, bringing up a large list of items.

"We'd prefer you didn't," the left guard said.

"We'd also prefer you not access your Freeborn shard. Won't do you much good anyway, we're jamming your transmissions," the right guard said.

He tried opening a feed to Linasette, then to Beskin. Nothing. Where he would normally simply think about opening a feed and having his built-in neural interface do the rest, he simply drew a blank. It was like trying to remember an old friend's name but not being able to come up with the right sounds. He did, however, receive Camlo's subsequent scream through his audio feed quite clearly.

"Kaha, Nace! They killed them! Oh, kaha kaha kaha..."

"Calm down, Cam. Tell me what's going on."

The guard on Nacen's left grabbed the pistol on the table and leveled it at Nacen's chest.

"It's useless to transmit through your shard, Freeborn. We're currently tracking down your remaining crew. They will be detained shortly. Now if you'd kindly come with us, Raul Omgar would like to ask you a few questions."

Nacen became very aware of his plasma pistol currently magnetized on his right hip. His hands were placed on the table though, and despite his confidence in his own reflexes, he wouldn't bet on himself with the left guard currently aiming a mag pistol at his chest. The guard on the right brandished a short black rod with a grin.

"Stand up, hands forward and on the table, Freeborn."

Seeing no other option, Nacen did as he was told. He rose slowly, glancing around as if to ask for help. Many of the patrons backed away from their table having noticed the guard's mag pistol. Many more were filtering out of the establishment. The right guard slammed the black rod down on Nacen's wrists and the baton went limp momentarily. In an instant, it lengthened and twisted around the vardosi's slender wrists, then tightened firmly. Nacen initially struggled against them, but ceased when he realized his efforts were futile. The metal was strong, possibly tungsten or titanium, and nanite reinforced to conform to his wrists.

"Typical Freeborn scum. You come into our station and don't care who gets hurt in the attempt," the guard on the left said, still brandishing his mag pistol. He appeared to be the senior guard here. Nacen addressed him.

"Getting hurt? You're the ones who slapped this iron noodle on me. Look, earlier I talked to Raul about C3 possibly being on the Crab. I have reason to believe there's been some kind of military breach. Check the temporary hold in ventral-"

Nacen was interrupted by a crippling electric shock from his restraints.

"You're not talking your way out of this one, vagrant. You'll answer to Raul directly for what you did to Talc and Igno."

"Talc, Igno – who? Are these... Boromites? Your friends?"

The guard with the leveled pistol nodded once.

"Station security. I'd have killed you where you stand if

Raul hadn't given me very explicit orders. Now move."

The guard on Nacen's right positioned himself behind him and shoved Nacen toward the front of the bar. The place had been completely cleared out now. The senior guard with the pistol began to take long strides back to the bay where Nacen had come from.

The high-pitched whine of a mag rifle echoed far off down the hallway in the direction the guards were leading Nacen. A panicked frenzy arose in the crowd, raised voices and screams passing through the throng like rocks triggering an avalanche. Nacen heard the hissing retort of a plasma beam from the same direction. It was answered in turn by another intense battery of mag round fire.

"We have more forces down in the ventral bay," the leading guard proclaimed. "Raul is requesting reinforcements. Let's move."

A bright blue beam stabbed out of a nearby shop to their right and narrowly missed the Boromite. Nacen's vision darkened as it reacted to the plasma fire erupting all around him. He was thrown behind a solid marble bench as another bolt lashed out at him. Smoke and bits of marble were hurled into the air. Nacen became aware of a loud alarm blaring throughout the station.

Nacen blinked and tried to get his bearings. The guard who shoved him was currently kneeling behind the bench that Nacen's back was against, returning fire on the shops across the bay. To his right, Nacen saw that the lead guard had gone down, severe burns still smoldering on his uniform. In some places, Nacen could see the plasma bursts had completely burned through the Boromite's body.

"You've got to take these restraints off me!" Nacen yelled to the guard beside him.

"Not a chance," the guard grunted. He leaned over the top of the bench and let loose another half a dozen accelerated armor-piercing rounds into the shops.

"Listen, that is not my crew! They use mag rounds like you."

"Like I care," the Boromite said bluntly. He stood to unleash another salvo of his pistol, but he ducked as a withering hail of plasma shot over their heads.

"These are plasma carbines. Therefore, not my domari," Nacen emphasized again.

There was a look of skepticism on the Boromite's jagged features, but the expression quickly gave way to desperation. The guard touched the restraints with the butt of his mag pistol. The weapon emitted a high-pitched whine and Nacen felt the restraints loosen. They snapped back and clattered to the floor. Nacen grabbed for the plasma pistol on his thigh and was relieved to find it still there. He leaned out to the side of the bench and looked out across the bay. Two humans clad in thick green and white uniforms crouched behind counters roughly four yan away and were firing intense bursts of plasma. Nacen spotted a third taking aim from a storefront on the second level of the interior of the bay. He ducked back as more bursts of plasma fire seared the bench.

The Boromite looked over and fired nine more rounds at the men behind the counters. Nacen looked over and took aim. One had disappeared behind the counter in response to the guard's returning fire, but one continued to lay down bolts of plasma. Nacen fired two bursts from his own plasma pistol. The first shot went wide to the left. So did the second. His pistol was not going to be effective this far away.

"Listen, we need to get closer if-"

Nacen's suggestion was cut off by a plasma bolt whizzing into the guard's head. The Boromite collapsed in a heap. Nacen heard a voice shouting at him then. A female voice. He realized it was Linasette. His squad shard was no longer being jammed.

"...in, Captain, come in. We are en route to your last known location."

Beskin's voice rang in his ear next.

"Lina was right, Camlo, it's C3 strike troops. A whole squad. They're wearing hyperlight armor under green and white robes. Stay in the holding bay, we'll come get you after we find the captain."

"Chodra to the captain, he's probably already dead," Nacen heard Shukernak say over the audio feed.

"Not yet, I'm not!" Nacen shouted.

Beskin's reply was lost in a burst of plasma directly over

Nacen's head. One of the guards had made a run to the nearest set of benches by Nacen and had opened fired at his more exposed flank. Nacen leaned around the corner and let loose a salvo of his own bolts. He saw the plasma shots connect, but a dazzling display of lights deflected the bolts harmlessly around the man. Hyperlight deflection armor. Definitely C3 strike troops.

Nacen heard a brief shout emanate from the interior shops, followed by the concussive thuds of mag rifle fire. Looking over the bench, he saw the black reflex armor of his domari as they began taking up positions in the shops below. He caught a glimpse of Beskin's crimson impact cloak for a brief moment as the vardanari emerged from a hallway and dashed behind the counter where the C3 trooper had been a moment before. More mag rounds erupted, this time much closer to Nacen. He saw the robed man who had tried to outflank him go down in a burst of armor-piercing rounds, the hyperlight shielding crumbling under the sheer quantity of projectiles.

Nacen raised his plasma pistol and fired at the trooper on the second floor, who was now pinning down his crew. Dashing out from behind the bench, Nacen let loose three more shots. One connected, but once again was deflected by the hyperlight armor. The distraction was all Beskin needed, as the vardanari fired a concentrated salvo from his own plasma carbine. The trooper was slammed back against the railing and sunk down onto the balcony, his armor burned beyond any recognition.

"Any longer and I might have started to worry," Nacen called out toward the shops.

"C'mon, we'd never let these C3 dogs bite our captain too hard," Merripen shouted back as the domari emerged from the shop. Nacen ran the rest of the way. He was relieved to see Linasette emerge from the hallway, appearing unharmed.

Nacen turned to his pilot. She looked shaken up, her blond hair a complete mess and parts of her acceleration suit torn up.

"Glad to see you're okay," he said.

"Likewise, Captain. Listen, the ship is secure, but I'm not sure how long it will stay that way. I'm reading heavy munition expenditure coming from the ventral bay."

"What's happening down there?" Nacen asked.

"Not sure, but there's definitely more C3 holed up somewhere. I've been trying to access the station security shard to get some video or audio on them but I haven't been able to."

"Could you issue a communication request to the station's shard instead? We need to clear the air with Raul so no more guards attack us on our way to the temporary docking bay."

"I'll try, hold on," the pilot said.

Glancing to his left, Nacen could see dozens of ships departing from the docking tendrils. Dozens more were already barely perceptible specks fading into the blackness of space. A familiar rumble soon came over the squad shard. Nacen thought it was a far off explosion at first, deep within the Crab. Then he recognized the Boromite's voice.

"You had better have a good explanation for this, Freeborn," Raul Omgar demanded, his voice flooded with rage.

"The assailants are Concord Combined Command, we've confirmed it."

"C3 launch an attack on my station? Impossible."

"I'm not debating what's possible or not possible, I'm telling you what's happening. As far as we can tell, a C3 squad entered the station under the guise of an agriculture freighter crew and unloaded six hyper-compressor crates into the same holding bay as you put our crates in."

"Why would they do that?" Raul asked, some of his fury being displaced by frustration.

"We're trying to find that out ourselves. It would help us out if you gave us full access to station security feeds."

There was a momentary pause before Raul spoke again. "It's yours. Now go figure out what's going on. I've ordered my men not to fire on you."

"I appreciate that very much."

The next transporter pad was coming up. This one would take them to the final bay before the long hallway that led to the rounded chamber where the Carmine was held, and where Camlo had given his last transmission. Linasette shouted for Nacen and Beskin to stop. Nacen did so, and Lina nearly collided with him.

"Captain, I have access to the entire station. It's incredible. So much data, it's overwhelming."

"Well, sort it out and tell me what's happening by the Carmine."

The pilot took a few deep breaths and closed her eyes.

"The Carmine is clear," Linasette reported, visibly relieved. "A few new scorch marks, but nothing serious. There's a few short corridors that lead to the temporary holding bay. Okay... let's see."

There was a sharp intake of breath and the pilot's eyes flared open.

"Oh. I... They're all, they're all..." she began despondently.

"Focus, Lina. I need a clear report."

Closing her eyes, Linasette nodded and continued.

"There are nine confirmed dead station guards leading up to the temporary holding bay. I see two strike troopers in the hold itself. They appear to be working on one of the crates."

"Alright, that's five strike troopers accounted for. Now where are the other five?"

"Contact!" Jeta bellowed from behind a nearby line of colorful bushes. She took aim down her mag rifle, using its zoom feature to keep a sharp eye across the massive room. "C3 in the previous bay, coming up fast!"

Two strike troopers had taken up positions on either side of the arch now and were taking blind shots around the corner at the domari's entrenched positions. Nacen grabbed Linasette and hurried to the interior wall. They leapt through the entrance of a restaurant and ducked behind the low wall facing the bay.

"Stay here. Keep plugged in to the security shard, and give us live updates on the C3 position. Can you handle that?" Nacen asked, forcing a calm demeanor to reassure the pilot.

Linasette nodded.

"Good. Beskin, on me. We're going to advance up this building district and get a better position to protect the bay entrance."

They leapt out of the window, and crouching low, began to make their way through the courtyards of the station structures. Nacen looked to the entrance of bay delta-two. Under a punishing barrage of mag rounds, three strike troopers materialized on the transporter mat. A small drone appeared behind them. The domari redirected their fire onto the newcomers, who began sprinting toward the buildings Nacen and Beskin were headed to. The mag rounds impacted harmlessly on a scintillating blue surface curving in front of the troopers. They were making good progress to the buildings, faster than Beskin and Nacen could hope to.

The strike troopers peaking around the entrance fired upon the domari with renewed vigor, spurred on by the advance of their allies. Plasma bolts connected with Merripen and the domari gave a shout of pain as she fell, three scorch marks searing into her leg. Ruslo took a direct hit to his black reflex armor and his torso evaporated as the bolt flung him back.

"Captain, something big is coming," Linasette announced.

She was right. The hum of powerful reaction thrusters emanated from beyond the arc where two strike troopers were still firing on the domari's position. Plasma fire now began to pour from the adjacent building as the C3 soldiers began to take aim at the domari around the bay. The humming reached a crescendo as a massive M4 combat drone flew in through the open arch. The sleek green vehicle measured nearly a yan long, and hovered effortlessly half its length above the ground. There was a moment of stillness in the bay as the drone shifted course, turning against the domari positioned behind statues, benches, bushes, whatever cover they could find. Then the plasma support gun in the front hull of the drone opened fire.

The nearby statue concealing Tobar was torn to pieces, the self-repairing effect of the nanites rendered useless by the torrent of plasma fire. Tobar was ripped to shreds by the weapon, and the drone revolved to face its next target. The plasma cannon situated atop the M4 emitted a sharp whine and let loose a massive pulse of energy that tore into the building directly behind Nacen and Beskin.

"Kaha!" Nacen shouted to his squad. "Forget the troopers, we have to take out that M4 now!"

Mag rounds poured into the drone, but each was countered with a flash of light as it was halted by the kinetic shielding. Desperate to relieve themselves of the rapid plasma support gun fire, the domari tossed their only plasma grenades. One landed in front of the drone and detonated harmlessly against the kinetic shielding. Another overshot the drone and thudded against the clear wall of the bay. The resulting blast blew a small hole into the curved transparent surface, exposing the bay to the vacuum of space. A howling gush of air poured through the hole as the station nanites sealed shut over the course of a few seconds.

"I have an idea, Beskin. I'm going to need your grenades."

The vardanari placed them in Nacen's open palms without hesitation.

"Good. I need you to go take the troopers in that shop next to us so I can make a clear sprint to the drone."

"Nacen, as your vardanari I must object to-"

"I don't want to hear it. This is just as dangerous for you as it is for me. Now go."

Nacen's last words were lost as another pulse of the M4's main plasma cannon ripped a hole into the buildings, flinging the two vardosi to the ground.

"Move!" Nacen shouted, scrambling to his feet. He jumped over the railing of the courtyard and darted behind the bushes where Jeta hid.

"Domari, do you still have any explosives?"

"One grenade, Captain!" She shouted.

"Alright, get ready to move on my command."

Nacen waited for the plasma cannon to fire again. His domari were still being pinned by the relentless fire of the support gun, but no more had fallen prey to its lethal spray. Once again the plasma cannon roared. He heard several of his domari shout as nanite composite marble was turned to shrapnel on them. The cannon glowed and the air around it simmered from the massive heat exhaust of the plasma coil.

"The cannon is plasma faded, go now!" Nacen shouted and leapt over the hedge.

He sent the beam of his plasma pistol into the batter drone at close range and overwhelmed its shield. The drone detonated in a flash of light and screeching metal. Jeta, following close behind, fired her mag rifle into the now exposed trooper behind the entrance to bay delta-two. He returned fire on the domari but his shots went wide as he fell to the ground, several mag rounds having found a resting place clean through his armor. The remaining strike trooper fled into the bay.

Nacen flattened himself on the inside of the wide hallway of the bay. He knelt down and placed two plasma grenades against the support beam. Jeta took cover behind the corner opposite and Nacen tossed the remaining grenade to her.

"I set it to remote detonate on my command," he told her. "Get out of here, now, and tell what domari are left to get ready to give that drone all they've got."

Jeta nodded and ran out of the entryway. The ground beneath her erupted in plasma fire from the second floor of the building Beskin was supposed to have cleared. She continued on, but took a direct hit to her left arm and side. She spun and toppled to the ground. Ducking behind the remnants of a marble statue, she unloaded the rest of her magazine into the upper floor of the building. She reloaded, bracing herself for the worst. Behind her, the drone continued to pummel the remaining crew.

"Domari," she cried, not knowing if any of her friends remained to hear her. "On my signal, throw everything you have at the combat drone!"

Plasma bolts erupted from the windows of the second floor of the building, keeping Jeta pinned. She zoomed in with her mag rifle to see Beskin firing point blank at the strike troopers. One flew back as the shots overloaded his hyperlight shielding. The other ran at the vardanari wildly. Beskin nimbly dodged to one side, his impact cloak absorbing the bone-shattering blow of the trooper's swing with his carbine. With one last shot, the trooper was silenced.

Jeta felt a hand on her shoulder. She wheeled around, prepared to smash her now empty mag rifle into her foe's skull. Her rifle connected with her captain's open palm with a soft thud. He grabbed her and they ran pell-mell to the row of buildings.

"Now!" They screamed in unison, and their voices were drowned in an intense volley of mag rifle fire. Some domari had survived after all. The combat drone lurched back under the weight of fire as the plasma grenades in the docking tendril behind it detonated. With a deafening roar the tendril came loose from the curved exterior wall of the station. It careened into another tendril and floated gently out into space. The nanites began to repair the wall, but a massive hole had been torn into the station. The drone was hurtled backward to the opening, pulled by the rushing air into the vacuum of space. By the time the drone's rear reaction thrusters reached the hole, it was nearly closed. The hull of the drone sheared along the edge of the wall, and as it lost momentum, the implacable wall of repairing nanites cut through the drone's reinforced hull. The entire front carriage of the drone collapsed to the floor with a tremendous crash.

"If that doesn't get you promoted to squad leader, Jeta, I can't fathom what will," Shukernak roared across the courtyard.

Nacen jogged to the center of the courtyard. He ran a quick diagnostic on his squad's status. Tobar was beyond saving, his torn remnants scattered beneath demolished marble, and Ruslo had suffered catastrophic damage to his chest. Alifair had been heavily concussed by the plasma cannon blast and had multiple shards of nanite shrapnel embedded all over his body. Merripen had been shot in the leg several times, and Jeta many other places, but they were otherwise unharmed. Beskin had taken several glancing shots to various places in his reflex armor, but looked none the worse for it.

"The medical drone is on the ship. Alifair, wait here with Jeta and Merripen and we'll send it to you as soon as we can."

"What about Ruslo and Tobar?" Merripen asked.

"Their names will live on in the vardos," Nacen said simply. "But now, we need to move."

Resuming their sprint through the docks, the group reached the corridors leading to the ventral bay and followed them into the large domed chamber where the Carmine Canotila still sat. Linasette remotely opened the cargo hold doors and a small buddy drone flew out and over their heads, obediently flying back the way they came.

"The medi-drone is on the way, Alifair. Hold on."

Nacen, Beskin, Linasette, and Shukernak crossed the chamber and entered the door to the temporary holding bay corridors. The scene in front of them was a massacre. The Boromite guards had been caught in the middle of the hallway by a tripod-mounted plasma support gun, an even stronger version than that of the M4 combat drone. With no cover to aid them, the guards had been cut down without mercy. As Nacen's crew approached the end of the corridor, they saw that the gun had been damaged beyond repair. A voice spoke up from behind them and Nacen turned in surprise to see a bloodied Camlo leaning against a Boromite.

"I got him, Nace," the young vardanari said weakly.

Nacen crouched down by his cousin and spoke softly back. "You certainly did, Cam. Well done."

"Do you think the Boromites would have appreciated it?"

"Of course."

Nacen made the gesture of loyalty to the Byzantia vardos against his right breast. Camlo could not return the gesture, having no arm beyond his shoulder to do so.

"Without wood, the fire dies," chanted Nacen.

"Where the vardos goes, wealth shall rise," returned Camlo, leaning his head back against the body he rested against. "He's gone into shock, but his own bionanites should keep him alive," Linasette said. "It's a wonder he isn't dead already, to be honest."

"He was always a stubborn one," Nacen said, standing up. "Beskin, proceed."

The narrow marble hallways continued for five yan around several sharp corners. It meandered down into the Crab, but on their right lay the door to the temporary holding bay.

"Ready for the serpent's strike?" Nacen asked Beskin.

"On your mark, Captain," the vardanari shot back, kneeling by the door.

"Lina, care to open the door for us?"

"Of course, Captain, ladies first."

"Go."

Lina used her station access to fling open the door. At the same time, Beskin threw in his last grenade, whose subsequent irradiation scrambled the occupants of the hold within.

Beskin burst into the room, Nacen and Shukernak following quickly behind. Bringing his carbine to bear against the pair of reeling C3 troopers inside, Beskin fired two rounds into the chest of the nearest armed trooper and he staggered back against a crate. The soldier's plasma lancer clattered to the floor. The remaining strike trooper cried out and threw her arms in the air. The attackers held their fire, but kept their weapons trained on her.

"Back away from the crate," Nacen said, gesturing to the crate the limp trooper was laying against. She obeyed, eyes darting between her motionless ally and the titanium crate.

"I must admit, Nacen, I'm curious as to what the C3 are trying to protect so desperately," Linasette mused.

"Well whatever it is, it better blow me away."

The sudden illumination of a green light signified the success of Lina's access into the hyper-compressor crate's shard, and the lid slid open with a barely perceptible hiss. Inside the container lay a massive Thorium warhead. Nacen's eyes widened.

"Kaha. They're trying to destroy the Crab."

An uncomfortable tension hung in the air between the vardosi, as tangible as the water vapor rolling back from the exposed crate.

"Lina, what's in the rest of these compressor crates?" Nacen demanded.

"Working on it."

"Good. Okay, you, down on the ground," Nacen said to the surviving trooper, who knelt down hastily. "Who is the demolition expert in your squad?"

"He was," the woman said, pointing to the trooper with several massive holes in his chest.

"Of course he was," Nacen said with a sigh.

"You sure you want to know what's in these crates?" Lina asked.

Nacen gestured for her to continue with an impatient hand.

"Each crate contains approximately twenty-thousand tons of hyper-compressed refined Thorium. If triggered with enough force, that's easily enough to turn this entire two hundred kiloyan wide asteroid into interstellar dust."

"I'll take your word on that," Shukernak said behind them. "Math was never my strong suit."

"Doesn't have to be with numbers that big," Nacen said

dryly. He turned to address the surviving trooper again. "Alright, we're going to unjam your connection to what's left of your squad's shard. When we do, and I need you to listen very carefully to this next part, I need you to deactivate this bomb."

The trooper nodded slowly.

"Alright," she croaked.

The warhead made a brief, high-pitched whine as the C3 trooper triggered IMTel communication with it.

"Tell me that was the sound of it deactivating," Nacen said to no one in particular.

Lina was bent over the crate, her eyes wide and locked in concentration.

"That was the sound of it deactivating," she said flatly.

"That wasn't very convincing."

"Well, I've managed to intercept the initiation command she sent to it, but I think I may have just delayed it. Give me a minute and I may be able to defuse it myself. Just need to decrypt the access codes she sent with that last signal."

Beskin and Shukernak stood rapt in what Nacen figured was either stoic discipline or paralyzing fear. Nacen smiled in an effort to hide his own panic-stricken expression.

"Now I thought you might misunderstand and try to set off this bomb," he said to the trooper. "Thankfully, you've given Lina here the access codes she needs to defuse it. I really wish we could've done it a little more easily though."

The C3 trooper made a desperate grab for her plasma pistol at her side. Nacen raised his own and fired, ensuring the woman would get no further. The trooper howled in pain, clutching her cauterized stump of a right arm.

"It's my own fault really," Nacen said. "I should have known you'd be willing to detonate this warhead with yourselves still on-board. You C3 are all backed up in Concord IMTel anyway. Of course, it's easy to back up a brain when it's as tiny as yours."

"By its very nature, the Concord adapts and evolves," the trooper said. "At a pace no others can hope to match. There can be no victory for those that play on the sidelines, content in their complacency to see how things turn out."

"I'll have you know, I get very torn up about my complacency from time to time," Nacen replied, leveling his pistol at the trooper's head.

The woman instinctively raised her hand and stump to shield her face. He released a low-energy pulse that didn't stop until it burrowed a finger's length into the simulated marble floor.

Lina clapped her hands together.

"I take it by the fact that I'm not space dust that you defused it."

"Quite observant of you, Captain," Lina said with the barest hint of enthusiasm.

Nacen released a sigh through a lungful of air he hadn't realized he had been holding in.

Nearly a half hour later, the entire crew of the Carmine Canotila was gathered under the ship's hull, absent the two fallen domari. Camlo was resting easy in the Carmine's medical bay, his flesh repairing itself over an artificial right arm of tungsten-reinforced nanite composites. Station Master Raul stood before them, surrounded by a dozen guards, mag pistols holstered at their side.

"The dedication of House Byzantia has been proven beyond a doubt today," he said, shaking Nacen's hand once more. This time Nacen was quite sure he would need some assistance from his medical drone once the Boromite released his hand. "You have my eternal gratitude, as well as the thanks of everyone aboard the station, and those who prosper from its existence for years to come."

"You are too kind, Master Omgar," Nacen replied, massaging his hand gingerly.

"I could have done without a docking tendril drifting into space and more than two dozen reported collisions from fleeing merchant ships, but the alternative scenario would have far eclipsed this damage. Of course, it goes without saying that your contract with the Attisan Trading Hub shall be renewed indefinitely."

Nacen nodded his appreciation. With one last round of handshakes and parting remarks the crew of the Carmine boarded their ship.

"What's with the memory chip?" Camlo asked as he

limped onto the bridge shortly after the Carmine Canotila had departed the station.

"It's a bargaining chip, to be exact," Nacen corrected flatly. "For when we inevitably run into the Concord again."

There would be plenty of time to reflect and learn from the events that transpired on the Crab. For now, as the Carmine propelled itself leisurely toward to gate leading to the Mu Arae system, Nacen contented himself with the fact that the entire ordeal was documented on the minuscule data storage chip he twirled between the fingers of his right hand.

Camlo rubbed the forearm of his new metallic limb with his own good hand.

"I still wish I could have my old arm back," he said.

"We took them for a lot more," Nacen reassured his cousin.

"Yeah, I guess it was a fair trade," Camlo acknowledged, a little forlorn.

Nacen Byzantia gazed absently at the chip as it danced between his fingers.

"A fair trade indeed," he muttered.

Leap of Faith
By Robert E Waters

Boromite Captain Hersh Ryza was surprised that Anka Qin-Rylish would allow him into her personal quarters wearing reflexive armor, a mag pistol holstered at his side, and a plasma carbine held tightly in his thick hands. He was equipped to kill. Why wasn't she afraid? Then again, why would she be? She was a Guild Mother of the Rylish Clan–his clan. Well, it used to be his clan.

"You may kneel," the Guild Mother said, her lavish evening robes flowing off her strong shoulders like bright red lava. Her face was a rock of confidence. Of course she wasn't scared. Ryza could see the half dozen dark glass panels on either side of the room, hiding her personal guard. A dozen carbines were trained at his head.

He slung his rifle onto his back and knelt, though he was loathe to do so. She did not deserve his respect. He lowered his head, as tradition dictated, and revealed his empty palms as a sign of peace and submission. He gritted his teeth and said, "I am honored to be in your presence, Guild Mother. May I know why I have been summoned?"

She hesitated, though he could feel the heat of her gown emanate throughout the room. She was purposefully trying to make him uncomfortable, perhaps hoping that he would err and spring those carbines behind the smoky glass. *This is a trap,* Barome, his advisor on political matters, had said before he had accepted the summons. *Do not go.* Ryza was beginning to see the wisdom of that council.

She moved closer to him, her feet invisible beneath her dress. She floated across the room, her posture as perfect as the rubies dangling from the ornate golden rings attached to her ears. It was uncommon for Boromites–even females–to wear such ostentatious wrappings. But she was a Guild Mother, and this was no normal meeting. He kept his head low and still, his eyes on the carbine at his side.

She laid a gentle hand on his shoulder. "I want you and

your brothers to return to the clan."

Ryza's powerful heart leapt into his throat. It had been almost one hundred years since their exile; he had been there to witness it. Why now?

He swallowed. "May I know why?"

Qin-Rylish withdrew her hand and swayed backward, giving Ryza the opportunity to look up in supplication. She smiled. "I want to be as honest with you as I can, Hersh.

"As you may, or may not, know, the Rylish Clan is without a mining contract. Our numbers grow small, our resources and status within the Boromite sphere have diminished." She paused, looked away as if disgusted with her own admittance. She cleared her throat and continued. "It is necessary, therefore, to ask you to rejoin our clan—your clan—for the benefit of all."

Ryza suppressed a snicker. He found the courage to stand and face her. He was taller than the Guild Mother. It was her turn to stare up at him. "So, after banishing us in disgrace, you now need our help. How the tables have turned."

"You are not standing on a rich vein either, Hersh," she said, using his first name again, as if they were old friends. "While you've remained alive, your brothers die, scores of them, to the point of no recovery. One engagement after another, an infinite series of battles against the Ghar, the Senatex, the Concord. Victories and glory all around. But for how long? You have no way to replenish your stock, and your ranks grow thin. There will come a day when your brothers breathe no more, when their hammers find no rocks to break. That day draws close. I think you know that."

There was an arrogance, a self-assuredness, in her voice that angered him. But she had him, he knew. No matter how difficult life was for the Rylish Clan these days, nothing compared to the impending doom of Ryza and his exiled brothers. Doom? A bit melodramatic, indeed, but not far from the truth. Their last engagement with the Senatex had cost them a third of their strength. Another fight like that and, well, he wouldn't be standing here staring down a Guild Mother. He'd be dead.

Ryza stared into Qin-Rylish's dark, forceful eyes. He did not care about his own well-being. He could die today, and his exile would not have been a fruitless time. He had learned a lot about life, about the nature of the universe, in having to strike out on his own, to find his own way through the morass of Antares gateways, without the constant need to please the clan or its Guild Mother. There was a certain pleasurable hedonism in exile that he had grown to love. Exile was his life now, and he did not care about losing that life. But what about the lives of his brothers? As their captain, their Rock Father, they had given him authority to speak for them, but he could not choose exile and death for them all. He could not be so arrogant, so selfish. He had to give them a chance to live and to excel. They deserved that much at least.

Hersh Ryza sighed. "It is an offer that I must discuss with my brothers, you understand. What is the catch?"

Qin-Rylish's strong, expressive face pinched as if she had eaten something sour. "Pardon?"

"Come now, Guild Mother. Share with me some of that honesty you professed but a moment ago. You did not summon me here to simply invite me and my brothers back from exile. There is a condition attached to your gracious offer. What is it?"

The Guild Mother stared for several minutes, then allowed herself a smile. "You are smart, Captain Hersh Ryza. And correct. There is a condition, and it is this. To rejoin our clan and have the blight of exile removed from your names, there is a mission that you must undertake. And allow me further honesty, my good captain. This mission is dangerous... very dangerous."

***

"I reiterate, Captain," Political Advisor Barome Ashute said, his voice raised in agitation. "She is leading us into a trap."

Barome Ashute's hide was the traditional Boromite slate grey, but he had personally inked his skin black so that the bony nodules running along the length of his spine stood out like flat, battered teeth. With a dull blade, he had scraped off the Rylish dragon head from his chest. It now looked like a dull red scar of paint with a line of fire through its heart. He had taken their exile harder than most.

"You say that about everything, Barome," Ryza said, using the first name because they were friends. "If I said I was going for a drink, you'd warn against the wetness of the water."

"Mock me all you will, but the Guild Mother is not to be trusted, and you know that. She exiled us once already. This is a ploy to finish what she started."

Ryza found it hard to remember anymore why he and his brothers had been exiled in the first place. The details were fuzzy, but his entire battalion had been on operations under the employ of the Senetex against the Concord. For some reason, their commander chose to switch sides at the height of the battle, and for a few short moments, Boromite fought Boromite. Ryza, then only a simple soldier in the ranks, remembered vaguely gaining a foothold in a town once controlled by the Rylish clan. It was all a daze. He had just been following orders, but when Qin-Rylish learned of his battalion's treachery, she exiled them all, including those like Barome Ashute who had pleaded that when he saw the deception taking hold, he had thrown down his weapon and walked away. That did not matter to the Guild Mother: they were all guilty in her eyes, all equally deserving of their punishment. Barome's hatred for the Guild Mother was deep.

"It's a mission," Ryza said, refocusing his thoughts on the matter at hand, "like hundreds of missions that we have gone on before. If the Algoryn had approached us personally, you would not be arguing against it."

"But they did not approach us," Barome said. "They are working through the Guild Mother, and as your political advisor, I strongly recommend reconsidering your decision."

Ryza nodded. "Thank you, Barome. But the decision is made. I've taken the measure of our brothers, and they are in favor of the try. And at the end, if we succeed, you may decide not to rejoin the clan. That is your right, and I will honor that decision. But we are going forward." Ryza moved so that the three dimensional display of the Algoryn world of Ephra floated at chest level among a sparkling display of stars and dust. "Now, do you wish to know the mission in full?"

Barome sighed, the muscles in his face pulling back in agitation. Despite his inked skin, his pallor brightened. He fidgeted in place, and Ryza could see that his advisor wanted to argue some more. But he held his tongue, settled beside the stellar display, and said, "As you wish, Captain."

Ryza cleared his throat and began. "The Du'rel Optimate Moch of the Algoryn Prosperate has hired the Rylish clan to investigate a missing Algoryn fleet that entered this gate..." Ryza punched a few buttons near the display, and a thick red pulsing sphere appeared near Ephra. "...and has not returned. Naturally, this is of great concern since this is the second gate to open in the system, which is a rare phenomenon, and one not to be taken lightly. That is where we come in. We have been asked by the Guild Mother to enter the gate and determine the fate of said fleet."

Barome shrugged. "Why doesn't the Guild Mother simply order her own fleet into the gate? She has ample Rylish assets at her disposal without involving us."

Ryza nodded. "Indeed, but this is our way of re-establishing our loyalty to her and to the clan. She also believes that our ship, a light, sleek model with strong counter-measures, will provide a smaller footprint than anything that she can muster."

"So we are expendable," Barome said in a huff, allowing his frustration to show. "We go in, and we may never come out."

Ryza nodded. "Yes, that is possible."

"Why didn't the Du'rel send in an explorer probe first? That's protocol on all newly appearing gates."

"They did," Ryza said. "Three, in fact, when the first two did not return. The third reported all clear, so they sent in the fleet for further exploration. It's not been heard from since."

Barome grunted. "Sounds like the Algoryn were duped." He rubbed his face, which was growing whiter by the minute. He seemed physically ill by the data. "So what did the Algoryn give–or promise–our exalted Guild Mother for our blood and sweat?"

Ryza punched a few more buttons on the display and Ephra was replaced with a long, healthy belt of rocks and dust surrounding a bright sun. "The Rylish Clan will gain exclusive mining rights to their Bu'tyk Asteroid Belt. It is a boon for our clan and will ensure our prosperity for millennia."

The thought of it made Ryza's face flush. He tried containing his excitement. It was unseemly for an exiled captain to be so in favor of reunion. He didn't need to be obstinate like Barome, but he sure as hell needed to show some decorum. The mission was dangerous, and a part of him even agreed with Barome. It could be a trap, and it probably was. They might enter this mysterious gate and never return. But then, would they be any worse off than they were now?

Ryza paid Barome the courtesy of waiting for a response, without speaking, without trying to influence the old man any further.

Finally, Barome said, with more sincerity than Ryza had ever heard his advisor use, "It's a suicide mission, Captain."

Ryza shook his head, laid his hand on Barome's massive shoulder. "No, it is a leap of faith, and I'm asking you to leap with me."

Barome looked at the display, ran his finger through the speck of light given off by the asteroid belt. He nodded. "Okay, Hersh. If you think it is that important, then I will help see it through. When do we start?"

***

The Du'rel provided them with the appropriate resonant signal, and the target gate they approached received it and responded in kind, pulling the Proudly Exiled into its trans-dimensional tunnel. Hersh Ryza hated this moment: the initial entry into a gate. His stomach always turned, his head felt light. He could be in a daze for minutes, even hours, depending upon the manner in which the tunnel drew them in. And how long they would travel through it depended upon the gate itself. There was no maneuver, no course correction to be taken while in flight through a trans-dimensional tunnel. It could be minutes, hours, days, weeks, even months before they reached the exit. Ryza put in his mouth guard to keep from biting off his own tongue during entry, sat back comfortably in his impact seat, buckled in, and closed his eyes.

Three days later, they emerged.

"Scan the area, standard protocol," he said to helm.

"Yes, Captain."

The system they had entered was not unique or unusual. It contained a standard G-type star with five planets, a small asteroid belt between the fourth and fifth planet, and two smaller proto-planets on the perimeter, locked in each other's orbit. What was unique was the swirl of ship wreckage that dipped deep into the asteroid belt.

"The Guild Mother's Mercy!" Ryza heard the muffled prayer over comm.

"Be still, now," he said, the prayer on the tip of his own tongue, but he did not speak it. "Move us in closer, helm. Get us to ten kiloyan of the epicenter."

Ryza opened the view window on the starboard side of his cabin to get a better look at the wreckage hanging in space. Algoryn ships, definitely. Scores of battered pieces floating cold in space, encircling the debris of the asteroid belt, mingling with the rocks as if they too were mere space detritus. There were no exposed interiors popping and flashing with electrical systems shorting out in vacuum, so it was clear that whatever had done such damage had done it quite a while ago. Everything was cold, solid, and dead. Was it the missing Algoryn fleet? There was no evidence against that, and the system that they had entered was uncharted as far as the scan was concerned, so there was no real possibility of it being anything but that missing fleet.

"Whoever did this," Ryza said, "the devastation was total."

Nearing the epicenter of the debris field, Ryza began to pick out hull remains of other ships. He zoomed the view screen in closer to try and pick out the white and red markings on the shattered hulls. The markings came in crystal clear, and they were not Algoryn symbols.

"Ghar, sir," helm said.

He recognized them immediately.

The shattered Algoryn and Ghar hulls were locked in a cold, frozen dance. It was clear from the disposition of the wreckage that the Algoryn had been on the attack, many of its prows sticking deep into punctured Ghar ships. It was almost as if the Algoryn were purposefully sacrificing themselves to take out this errant Ghar fleet, which seemed to have been comprised primarily of destroyers, cruisers... and was that the hull of a battleship? It was hard to tell from this distance, and intervening wreckage was making it difficult to ascertain the full Ghar complement. But whatever the case, the fighting had been close-in and desperate.

"Well," he said over comm, so that everyone listening in could hear, "we know now what happened to the Algoryn fleet. I see no reason to stay any longer. Helm, turn us around and—"

"Sir, we're picking up a distress beacon beyond the debris field," helm said. "About three hundred kiloyan beyond. It's weak, but consistent."

Damn! He could already sense annoyance from Barome. He hadn't said anything during their debris field sweep, but he was listening, and Ryza could feel the temperature of the room plummet.

"Okay, helm," he said, quietly, "take us around the field. Slowly, with stealth and counter-measures at full throttle. Shielding as well."

"Yes, Captain."

The Boromite were not known for their space fleet prowess. Their infamy had been shaped by their skills on battlefields planetside, but the Proudly Exiled had been commandeered early in their history and refitted over the years with many improvements that made her nearly invisible to common scanning technology. Helm could move it through the wreckage with such skill that, if anyone were scanning for life signs, they would interpret the ship's footprint as nothing more than fast floating debris. It was an advantage that had not been missed by the Guild Mother. That was why she had sent them on this mission. But their duties had concluded, hadn't they? They had only been tasked with discovering the fate of the Algoryn fleet, and they had done that. Nothing more. So why was he pushing the mission further with more investigation? He didn't know for sure, but perhaps the answers lay in the weak distress signal.

They emerged from the debris field to discover a line of wreckage swirling down into the ionosphere of the fourth planet. To Ryza, the swirl resembled the mass transfer stream between a red giant and a white dwarf. Both Algoryn and Ghar wreckage formed the stream. The signal was emanating from the planet's surface.

"Can you determine the ownership of the distress beacon?" He asked helm.

There was a pause, then, "Yes, Captain. It's Algoryn."

"Sir, we do not know if there is anyone alive on that planet." Barome's voice, and opinion, came through loud and clear. "Could be an empty escape shuttle damaged and sending out pings randomly."

Ryza nodded, though no one was there to see it. "It could be. It could also be survivors."

"Ghar could be down there as well," Barome said, "judging from the wreckage swirl."

"You are not afraid of the Ghar, are you, Barome?" Ryza's battle advisor, Plaxyn Mosh, said indignantly.

"Much less than you are," Barome replied, his voice lowering, "judging from our last encounter with them."

"Gentlemen," Ryza cut in, before tempers flared any further, "enough! If there are survivors, they need to be found, because it isn't enough to know that the Algoryn fleet was destroyed, much to my regret. We need to know the nature of their engagement with the Ghar. We need to know everything."

He looked toward the swirl of wreckage once more, listened again to the distress beacon. Barome was correct. There was no way of knowing what lay on the planet. But that did not matter.

Ryza darkened his window, turned off his view screen and said, "Get a force ready, Mosh, and leave a spot for me. We're going down."

***

The surface of this planet was not unlike any number of planets Ryza had visited and fought on over the past one hundred years. Mixed density foliage, hills, rivers, long stretches of golden grass veldt's, deserts, jungles, swamps, and mountains. An ample ocean divided the two main continents, and tiny ice caps lay far away at the poles. It had a slightly higher oxygen level than he preferred, and thus he expected to experience higher growth rates in the forest and jungle regions; the amount of desert and grassland surprised him. But he suspected that the actual oxygen level had been declining over the past several millennia as surface changes continued. They were setting down on a planet in physical transition. That was fine with him. Oxygen levels were higher than normal, indeed, but well within a Boromite's ability to handle.

What concerned him the most was the Algoryn wreck that scarred the landing site. A massive destroyer had cut a swath four miles long, leaving behind it a chasm that would now forever be part of the planet's surface. A wreck that size was troubling. What was even more troubling was the smaller, though equally deadly, Ghar assault pod that lay in scorched ruin nearby.

"There could be hundreds of survivors," Plaxyn Mosh said as they swept forward twenty-five strong, fully kitted out in reflective armor, plasma carbines at the ready, with shield and spotter drones in forward deployment.

"Thousands," Ryza replied, and if that were true, there could be no rescue mission. Well, not for every Algoryn survivor. Their small assault craft was only capable of holding a handful beyond its normal capacity. Getting thousands of survivors off-planet would take a long, long time, and besides, the Proudly Exiled did not have that kind of cabin space. Hell, they didn't even have enough space to stack survivors into corridors.

"Over there," Plaxyn said, pointing his carbine toward a line of trees that edged the sea of light-green grass that lay all around them at waist level. It had been trampled flat in the direction Plaxyn pointed, a long winding path toward the tree line.

"Could be a herd of grazers," Ryza said.

"Unlikely," Plaxyn replied, "given the pattern. Recommend following."

Ryza nodded and the unit shifted toward the path.

Three troopers and a shield drone were left behind to scour the wreckage, to search for wounded, with strict instructions to report surviving Algoryn, and to kill all surviving Ghar.

"Keep it low and tight," Ryza said, crouching as they quickened the pace. Along the way, dead Algoryn troopers could be seen moldering in the thick grass, their reflexive armor ripped open, their carbines and mag guns broken and tossed aside. The local fauna munched on the remains of one, and a Boromite trooper kicked the rat-like beast for fun. It screeched and scurried away, seemingly unharmed.

"A fighting withdrawal?" Ryza asked Plaxyn.

The tall, thick Boromite commander shook his head. "No, they were moving toward the fight. The kill pattern is consistent with an assault." He stopped quickly, held up his arm, crouched in the grass. Everyone stopped and knelt as directed. Even the drones dropped below the grass top. "And now we know for sure who they are fighting."

At Plaxyn's feet lay the battered, charred remains of a Ghar Outcast Trooper, partially trampled into the soft ground. It still held a lugger, its trigger finger black, stiff, and pressing down tightly.

"At least it went down fighting," Ryza said, poking at the remains with his carbine. "The first assault occurred here, no doubt. But how long did the Algoryn push forward, I wonder? And where are they now?"

"If we move any further afield, Captain," Plaxyn said, "we'll find out for sure. And there will be no turning back. Our brothers are prepared for a fight. It's been too long since these hands, this gun, have tasted blood. I need to take the edge off. We all do. But it's your decision. Do we press on, or go back?"

It was a ridiculous notion for a Boromite to even consider retreat, though falling back now would not technically constitute an official withdrawal from combat. They had not engaged with an enemy yet, but Plaxyn was right; it had been too long between fights. Too, too long.

Ryza nodded, and said, "Forward."

They pressed on, and roughly three klicks later, they heard gunfire. The spotter drones picked it up first and relayed coordinates back to the main body. Another klick forward, and the battle commenced.

A plucky Ghar combat unit had established a redoubt along a natural ridgeline, reinforcing it with crude wooden spikes, piled rocks, and Ghar dead in heavily damaged battle suits. The Ghar fighting force was comprised primarily of outcast troopers with weak lugger guns, although there did seem to be a few Ghar battlesuits still operational and still pumping out horrifying strikes with scourer cannons. They were making a fight of it, but their opposition had them surrounded.

On three sides, at least. Algoryn survivors scattered through hillocks of tall grass, small patches of wood, hastily established defenses behind splintered logs, piled dirt, and Algoryn dead. Their weaponry was comprised of plasma carbines, mag repeaters, D-spinners, and a few spotter drones. To Ryza, it was clear the siege had been going on for a long time. But he wondered why the Algoryn hadn't been more successful in breaking it.

"We need to find a leader, if they have one," he said.

Ryza led the unit toward the other side of the siege line, where they found a young Algoryn, tight-pressed, with anger flaring in his eyes.

"I am Ensign Karlyle," the young Algoryn said, gripping his carbine tightly. He seemed spent, exhausted, his face wet with sweat and blackened scabs of dirt and blood. "I am the highest ranking officer with operational status."

Ryza huffed. "That explains why this siege hasn't been broken yet."

Ensign Karlyle ignored the insult, though Ryza could see the Algoryn's jaw muscles clench. "It has not been broken for three reasons. First, radiation and pollutants from Ghar weaponry are too great at the redoubt point. Second, and you should know this, Boromite, our nano-based technologies cannot function properly within radiation fields so strong. I assure you, if either of those two factors did not exist, we would not be having this conversation. The Ghar would already be dead."

"What's the third reason?" Ryza asked.

Ensign Karlyle cleared his throat. "They have a prisoner. Admiral Shin Bak Bukara. His signal is weak. We do not know if he is even alive. We cannot go in at full power because, alive or dead, his body must be preserved. We cannot risk an assault that might see the Ghar, as a last desperate act, annihilate him."

"Why?"

"Because his internal data nano-storage contains the

Ghar invasion plan for Ephra."

Ryza nodded, pointing to the sky. "I assume that shattered Ghar fleet up there was the invasion force?"

Ensign Karlyle nodded. "But only a portion of it, the initial deployment. Their plans call for three times that number of warships with tens of thousands of Ghar battlesuits, and even more Outcasts. It's perhaps the largest Ghar force that Algoryn have ever faced. And they'll use that new gate to pop into our system."

"A surprise attack, eh?"

"Indeed. They did not expect us to send in an entire fleet, risk that much steel, for a simple reconnaissance of a new gate. That is the weakness of the Ghar: tough and savage on the field of battle, but simple-minded strategically. We surprised them. As far as we know, those Ghar in the redoubt are the last of that fleet. The ideal situation would be to kill them all, but the priority is to reclaim Admiral Bukara."

"I don't see why his body matters so much," Plaxyn Mosh said derisively. "You know they are going to attack. Relay word of that back to Ephra and be prepared."

"Are you dense? Communication cannot occur through a gate. Besides, details matter, Captain," Ensign Karlyle said, raising his carbine to chest level. "There is more in the Admiral's storage than a strategic overview. There are timetables, fleet dispositions, weapon types and numbers, unit designations, and scores of other details that no one else possesses. We need to get it, and before the radiation eats away at his body and destroys those details. Our plan is to extract the admiral, attempt to resurrect one of the damaged shuttle craft in our wreckage, then get the hell out of here. That's the plan."

Ryza considered. He looked toward the redoubt again, surveyed the sporadic gunfire being placed upon it by Algoryn troopers. He huffed and shook his head. Theoretically, this standoff could keep going for days, weeks even, or whatever constituted days or weeks on this planet. Eventually, ammunition and power sources would run out, and more likely, it would be Algoryn weaponry that would stop firing first. And by then, none of it would matter. The Ghar would have arrived in-system with the rest of their fleet and Ephra would be burning like a candle.

If that happened, Ryza knew for certain, that the Algoryn would not give them their exclusive mining contract, and the Guild Mother would not let him and his brothers back into the family. For all of that to happen in the proper manner, the siege had to be broken, and the admiral had to be saved.

Ryza took two steps toward Ensign Karlyle. He spoke low, as if he didn't wish anyone else to hear. "Okay, Ensign. I have a plan. We can break this siege, but it'll require a great sacrifice on your part."

The ensign stared at him. He swallowed. Ryza could see determination, but also fear, in the young man's eyes. He nodded. "Admiral Bukara is all that matters now."

"Very well. Then listen up. Here is what we're going to do..."

***

The red sun was setting and the Algoryn attacked in force.

Led by Ensign Karlyle, they came out of their defensive positions and exposed themselves to furious Ghar counter-fire. Ryza was impressed.

He and his brothers waited in the tall grass on the left side of the siege line, waited until the Ghar seemed convinced that the Algoryn were making their final assault on their redoubt. It wasn't a long wait, but to Ryza, it seemed interminable. Everything came down to this plan of his. The men were up to it, or at least they pretended to be. Some would die trying to save the Algoryn admiral, never having the chance to live a life out of exile. Was it worth it? Yes, Ryza nodded to himself, as he watched Ghar gunfire rip through the assaulting Algoryn line.

"Now!"

His small force of twenty-five rose from the grass and attacked, hitting the left side of the Ghar redoubt, while the Algoryns continued making their faux frontal and flanking assault, with strict orders not to enter the radiation field. Ryza lay on his plasma carbine, not caring anymore about exposing himself to Ghar fire. A tiny Outcast scampering about in the redoubt suddenly realized the Boromite force rising out of the grass. It shrieked the alarm, and lugger fire whisked through the grass, some pelting the Boromite reflexive armor and bouncing away harmlessly. But that would not last, Ryza knew. The closer they drew, the more deadly the Ghar defense would become.

A lucky lugger shot splintered the armor of a nearby Boromite soldier, and he fell dead at Plaxyn Mosh's feet. The military advisor stepped over the body without a care and shouted, "We're coming into the radiation field. Keep it tight!"

Radiation was invisible, but it felt like they were walking into the shimmering heat of a desert. Ryza could almost see the radiation coming off the stacked Ghar battlesuits that protected Outcast soldiers taking refuge within those rendered remains; he activated his scope and took aimed shots wherever he saw red eyes glaring through the pile. He responded to Plaxyn's order with his own. "Aimed shots! You hear? Aimed shots! No spray or anything that might harm the admiral."

He did not know where the admiral was in that redoubt. And if he were alive, Ryza certainly didn't want errant carbine fire to take him out. Ensign Karlyle was right: all that mattered was recovering the body, dead or alive. But a live admiral would be a much sweeter find.

A lugger round struck Ryza's shoulder. It threw him back a few paces. He responded with fire of his own, pelting the discarded battlesuits in front of the Outcast who had committed the strike. The remains of the battlesuit shifted under intense plasma strikes, but held firm, and the Outcast continued to fire.

The effects of the radiation were beginning to take their toll. His men were still moving forward strongly, but Ryza could feel his heart rate and breath quicken as the deadly heat from both the suits and setting sun drew drenching sweat from his face and body. He was beginning to feel a little light-headed as well. He shook away the sensations, laid on his carbine trigger, and leapt forward into the battlesuits.

He and Plaxyn hit the redoubt's edge at the same time. They reached out together and tore chunks of battle armor away from piles of logs. Lugger fire pelted the space around them, in fact, unintentionally helping to break up the barrier. Another yank and the entire defensive wall collapsed. The wave of ruined metal and molded plastic toppled down the bank, taking several Boromite soldiers with it. Ryza held firm, digging his strong fingers into the embankment and letting the avalanche roll over his back. It hurt like hell, as sharp metal tore through exposed flesh on his arms and legs, but he held firm and waited.

Then he rose. He could see into the main platform of the redoubt, where the Ghar had hastily erected a command center. No Ghar commander, however, was sitting back, dolling out orders. Apparently most had already died in the initial Algoryn assault that had occurred days before. But there were two Ghar commanders still fighting, both of them in battlesuits, holding firm the line against the new Algoryn assault.

Ensign Karlyle had pushed further forward than planned. Brave, indeed, but foolish. Now Ryza could see a wave of Algoryn troopers hit the redoubt edge and try to tear away the Ghar defenses. But the radiation exposure was taking a huge toll on their assault, and they were getting hammered by Ghar weaponry.

"Go!" Ryza screamed to his brothers, as he pulled himself up and over the remaining Ghar defenses.

They attacked the command center in strength, bowling over the weakened Outcast defense. Ryza smashed the face of one Outcast with the barrel of his carbine, blew away another with a plasma round in the gut. Three more struck him at the same time, jumping on his back like monkeys. In desperation, one bit at his ear and tore away flesh. Ryza howled, reached up, and grabbed the runt and used him like a club against another more determined Outcast that was trying to stab a combat knife between the gaps in Ryza's reflex armor. He did not succeed, however, as Plaxyn's beefy fist crushed the little fellow's spine with one strategically placed shot. The third Outcast scampered away in fear.

"Find the admiral," Plaxyn said. "I'll hold them off."

Ryza nodded and began shuffling through piles of equipment and boxes and various other Ghar items and weapon caches. The smell of rotting Ghar flesh was quite pronounced, as Ryza stepped over bodies that had been decaying in the hot sun for days. It would seem that the Ghar intended to fight to the last, to die in place. Discarded food containers and foul excrement lay everywhere. Ryza walked through it all, trying to steel his mind away from the putrid odors.

Two Boromite soldiers joined him in the search, and soon they found a small, metal cage. In it lay Admiral Bukara, heavily bound with rope and cable ties. His mouth was covered in a thick tape. His naked body was covered in lacerations and red radiation whelps.

"Bastards," a Boromite soldier said, his eyes showing full disgust and anger.

Ryza reached through the cage bars. He touched the admiral's shoulder. "Still warm. He's alive. Barely."

He stood up and grabbed the handles on the cage. Another soldier gripped the handles on the opposite side, and together, they hoisted the cage up and out.

The fight was still on. Ensign Karlyle stood beside Plaxyn Mosh as they poured fire upon a huddle of Ghar soldiers who were seeking refuge at the base of the redoubt. The Algoryn dead piled high, along with some Boromite brothers. Ryza did not like seeing that, but there would be time for grieving later. They needed to get the admiral to their ship.

"Go!" Plaxyn yelled and waved to him as he stood his ground against a Ghar battlesuit. "We'll follow!"

Ryza nodded, turned, and slammed into the waiting chest of another metal monstrosity.

The massive trooper swung at Ryza with its plasma claw, but the quicker Boromite captain dropped the cage and ducked. Sparks flew as the claw scraped across his armored shoulder. The Boromite soldier on the opposite side of the cage tried to respond with carbine fire, but the battlesuit tore a black hole through his chest with a strike from his scourer cannon.

Ryza kept his balance, pushed hard upward through his legs, and slammed his shoulder into the battlesuit. He managed to raise it off the ground for a moment. It then came crashing back down by driving one of its spiked legs into his boot. Ryza howled, fell back, recovered against the cage, and punched the Ghar's metal face. The Ghar stammered, but the strike did more damage to Ryza's hand. He felt a spear shot of pain leap up through his arm. He fell back again, tried raising his carbine to take a shot. The battlesuit plucked the gun away from his hands like it was picking flowers.

The battlesuit aimed his scourer cannon to fire again. Fighting through his pain, Ryza reached out and grabbed the cannon with both hands. It fired wildly off to the right. It tried firing again. The same result. Ryza refused to let go, despite the battlesuit's plasma claw nipping away at his armor. It was in tatters, and if the cannon could ever be brought to bear, Ryza knew he'd be blown away.

But that didn't happen. Instead, Ensign Karlyle, his face a smear of bloody lacerations and red blisters, came up to the right and hammered the battlesuit with his plasma carbine. The spray of plasma struck the suit and forced it to abandon its cannon fire. It fell back, almost to the edge of the redoubt, but recovered and struck out with its claw. It took Ensign Karlyle straight in the face and clipped his jaw in two.

Plaxyn Mosh answered from the left, throwing his body into the suit. The sheer force of the strike took them both over the embankment. Ryza watched them tumble down the ledge, Plaxyn on top, using his carbine like a club, pounding the Ghar battlesuit. Ryza's instinct was to follow, to save his battle brother, but he paused, remembering why they were here.

He turned and stared into the cage. Admiral Bukara looked dead. He probably was. But there was no getting him out of here in that cage. Too heavy, too bulky.

With his good hand, Ryza picked up his carbine, aimed it at the cage lock, and fired. The lock melted away. Ryza reached in, pulled the admiral free, swung him over his shoulder, and ran.

The sounds of battle quickly diminished as Ryza reached the perimeter of the Algoryn defensive line and into a sea of grass. He didn't bother to look back. He kept running, and in time battle sounds disappeared altogether. He breathed a sigh of relief, then felt panic as he suddenly remembered the brothers that he had left behind. Were they dead? Many for sure. What about Plaxyn Mosh?

He put the terrible thoughts out of his mind and kept running. He radioed ahead to the three they left behind to survey the wreckage. His comm link was in tatters, and his message was cut off, but hopefully they got enough of it to be waiting, with the shuttle's engine hot and ready.

A cannon round soared over his head, hitting the ground in front of him. The plume of smoke and fire that erupted forced Ryza to turn left. More gunfire erupted, and another cannon round split the grass as it flew harmlessly to the right. Ryza dared stop, turn, and see who was in pursuit.

A Ghar battlesuit.

His lungs were at the breaking point, but he ran even faster, not caring anymore about holding Admiral Bukara gently. The puncture wound in his foot began to ache with each step, but Ryza zigged and zagged, keeping the Ghar guessing as to where he was going. Round after round struck near him, until the very air he breathed was choked with smoke and fire. At one point, he stumbled, fell to one knee. He held there a moment, listening to the wind, trying to divine where his pursuer might go. Perhaps he could lie quietly in the grass, wait until the beast had passed him, then strike. But no. He was too weak for that, and the admiral would surely be killed in the scuffle. He picked himself up and kept running.

"Ghar in pursuit," he screamed over comm. "Get ready. Get ready!"

He reached the edge of the grassland, making a point to stay out of the well-worn path that they had traveled earlier. Why give the battlesuit an open target? He ran another one hundred yards across an opening, and then he saw his shuttle and the three Boromite soldiers, protected behind defensive positions, held carbines aimed in his direction.

Another cannon round hit near the shuttle, knocking it sideways, but it didn't collapse. Ryza kept running until he found shelter behind it. He lowered Admiral Bukara to the ground, not bothering to remove the Algoryn's bindings. He had more important matters to attend to.

A soldier threw him a carbine. "Do we take off, Captain?"

Ryza caught the gun and shook his head. "No, it's too close. We have to pound it with gunfire. We have to protect the shuttle!"

He lay down in a rut in the ground caused by the destroyer wreck, trained his carbine on the field, and waited.

They could see the Ghar battlesuit coming at them as

it ploughed through the grass. It was fast, it was wild, it was angry. He could hear its metal parts grinding together as it reached the grass line. It emerged, scorched and pock-marked with plasma fire, its claw inoperable. But its cannon worked. It raised its arm up, took aim, and—

A shower of sparks erupted out of its belly. Its cannon fire flew harmlessly into the sky. More sparks and smoke burst from the battlesuit. It stood there as if it couldn't understand what was happening. It looked down at the long metal bar sticking out of its body. It tried moving its claw to the bar as if to try to rip it out, but the bar was twisted from behind, once, twice, until the wound gave out a final belch of fire, and then the battlesuit fell forward into the soft dirt.

Plaxyn Mosh stepped up onto the back of the fallen, his hand on the metal bar as if he were planting a flag. Ryza lowered his gun and breathed deeply. "That was close!"

Plaxyn nodded. "I told you I was right behind you."

"What's our situation?" Ryza asked.

"Grim," Plaxyn said. "We need to get out of here, now. More Ghar are coming."

Another eight Boromite brothers emerged from the grass. Ryza was thankful that some of his men had survived, but it had been a costly fight.

"Admiral Bukara is dead," Ryza said, as he felt no pulse on the man's neck. "Damn! All that running for nothing."

"But we have his body," Plaxyn said, "and that's what matters."

Ryza nodded. "Let's get him on the shuttle," he ordered, "and let's go home."

"What home would that be, Captain?"

Which one indeed. Ryza considered. They had done all this to be allowed back into their clan, and was it a trap like Barome Ashute had warned? No. The events that had transpired had convinced him that it wasn't a trap. The Clan Mother had been sincere in her offer. But would he accept? At the end of the day, he could still refuse, and his brothers – those still alive – would respect his decision, and they could go on and on as they were. The benefit of their exile had been autonomy. In their current situation, they could do what they wanted, serve whomever they wished, accept and decline any and all missions. If they returned to the clan, that freedom would be gone. He remembered asking Barome to take a leap of faith. As Ryza stood there, looking into Plaxyn's battered face, a dead Algoryn admiral at his side, he knew the answer immediately.

They all needed to take that leap, and take it now.

"Lift off," Ryza said, as the shuttle doors were being shut. "Lift off, and let's go home. The clan, and our mother, await."

Subver/ion
By Dave Horobin

Concord Integrated Machine Intelligence provided steward-ship for all of the history of the planet Votune, affording it with peaceful protection and guardianship for each and every citizen. Comforted by this safety, one inhabitant, Ryson, slept comfortably in one of the hundreds of thousands of apartments, blissfully unaware that his home was housed in one of many giant habitation towers scattered across the planet's surface. During the course of his slumber, the microscopic nanodrones set to work, repairing biological cells and stimulating relaxing hormone production. Ryson was not unique in this, as this was standard for all societies that had been bound to the IMTel, an intellect shared between man and machine, interfacing through the medium of nanospore. It also served as a power source and a communication tool merging the thoughts of civilized societies together on their respective planets within the PanHuman Con-cord, each forming its own unique shard. The planet of Ryson's abode was not remarkable when compared to many other plan-ets belonging to system gates in this part of the Western Inter-face around the surface of the great Star-Gateway of Antares. There had been no wars, no invasions, and no disasters. This sustained the serene nature of the populace.

Ryson was content. Ryson was satisfied with every aspect of his life. There was nothing that Ryson desired. The thoughts flowed through his mind as he lay on the sleep-bunk, wearily blinking his eyes after another restful night's sleep, thoughts easily mistaken for his own. As he flickered his eyes open to adjust to the increasing light, he glanced around the room; his hab-apartment was plain and not very big, the gentle off-white of the walls making the small box style apartment appear larger than it really was. Everything Ryson required was accessible on demand within the hab, although the emptiness of the room hid this reality.

Today was much like any other day. Ryson rarely left the luxury of his sleep-bunk immediately upon waking, the comfort provided by the suspensored bedding unit matching exactly the level of support required, tailored specifically to himself. Ryson did as he normally did and lay gazing at the ceiling, allowing the shard's Integrated Machine Intelligence permission to flood his mind with wondrous and pleasing swirls of color to appear before his eyes. Gentle pastel shades danced around his vision during these intentional daydreams that he found both soothing and calming. Not that there was much need to be reassured, but nonetheless it was a pleasing experience. Besides, he did not need to visit his brother until later.

Time progressed, much to the ignorance of Ryson who, after his regular daily activity of semi-consciousness, slowly regained focus and awareness of his surroundings. He noticed that a table and seat had appeared on the opposite wall to his sleep-bunk and the sensation of hunger rippled through his mind. Yes, he thought to himself, definitely time to eat. As he stood up from his resting place and walked the few paces to the chair, the bunk sunk to the floor and into the inter-wall space, an area controlled by self-aware suspensored drones and the hyper-fluidic nature of the boundaries of the rooms. It was here where all belongings were stored in hyper compression while not in direct use, following the owner around unseen, ensuring that whatever object or item was required, the IMTel would provide immediately.

Ryson sat at the table and a bowl and spoon were delivered through the surface. The bowl contained a nutritious meal, personalized for Ryson to ensure that the correct nourishment and quantity would be consumed. He spooned the first mouthful of the grey nutri-paste into his mouth and the sensation of flavors and textures in his mind replaced that of the tasteless, viscous fare. Further spoonfuls would vary the flavor, but never once did Ryson question how the taste changed from the same bowl; he never had: the thought had never occurred to him.

With the meal completed, Ryson stood up away from the table and it rippled through the hyper-fluidic wall, the suspensor fields closing behind it to give the appearance of a smooth solid wall where nothing had ever passed through. It's time to leave, he thought to himself. Each day after taking his meal he would go into The Garden and meet his brother; today would be no exception. Two ripples emanated around the room as a transmat pad moved up from the floor and a collection of garments on a rail appeared through a wall. Warm and sunny with a slight breeze, the IMTel projected the external weather into his mind. He changed into his functional outerwear, hesitated about taking the coat, and ultimately left it on the rail. It withdrew back into the wall as he stepped onto the transmat.

***

The destination pad was in what everyone referred to as The Garden. The gentle afternoon sunlight broke through a row of trees and caressed Ryson's cheeks as he appeared on the transmat. The localized climate for this shard had been set to mild-temperature and had been for quite a while. A thought about the weather changing almost coalesced in his mind but never quite came to pass as the desire to get to The Café, the usual rendezvous, grew stronger. He began his journey through The Garden along a tree lined pathway running from the local shared transmat pad through a peaceful parkland that ended in grassy embankments, just too high to see over. I wonder..? Ryson began thinking to himself, but he lost his train of thought as he carried on his way. There were many other people bustling their way through The Garden, all some type of PanHuman. We are all so different, yet all so the same, protected by the IMTel. After a short time weaving between the crowds, he reached the end of the tree-lined pathway, which gave way to a built up area with a collection of regular style perma-structures, buildings that had fixed walls and permanent furniture; a quaint throwback to a simpler era.

Inside The Café, Ryson saw his brother sitting at the same table, in the same chair, as they always sat. On the table were two cups, with the same steaming beverage they had taken each time they met.

"Long time no see." Ryson smirked as he sat into the chair. His brother's fist playfully impacted onto his shoulder.

"You say that every day." Dorath rolled his eyes and made a face that only a big brother could make to a younger sibling. "How are things?"

"Since yesterday? All okay, I suppose." Ryson grinned, he took a sip of his drink and an interesting flavor of mint Neotea stimulated his senses. "But you know, take each day as it comes."

Dorath's facial expression took on a more concerned demeanor, one he tried to hide each time he brought up the subject. "We're still worried about you."

Ryson's shoulders sank, he had heard this conversation so many times before...

"You have continued to spend so much of your time Stimming, have you found no long-term role yet?" Dorath continued, carefully watching his younger brother's reaction. Ryson never liked discussing this specific subject. A heavy and uncomfortable silence fell around their small two-seater table. The noise of other patrons washed over them, idle chatter, crockery, cutlery, and music putting a distance between the stares of the two brothers.

"It's just harmless daydreaming, no one has ever been proven to have been harmed by it," Ryson eventually protested, his brow furrowing in disagreement. He caught the eye of his brother. Dorath raised an eyebrow and the tip of his mouth curled gently upward. Ryson continued to object, "I, I need to do this. It's my way of helping and feeling useful. I know it is not much, but at least I feel that I'm helping the shard maintain our society." The elder brother lay a heavy hand on the younger's shoulder, a heavy silence settled between them again.

"Yeah, I know." Dorath's voice cracked quietly. Silence once again crept around the table. Stony glances darted between the two. Eventually Dorath stood, "It's been good to see you." A smile crept across Dorath's face as he emptied the last of his Neotea from his cup and placed it back on the table. "I'll be seeing you again tomorrow, don't over-do it." He winked at his younger sibling and took his leave.

Ryson remained seated for a while. All the civility of meeting his brother in such a bustling area always left him feeling fatigued. He drained the remnants of the Neotea and wistfully sighed to himself. He loved his family and wanted to protect them. He looked around The Café, noting all the other people that he knew indirectly through the IMTel. He wanted to protect them all.

His walk back through The Garden was dimly lit by the setting sun. The hum of a lumiglobe's suspensor caught his ear, which cast its light around him. The only reason for this drone's existence was to provide light to members of the shard while out after dusk, to protect them from the unknown lurking dangers in the dark. Not that there were any dangers here, Ryson thought to himself, but he could completely empathize with the lumiglobe's plight. The tramsmat took him back inside his hab. Perhaps not the same one he had left a few hours earlier, but that did not matter. All of the rooms were identical in the tall building, with personal possessions being moved around by the intelligent suspensor-borne compressor drones within the wall space, so no matter which hab was assigned upon returning, belongings were always there available. A table and bench protruded from a wall as the transmat shimmered back through the hyper-fluidic floor. A bowl sat upon the table, filled with the same grey nutri-paste as before. Ryson sat and ate, found the alternate flavor of his evening meal to his liking, the tiny nanospores pervading his mind stimulating different parts of his senses, generating an alternate taste. The table and bench extracted themselves from the room and a cleanse-booth appeared, ready for Ryson's evening preparations before the next sleep cycle. He thought about what his brother had said; it always bothered him each time Stimming was mentioned. With the cleansing process completed, the sleep-bunk's gentle suspensor hum announced its arrival through the floor. Ryson lay down and closed his eyes. The faint white noise of the suspensors helped him clear his mind and he felt at peace again. He felt relaxed. Most of all, he felt content.

***

Ryson was content. Ryson was satisfied with every aspect of his life. There was nothing that Ryson desired. The thoughts flowed through his mind as he lay on the sleep-bunk, wearily blinking his eyes after another restful night's sleep. Today was much like any other day. Ryson rarely left the luxury of his sleep-bunk immediately upon waking. Ryson did as he normally did and lay gazing at the ceiling, allowing the shard's IMTel permission to flood his mind with wondrous and pleasing swirls of color to appear before his eyes. Gentle pastel shades danced around his vision during these intentional daydreams, soothing and calming shapes and swirls, reassuring. The shard would reward Stimming with these sensations to compensate for using the brain's biological processing capacity, and to offset the discomfort it caused. All members of the shard would be affected in this way, but usually while sleeping. Few actively opened their minds while awake and invited the IMTel to utilize their capacity. Ryson enjoyed the sensation delivered directly into his mind. There was much to be reassured about during Stimming, it was a pleasing experience which took up his spare time. Spare time being something he had in abundance.

Time progressed, much to the ignorance of Ryson who, after a while of his regular daily activity of semi-consciousness, slowly regained focus and awareness of his surroundings. His thoughts turned to what his brother had said the day before. Ryson had always felt that Stimming was his way of adding something to society. He would willingly offer the nanosphere the extra capacity of his mind, if it meant that he could help it to maintain order. This planet felt so important to him and he would do whatever he could to maintain the peacefulness that a well ordered society could offer. Many a time he had spent trying to think of what else he could do, but no thoughts had ever come to him about a long-term role in the shard.

The bowl of grey nutri-paste tasted as good as ever and the empty bowl slid with the table and chair back into the wall. It was time to visit his brother. The weather appeared in his mind: sunny again. He fought the urge to retrieve a coat from the outerwear rail and passed through the transmat.

***

A thin cloud overhead obscured the destination pad from being bathed in direct sunlight. He made his way through The Garden, the trees gently swaying in the warming breeze. A memory of running up the grassy hills behind them popped into his mind before vanishing away and pushing him onto his destination quicker. The pathway took Ryson directly into the perma-structure area and he turned to enter The Café.

Inside, Ryson saw his brother sitting at the same table, in the same chair, as they always sat. On the table were two cups, with the same steaming beverage as they had taken each time they met.

"Long time no see." Ryson ironically smirked as he sat into the chair. His brother's fist playfully impacted onto his shoulder.

"You say that every day." Dorath rolled his eyes and made a face that only a big brother could make to a younger sibling. "How are things?"

"Since yesterday? All okay, I suppose." Ryson grinned as he took a sip of his drink, an interesting flavor of mint Neotea stimulated his senses. "But you know, take each day as it comes."

Ryson and Dorath sat chatting, as they did each day with the brotherly affection and warmth they were akin to sharing, which usually consisted of them taking turns, back and forth, teasing one another.

"It's been good seeing you again," Dorath said, finishing his drink and placing the cup back on the table. "I'll be seeing you again tomorrow, don't over-do it." He winked at his younger sibling and took his leave.

Ryson remained seated for a while. All the civility of meeting his brother in such a bustling area always left him feeling fatigued. He eventually drained the remnants of his Neotea and sat quietly. He was alone, but not, as he closed his eyes and felt the flow of the thoughts of others residing in the hyper-fluidic building beneath wash through his consciousness. Every one of them protected, all of them safe. There had been no wars, no invasions, and no disasters.

Ryson jolted out of his musings and quickly came to his senses as he realized he had been in The Café much longer than usual. The place was deserted. He eyes darted toward the doorway and was confused to see that it had gotten dark outside, much darker than when he usually headed home. He left and once more heard the familiar sound of a lumiglobe behind him as he made his way through The Garden. As he walked, he picked out the pinpoints of starlight against the backdrop of space. No, not starlight, he thought to himself, not all of them, some of them are moving, are they ships? He remained stationary for a moment, excitedly transfixed on the tiny points of light hanging in the sky. He watched them silently dance around each other, swirling trials luminescing as they mingled and intertwined. A flutter of apprehension ran through him turning his stomach. It was a reflexive feeling he was unfamiliar with. Was it a battle? Are those ships fighting? The feeling faded and stable rationality replaced his natural impulses. Perhaps it is a display for a dignitary. He squinted his eyes as if to provide additional length to his vision in the dusk and continued to watch the points of light. There appeared to be a single larger ship, but it was difficult to tell from this distance. This must be the important ship as a multitude of smaller ships sped around it. Some would twinkle brightly and fade, others would launch a dazzling array of eerily mute pyrotechnics into the path of the largest ship, which would glow brightly for several moments as its shielding reflected the impact energies. Yes, must be an important dignitary for all of that ceremony. As the number of smaller lights dwindled, the performance slowly weaned. He could see the dignitaries' ship approaching the planet closer now, making a path to what was considered the administration center. He watched as light from the ship's engines vanished below the horizon, then Ryson completed his journey through The Garden and onto the transmat.

***

Back in his hab, Ryson proceeded to go through with his usual evening routine. Even as a child he performed the same actions in the same order, the repetitive nature bringing self-assurance that the tasks had been completed correctly. His mind briefly flickered to the events he had just witnessed in the night sky, but he paid no further thought to it as the sleep-bunk issued from the hyper-fluidic wall and he settled down to sleep.

But sleep never came. Ryson was restless and much warmer than normal, causing him to feel irate. He felt uncomfortable within his own skin. He had never had this sensation before. Anxiety flashed through his entire body as his mind wondered why he felt this way, suddenly feeling very alone and isolated from the normal buzz of the idle thoughts of others in the shard. A perception of being trapped within the confines of what was a very small room flitted around his head, closely followed by indecision born of panic due to imagining leaving the room only to end up in an unexpected danger. He tried to relax, he knew Stimming was a good relaxation technique, yet the patterns and swirls this time were worryingly vibrant and harsh. He willed the patterns to calm, for the hue of the colors to soften. Much to his relief, and only after great effort, he slowly matched the flow of the colors and patterns. Although not fully relaxed, he felt much less agitated and attempted to sleep again. He allowed the faint noise of the suspensors in the sleep-bunk to fill his ears, and Ryson eventually managed to sleep.

***

Ryzon chose not to get up, he never liked to get out of bed too quickly. His sleep had not been great, he still felt uncomfortable, but much less so now. He lay dreamily gazing at the ceiling of the room as he often did after waking. He permitted his mind to wander; as it did so the vibrant colors and patterns from the night before came back. Ryzon was prepared for the change this time and was comforted by the new pattern created within his vision. He was not aware of how long he had lay there, semi-conscious of his surroundings. Finally, his mind regained focus, and awareness of his limbs returned. The desire to eat overcame him.

Ryzon stood and walked over to the table as the sleep-bunk went back into the wall-space storage. He tucked into the nutri-paste which, fortunately, tasted as good as ever. With appetite sated, his mind turned to leaving the hab to visit his brother. The outerwear rail appeared, the imposed thought of sunny with a chilled breeze did not persuade him to take the coat. He stood on the transmat. Nothing happened. As he was about to step off and try again, the transmat flicked him outside. A slight delay, he pondered to himself and paid it no further thought as he began his daily walk through The Park. His eyes were drawn upward and he imagined the visions he had seen the previous night. Another person pushed into Ryzon as he walked, unpleasantly snapping him out of his reminiscing. By the time Ryzon had realized it had happened, the offender had already reached the transmat and vanished. He continued his journey to The Café, paying more attention to the other people around.

Inside The Café, Ryzon approached the usual table, but he did not recognize the person sat in his brother's chair. Ryzon checked the time and it was as expected. He glanced around the room, could not see his brother anywhere, and so slid into his usual seat and smiled passingly at the person in his brother's chair. The stranger glanced at Ryzon and politely smiled back, then turned back to nurse the drink in front of him, periodically glancing around toward the door expectedly.

The awkward silence between them continued, though The Café was noisier than expected, given the small number of patrons. Perhaps it just appeared that the fewer people were spread out more than normal.

Ryzon was not certain if the cup in front of him was meant for him or not, so he just stared at it. Watching the liquid inside cool. Ryzon noticed that the drink was his normal Neotea that his brother would get for him. Had Daroth already visited and bought this drink, then left?

Without ceremony, the stranger stood and left, leaving his cup empty on the table. Ryzon waited until he was out of sight before he felt he could relax. He took a sip of the drink in front of him. It was mostly cold, but the nanospore stimulated the area of his brain to make the drink appear to be a pleasing temperature.

After draining the cup he looked around. It was still reasonably noisy considering how few people were left. With no sign of his brother and the time getting late, Ryzon took his leave and proceeded to the door. He was almost pushed over by another individual hurrying inside, oblivious to Ryzon, almost as if he was not there.

He continued his dimly lit walk back to the transmat when the absence of a familiar noise registered. The sky was shrouded in darkness; the sun had set, but there was no lumiglobe following him. He could see the light from lumiglobes following others, but not him. *Not my night tonight.* He reached the transmat and after a moments delay was transported inside.

His evening routine took slightly longer than normal. He stared at himself in the mirror protruding from the hyper-fluidic wall. Something was unusual today. He could not work out why, but something was unequivocally amiss. His brother had never missed their daily meetings at The Café. *Was Dorath okay?* He had always been so relaxed and comfortable in his own little world that had always known peace, he had never considered doing anything other than Stimming to assist the shard. *Perhaps I need to play a more active role in society?* He continued his cleansing routine before settling on the sleep-bunk.

***

Ryzon was content. Ryzon was satisfied with every aspect of his life. There was nothing that Ryzon desired. The thoughts flowed through his mind as he lay on the sleep-bunk, wearily blinking his eyes after another restful night. Today was much like any other day. Ryzon rarely left the luxury of his sleep-bunk immediately upon waking. Ryzon did as he normally did and lay gazing at the ceiling, allowing the shard's Integrated Machine Intelligence permission to flood his mind with wondrous and pleasing swirls of color to appear before his eyes. Vibrant hues danced around his vision during these intentional daydreams, and he found them invigorating and empowering. Not that there was much to be excited about, but nonetheless it was a pleasant experience. Besides, he did not need to visit his brother until later.

Time progressed, much to the ignorance of Ryzon who, after a while of his regular daily activity of semi-consciousness, slowly regained focus and awareness of his surroundings. He became aware that a table and seat had appeared on the opposite wall to his sleep-bunk and the sensation of hunger rippled through his mind. *Yes,* he thought to himself, definitely time to eat. As he stood up from his resting place and walked the few paces to the chair, the bunk sank into the floor. The nutri-paste was as good as ever, and with the meal completed, the table and chair receded back into the hyper-fluidic wall.

It's time to leave, he thought to himself. Two ripples developed around the room as the transmat moved up from the floor and a collection of garments on a rail appeared through a wall. Cool and shaded with a slight breeze, the thought of the weather outside greeted his mind, perhaps the next agri-season is approaching. He changed into his functional outerwear, hesitated about taking the coat, and ultimately left it on the rail. It withdrew into the wall as he stepped onto the transmat.

Ryzon instantly found himself outside. No glitch or delay similar to the day before. He took a deep breath and paraded across The Park. Soft intermittent clouds gracefully drifted overhead, and the cooling breeze caressed his cheek as it brushed around him. There was no delay in his stride today on account of his purposeful pace, one much more brisk than usual. He passed by the trees lining the gentle green hills without much notice. Many other people were out on their business too, but Ryzon avoided incident. He had reached The Café in a much quicker time than normal, so much so that his brother had just sat down, carefully placing two cups on the usual table.

"Long time no see." Ryzon ironically smirked as he sat into the chair. His brother's fist playfully impacted onto his shoulder.

"You say that every day." Daroth rolled his eyes and made a face that only a big brother could make to a younger sibling. "I didn't see you yesterday, were you okay?" His brother's head tilted gently to the side, inquisitively.

"I didn't see you either," Ryzon replied, a confused frown furrowed in his forehead as his eyes narrowed. "But I was fine." He excitedly leaned toward his brother and his voice took on a hushed tone "Did you see the star ships dancing around the other night? They were putting on a display for some dignitary or something."

"No, I must have missed that. I was busy attending mother." Daroth's lips curved into a smirk, badly hidden behind the cup as he took a sip.

"Look." Ryzon's eyes narrowed as he glared at his brother, "if you've been discussing my life choices with that woman again-"

Daroth matched Ryzon's stare. "Please don't call her that, little brother. She regrets saying those things, but..."

"But..." Ryzon continued his brother's sentence, ire reddening his cheeks. "But she can't say it to me. I know, I know." He could feel his heart beating faster thinking about his mother discussing her thoughts about his lack of finding a role in society to the rest of the family; it made him uncontrollably irrational. Ryson's eyes fixed his brother's. "She's tried apologizing through you, she's tried apologizing through Dad, and she's even tried to apologize by gifting me that coat..." His voice tailed off as his raised a hand in the air and steadied himself with a calming breath. Composed once more he took a sip of the warm Neotea, holding it in his mouth for a moment before swallowing and swirled the remainder around in his cup thoughtfully.

"She does care, she just has an unusual way of showing it. She tried to reach out to you by getting you that coat." Daroth sighed and placed a reassuring hand on top of Ryzon's shoulder. "She just wants to make sure you're not wasting your life. I know that you have not found a role to your liking yet, but continually Stimming has never been good for anyone."

Ryzon's shoulders slumped. "You're right." He almost shocked himself with the unexpected words. "I'll find something that would make your mother proud."

Daroth's fist playfully met his little brother's shoulder as he stood up to leave. "She's your mother too. Don't forget that. See you tomorrow."

"Yeah, until the next time." Ryzon muttered to himself as he lost himself in thoughts that meandered through different roles he could perform to assist the shard. Perhaps they're right, he thought to himself. He drained the last bit from his cup as he stood and pushed the chair back under the table before leaving.

Back within a hab, his mind still drifted over potential futures while he continued with his evening routine. He recalled the good times he had growing up with his family, the time spent in the shard, the entire populace enjoying their life within it simply because it had always been so peaceful. He caught his own eye in the mirror for a moment and froze. A thought coalesced which escalated into a crescendo of images. In that moment he knew exactly what he must do, he had uncovered his desired role to assist the shard.

Ryzon finished his evening routine and the sleep-bunk gracefully rose from the floor. As he settled, preparing to sleep, his mind wandered. It is time to take action, I've spent so much time Stimming but that's such a passive activity, I need to be out there actively doing things. His last thoughts before drifting to sleep were decisive.

In the morning I will do what I can to protect my family, my shard, my planet and my home. I will enlist, I will ensure protection of this planet by becoming a member in the military arm of the planet Votune within the Isorian Senatex.

Slipstream
By Brandon Rospond

Brown eyes, hidden within an even darker, black, helmet scanned the battlefield and took in everything that the IMTel relayed to the soldier. Every shot fired, every explosion gone off, every step taken, every detail – from both enemy forces - was transferred through his squad's shard and passed to each of its members. The Algoryn and the Ghar had stubbornly fought from one end of the planet to the other; when one side seemed to win, the other would fight back twice as strong, chasing each in turns through the dense jungle.

Fenris Teyvirium was glad that they had the camo drone with them, keeping them cloaked even more than the thick foliage could. At that moment, the nano-veil was down, and he could see the five members of his squad hunkered down in their black bio-silicon armor, waiting and watching.

And then there was the other person, sat back on his haunches, observing through the sniper drone that was as much his weapon as it was a part of himself – a phase sniper. A soldier with his qualifications was not normally added to phase trooper squads, but as the unique cloaking drone also proved, this mission called for some unique exceptions.

"They're on the move again, sir."

The squad leader nodded to Zyler, the phase trooper beside him; he had known through the shard before the words were uttered. His mind, linked with the drone hovering to his right, activated the cloaking tech to conceal them once more. The Isorian commander moved forward, keeping at a pace that allowed them to move quickly as a unit, yet not as much so that any would fall behind and sever the veil's connection. Another drone hovered closely to his rear left; the sniper's. Even though the machine felt strange from the lack of a shared connection, the phase sniper, Daveen, had caused no discomfort in the unit. The feeling through the shard was neutral, if not welcoming, on the added presence. The silent soldier followed every order Fenris gave without hesitation; he connected with the shard so well that he could predict the commander's every decision almost as quickly as the others could.

"There's no way they could have found it already, is there?"

Fenris shook his head at the voice that hissed into his mind through the connected neural network; it belonged to his second in command, Basch'ra.

"Negative. The battlefield is moving in that direction, but there is no indication either side has found the objective yet." The firefight was spreading toward them from the west, but they were still ahead of the enemy forces. "If we keep this pace up, we'll be plenty of kiloyan ahead of them. Let's just hope they don't obliterate it in their careless warpath."

A feeling of understanding and agreement spread throughout the shard, echoed by silence. The Isorian IMTel had been keeping a close eye on the lush vegetative world of Pfytorus, steadily watching as the Algoryn and Ghar fought over dominance for years, slowly devastating the greenery with every planet-side clash. After sending in drones for closer analysis, they discovered the planet was scattered with remains of technology from a Fifth Age society! It was doubtful that the tech would provide any immediate benefits, but to better understand a society now defunct from two ages ago might prove beneficial to the Isorians as a culture in the wider scheme.

As their luck would have it, the largest grouping of the technology was in a settlement of ruins on the far reaches of the planet. It was near impossible to land anywhere near the target, as it was surrounded with a sea of forest greenery and the open area directly around it was too treacherous with ruins. The IMTel tracked the sporadic movements of the enemy and was able to time a landing on the far edge of the treeline when the fighting was elsewhere.

While the Algoryn and the Ghar had unknowingly destroyed many deposits of the old tech in their bombardments, these ruins still remained untouched. If Fenris could get his phase troopers to the location before the enemy, it would be a magnanimous boon for their cause.

"Squad, halt." Fenris held up an invisible fist that was traced in yellow lines by the IMTel as it flashed past his eyes.

Mag-fire from the Algoryn and lugger shots from the Ghar trickled in before them until it escalated to a full-blown firefight they were caught behind.

They remained still as the lights flashed around them. Occasionally, Fenris's phase-armor shielding would sparkle with luminescence as it deflected a shot. There was no point phasing through the fight; the enemies were not aiming at his unit, and all the same, he needed to be aware of the direction the battle headed in.

His eyebrows furrowed in a scowl. There must have been more Ghar and Algoryn units scattered than they had realized. With the lack of dispatchable drones, they were relying on the IMTel's last calculations, which the predicted percentages were not as hopeful as he would have liked. It had told him there was a slight chance he would run into scattered resistance, but he had not expected it to be from both sides.

Just as spontaneously as the fight began, the forest returned to its eerie stillness. Fenris ordered the drone to decloak to save resources as they trudged on.

"Damn Ghar," Basch'ra growled down the comms. "If it weren't for them fleeing halfway across the world, maybe this fight would have been over ages ago."

Ethar, the most tech-savvy of the group, chuckled. "Yeah, but if that was the case, would we even be here right now? Who's to say that one of the two wouldn't have found it once they had less distractions? Or what if we had to land the whole army here to contest it?"

"I doubt that," the feminine voice with the cold edge to it belonged to Tona. "The Ghar would have destroyed the planet to the core, looking for raw materials. The tech would have just been junk to them - stripped and scrapped. The Algoryn, with their outdated shards, wouldn't even begin to grasp at what they found. It would have gone under the radar until we or the C3 picked it up."

"Yeah, well we're not out of the woods yet – figuratively or literally. We still need to find-..."

Fenris's plasma rifle was aimed before he consciously acknowledged it; Daveen's warning spread through the shard without even uttering a word; contact. He stared into the eyes of a black face mask belonging to one of the Algoryn AI troopers as the enemy came through the foliage. His finger was on the trigger in a heartbeat and his crew followed suit; a wave of plasma came from the Isorians that cut fiery swaths through the dense leaves, exploding in waves of colors against the shielding of the Algoryn.

In that same instance, his body fell and rolled to the nearest thick tree, the order for cover spreading through his shard's neurolink. Coordination through the IMTel displayed an image in his mind of where his enemies should be and the most accurate spots to fire. Magfire rained down around him, trying to pick holes in his squad. Fenris reached his arm around to the right and squeezed two shots off. He heard a squeal before the voice was drowned out from blood. The IMTel never steered them wrong.

Another three, then four, went down from his squad's pinpoint accuracy before Fenris nodded to another one of his squad members, Laurice. The lead phaser leapt up from his cover, sprinting forward to the Algoryn AI. Mag fire peppered into the colorful shielding of his bio-silicon armor, and then the moment presented itself. The remaining four troopers popped their heads out, and the IMTel showed Fenris exactly where he needed to place his focus.

The four streams of energy came at Laurice in unison, and before they made contact, he stopped. His body almost seemed to vibrate where it stood, the shots passing right through him. The phasing technology was a wonder; it seemingly removed a person's body from the very bounds of space and time. Even though use for prolonged and constant periods of time could drive a person to the brink of madness, the Isorians, and in particular phase trooper squads like Fenris's, were trained how to properly manipulate the defensive technology for short bursts of time.

With practiced efficiency, Fenris raised his wrist to fire the x-sling at the distracted foes. Four grenades shot through the air, exploding in gouts of flame as they made contact with the targets.

Laurice's body stopped shivering and he turned to his commander, jerking a thumb at the flaming brush. "So can I assume we're all clear?"

Fenris stared at the flames as the IMTel checked for remaining targets. He opened his mouth to respond, but a red helmet popped up. A shot barked from the enemy mag gun, but not before a long, green laser burst his head like a ruptured melon. Fenris turned to the source, even though he already knew what caused it; Daveen nodded solemnly back to him once.

Something else cried across the shard, something non-human, that caused the phase commander to wince as he traced the enemy fire. Ethar was kneeling on the ground, carefully holding the camo drone in his arms as he inspected it. Fenris felt the annoyance of his group and fought every urge to contribute to it.

"Dammit," Basch'ra's gravelly voice howled. "That thing's not standard issue! Command's going to be furious when they find out the Algoryn turned it into scrap!"

"Basch'ra," Fenris raised a hand. "Enough. Ethar, damage report?"

"Well, it was a crippling shot, but it's not destroyed. I'm not sure if I can fix it, but given time, I can keep tinkering with it."

Fenris scowled, more furious with the luck of the enemy than anything his own squad had done. "Chance of success?"

Ethar took a moment to consult with the IMTel. "Four point sixteen percent chance of success."

Tona scoffed and there was a general wash of dissatisfaction that came over Fenris from the others.

"We can't stop to worry about it. Take it with us and work on it. We cannot let them get the Fifth Age tech."

* * *

Night had fallen and obscured the forests of Pfytorus in a thick darkness. Wherever the moon was above them, it shone no light down on the seven bodies of the phase trooper squad. Of course, that made no difference to Fenris, as he could see the others through the night vision of his helmet as if it were the middle of the day; it distorted the color slightly and gave the members thick outlines to solidify their presence in his vision. They had not made as much progress as he would have liked, moving a bit slower to make up for the lack of stealth. He knew his squad needed rest, if not for the sleep then to calm the tension they all shared; a few hours would be enough to still get them back on course.

His eyes traced the thick off-colored outlines of his squad. Laurice sat a stone's throw away, meditating. Even though they all had been trained in phasing, Laurice's thick frame yet nimble movements allowed him to most often be the volunteer for the trickiest of time-bending maneuvers. Phasing, while protecting the body, affected the mind in strange ways when used for long periods. It took the soldier completely out of the moment, phasing out of time entirely; and when they returned, it was as if they had not moved at all. Timing the activation and duration was a technique that took a great deal of patience and practice. And it was in moments like these that Laurice took time to steel his mind for the next bout.

Each of the troopers had their own way to achieve a personal zen. Tona leaned back against a heavy log, meticulously checking her plasma rifle and sidearm, almost as if to make sure not a single speck of dirt could invade any crevice of the weapons. Zyler found a branch to draw into the dirt with; it was hard to make out if he was writing to keep his sanity or drawing swirls to match the craze of his mind. Basch'ra passed an ancient combat knife across the knuckles of both hands, a family heirloom that his second brought as good luck. Ethar was pouring over the camo drone, a spark from his work rarely igniting the sea of pitch.

Further away from the rest was Daveen. The sniper was as still as the towering trees around them as he sat on his haunches, facing away from the phase troopers. The sound of exchanging fire was omnipresent, even through the black of night. The blasts were distant, but Daveen nevertheless scanned all around the group's encampment. His rifle would slowly sweep to one side of the forest, pause, and then carefully swing to the other. The man piloting the drone could easily have been mistaken for part of the machine.

Fenris wondered if Daveen found peace behind the barrel of his weapon, that calm being the reason for such silence.

His squad had been quite the veteran of combat, having

seen at least thirty-some battles. Thirty-nine, to be exact, the IMTel called up before his eyes. Even though none were as sensitive and crucial as this one, that experience with the other five, all linked to the same shard, had given them a sense of unity like nothing else. Every emotion, every action, everything that one person of the group felt, they all felt in unison. It seemed that beyond just the shard, they were in sync with one another's reactions and movements before they occurred. While that never stopped each person from acting as their own, they felt a collective unison that would feel hollow without every member there. Fenris thanked the IMTel's great knowledge for putting such a skilled squad together that still remained intact since their formation.

"Any luck, Eth?" Zyler mumbled, still tooling away at his art.

"Uh... Somewhat."

"Really?"

The heads of the squad members turned at once.

"Well, uh... No... Sorry." He shook his head as they each turned back to their tasks. "I mean... It's not completely broken yet, but it might as well be. I can get it to spark, as you've seen, but I can't get it to come back on-line. It keeps trying to reboot, but after a random percentage it just shuts down. I've seen it get as high as sixty-two, but then as low as three. Something's not clicking right, and I can't figure out what it is."

"Tona, you're good with guns." Basch'ra growled as he flicked the knife in her direction. "Can't you see if you can help the boy out?"

"Thanks but no thanks, Basch. I'm good with guns, yeah - firing them, cleaning them, kitting them - but my expertise ends there. I can tell you how to fire any sort of rifle, the distance a lugger can hit, how many plasma shots it would take to kill a Rock Father, and I can even disassemble one of those Algoryn D-spinners to rework them into a functioning x-sling," she made a swirl with her finger to emphasize her point. "Drones though? No idea how they work."

"Just how different could they be?" Basch'ra was a dependable man, the best second Fenris could have ever asked for, but there was always the hint of something in his voice that sounded as if he would get up to start a brawl. "A drone is a weapon too. Just hovers with the suspensors."

"More to it than that," the female trooper shook her head. "A drone's alive. It can think and react and make tactical decisions based off of analysis. Would you want Ethar to open you up and take a look inside you if your leg got blown off, just because he knew the inner workings of a drone?"

"Point taken," Basch'ra turned his head in the other soldier's direction. "No offense, lad."

"None taken," Ethar shrugged.

Fenris leaned back, crossing his arms as he looked over to the sniper. "Tona, you've got a good point. Drones are different than the standard weapons we carry - they are very much so more alive. That said, Daveen, any knowledge on the subject?"

There was a pause before the sniper spoke.

"What do you mean, Phase Commander?"

A sort of reverence warmed Fenris that he knew was more than his own. The sniper's voice, which he rarely heard, was soft with a regal air to it that did not match the general brusqueness of most troopers.

"Your sniper rifle is more than just a weapon, correct?"

"Yes. As you can tell, it is also a drone. The IMTel flows through it, alerting both it and I of targets, allies, natural wildlife, heat signatures, and any other points of interest. Together, we are one unit instead of two separate."

"Truly fascinating how a machine and a PanHuman can find such harmony. Is it possible that you might have information on drone schematics and diagnostics beyond what the IMTel is giving us?"

"Negative," the sniper shook his head. "If I knew of anything, it would have been fed directly to the shard. Even though my drone and I are one collective unit, we are still in the same way so very much different. I know as much about it as your tech-savant does."

Fenris nodded and turned back to the rest of his squad. "I figured that was the case. Ethar, keep trying what you can. Don't overwork yourself, though. Tona, try to help however possible. You at least are a little more versed in the subject than the rest of us. Basch, Zyler, Laurice, get whatever rest you can.

We'll be on the move shortly."

* * *

Even with the cover of the night, they treaded carefully through the maze of forestation. While their bio-silicon suits allowed them avoidance from most of the Algoryn and Ghar's primitive signature readers, if the enemy had any sort of night vision, the squad could still be visibly seen. As the traversed on, sunlight's golden rays started to seep in through the cracks of foliage above, which only added to their vigilance.

"Closing in on destination," Fenris breathed over the shard. "Stay sharp."

The exchange of mag and lugger fire grew louder, and to Fenris's chagrin, the neural display started blotting his vision with scattered red outlines. Whether the enemy knew what secrets the ruins held, whether one of the forces was using it as a defensive position, or the fates had conspired against the Isorian unit, the IMTel still gave them the same objective: recover the technology. Percentage of success: sixty-four point eighty-six percent. Not bad odds, but not at much as Fenris would have liked.

The treeline started thinning, and just past the last drooping branches towered a several hundred yan monument. He had seen the crumbling black obelisk throughout the duration of the mission, projected into his mind from the IMTel. Perched around various point of rubble were Ghar defenders supporting the ground troops and the Algoryn pressing the assault from spread angles in the field littered with black stone.

"Easy targets." There was almost a chuckle in Basch'ra's voice. "That is, of course, Commander, if we are heading into battle."

Fenris furrowed his brow. He ran several scenarios against the IMTel. Trying to duck and weave their way through the spread combat yielded unfavorable results; waiting until the combat ended seemed an abysmal choice, putting the relic and the tech in danger; however, not being seen seemed the IMTel's most favorable option. He looked at the drone hovering on a suspended platform in front of Ethar; there was no visible change that he could see.

"Drone status?"

Ethar shook his head. "Nothing yet, sir."

"Thing won't wake at all," Tona shook her head. "Between the knowledge we both share, we can't make heads or tails of how to fix it. Nor is the IMTel giving us any options. Just keeps saying the drone's rebooting. Maybe the connection's severed?"

"Well, then that only leaves one choice." Fenris picked his plasma rifle up, sighting up on the enemy lines. Daveen had already trained his aim, steady on his chosen mark; the others followed suit of their leader. "Pick your targets carefully. Make every shot count. There's a lot of open space between here and that doorway. If we're going to make it, we have to cause as much confusion and take out as much of the opposition that we can. When we move, find thick chunks of cover and hunker down."

Acknowledgment came through the shard from each of the members, including Daveen. He scanned through the targets, assessing which would be the most beneficial kill. He lined up with an outcast who had taken refuge by the doorway and tried to suppress the uneasiness from spreading through the shard. The Ghar were the less favorable of the two to take position in the ruins; the destructive minions were less likely to leave the technology unscathed.

He felt the others awaiting his command; three, including Daveen, had picked targets close to his own while the other three chose Algoryn prey. He waited for a calculation that he approved of, not for himself, but for the unit.

His finger quickly pulled the trigger in succession. Two light blue slivers of light shot through the air and struck the outcast; the first just barely missed the head and struck the wall behind while the second made impact and cleanly passed through the eye socket. The body slumped back against the foreign sleek black of the obelisk and did not get back up. The six others fired simultaneously. Some of the phase troopers fired three or four shots, but Daveen, using the power of his drone-rifle only needed one. Seven other targets fell; each trooper made their mark and Daveen's sniper shot pierced through one and then cleanly took another.

Fenris switched his aim down to the battlefield. There was more cover than he realized – if it could even be called that. The chunks of rubble were barely large enough to shield the Algoryn bodies, but enough to deflect most shots. He switched the plasma rifle from single shot to semi-automatic.

"Someone cover the defenders."

"Understood," Laurice aimed up at the Ghar outcasts.

"In my sights," Tona acknowledged.

There was a third response to his command, but it did not come in verbally; Fenris knew it was from the stoic sniper.

Before either side had known where the plasma shots had come from, another volley sounded out from the trees. Fenris let the shots bark from his gun in a wave of searing blue. It was less accurate of an attack, but it killed at least seven Algoryn AI troopers. Blips of red on his map readout showed several of the Ghar outcasts go down as well - more than he expected. The kill readout from the others attributed those, once again, to Daveen. Fenris smiled. Without the proper technology like what the IM-Tel provided, it would be hard for either of the opposing forces to detect where the fire originated from, standing at the side angle they were; they were too focused on each other to even suspect a third party. With less numbers of opponents and the element of surprise still on their side, the steadily increasing success rate told Fenris now was the time to move!

Fenris lowered his rifle and began sprinting forward, his pace increasing with every pounding step. He knew his squad was flanking him the moment he had decided to move. Each sure step took him through the woodland, past the grass, and into the dirt and rubble. They managed to make it several yan before Fenris noticed the mag fire licking at their heels. It was a slow trickle that could not keep up with the agile phase troopers, but Fenris still marked out the aggressors for the others to take note of. Raising his gun, he changed the rate of fire once more to automatic, and then unleashed a stream of plasma shots toward the Algoryn.

More guns turned their attention to them, and this time there were stray lugger shots in the mix as well. Lights would flare up here and there as shots peppered his shielding, rerouting the damage away from Fenris. With each hit that struck him, the phase commander's gun was up and barking across the field, echoed by the rest of his unit and the powerful blast of the phase sniper.

He managed to duck into relatively thick cover and checked on the status of his unit. Shields had taken a bit of a beating, but no one had suffered any real damage.

"Ethar, you doing okay with the drone?"

"Yes, sir." The soldier had ducked close by, spread loosely in with the rest of the phase troopers.

"Is it weighing you down at all?" Fenris raised his gun over the rubble and let the IMTel help him to find his shot.

"No, sir. It's strapped tight to my back and not going any-where." It was Ethar's turn to fire a burst out at the enemies. "Just as long as a stray shot doesn't find our little buddy again, hopefully he'll have enough time to reboot."

"Sir." Laurice moved in closer to his left. "Is it time?"

"Not yet," Fenris shook his head. "Too much fire still. I don't want to risk you not being able to keep phased."

"Well, we better do something soon." Basch'ra waved his hand at Fenris; the phase commander threw him one of his x-grenades which was then lobbed out at the enemies with a great explosion. "We're going to get pinned in here soon enough."

Before Fenris had a chance to answer, a blinking red blip caught his attention. He turned in cover and could see the IM-Tel was showing him something coming his way from the enemy position. He did not need the readings to tell him what was hurl-ing down. Fenris's first instinct, and what the IMTel told him to do, was to brace for impact, but the explosion sounded out before it ever reached the Isorian troopers. He looked toward Daveen, who was poised out of his cover, aiming with the sniper drone. The IMTel was never wrong – they really had needed a sniper for this mission.

Turning back to his lead phaser, he gave Laurice a nod. "Go, now! We'll keep you covered, but get up there and clear that entryway!"

The phase trooper bounded out from cover, his nimble steps propelling him toward the main structure. With a unified front, the others in the group sighted out from their spots, taking shots at those that presented obstacles in Laurice's path. The trooper did not have far to go, and Fenris planned to make sure that he was unscathed.

Keeping one eye on the enemies as he mowed down two Algoryn AI, he reserved the other one to watch the show Laurice was putting on. He had not stopped moving; when a stray shot found its way to him, he phased for a moment, and with the propulsion of his pace, it was like he was teleporting with every use of the technology instead of freezing in that spot in time.

The Ghar outcasts at the steps of the ruins did not know what to do with the plucky Isorian. They tried firing, but he was too quick and too in touch with his phasing. One tried to shoot him point blank, but the lugger shell went through the hologram-like being and into the back of another Ghar's head. Pulling back into reality, Laurice grabbed the rifle out of the putrid creature's grasp and smacked it in the head. Turning toward the others on the steps, he held down the trigger and eliminated all targets.

"Now, move it!" Fenris had already been in motion before he uttered the command. Laurice was not the only member of the group that knew how to skillfully phase. Each member of the group turned their attention away from the two battling forces and ran with all of their might toward the steps. Fenris knew they could feel every shot that would come their way, that they could sense each time that they were being fired upon, and each member knew just how to distort their bodies just long enough to avoid unnecessary damage to their phase-armor shields.

But then there was Daveen, who rarely used the Isorian suit tech. While the expertise marksman could shoot a grenade mid-air with unparalleled accuracy, the other Isorians knew how to get to their destination quickly and effectively – of course without losing their sanity. Perhaps that was what he feared, losing his sense of balance on the battlefield and connection with his drone.

Fenris nearly threw his body up the steep steps, turning back to fire a few sporadic shots at his opponents. He slammed his back into the wall once they crossed the threshold into the ruins. He exchanged nods with Laurice and made sure his approval was sufficiently fed through the shard.

"Good job as always, soldier."

"It's what I do best, sir."

One by one the other phase troopers piled in through the doorway, leaving Daveen the last one in to cover the entrance.

"Damn Algoryn, and damn Ghar," Basch'ra spat as he sent a couple of warning shots back out. "If only we had more troops that we could wipe the lot of them out."

"But we don't," Fenris took point, leading them in. "And we need to figure out if the Ghar are already inside. If they held the entrance, who knows how far they got in."

"IMTel doesn't seem to have exact coordinates for the tech," Tona muttered as she examined the narrow corridor. "This place looks a lot more intact from the inside than it does the out."

"The IMTel could not detect exactly where it was, but what drew it to Pfytorus in the first place was the discovery of an energy unlike anything else registered. The drones found the rest of the tech that was destroyed in or around similar ruins to this one. It could only see an orbital view of this particular set, as the fighting had been too intense to try and get a drone down here."

"So we have no way of knowing if the tech is actually here?" There was almost an ounce of panic in Zyler's voice, but Fenris knew him better than that. Fidgety and easily distracted, yes, but he was not one to lose control of his senses.

"The IMTel is never wrong," Fenris reassured, and the response that he felt in unison from them was one in the same. "We know it's here, it's just finding where in here."

"No predicted layout of the inner workings either," Ethar shook his head. "I keep trying to call one up, but the IMTel is only projecting our entrance. Everything ahead is... shadowed and unknown."

"Could there be something in this ancient structure blocking IMTel feed, Ethar?"

"I don't think so," the Isorian touched the obelisk-like walling with the fingertips of his suit as they walked on. "The building itself is clearly Fifth Age as well. I'm sure the data we're here to recover has schematics on it. Whatever civilization built this, we can hopefully better understand once we find it."

Fenris stopped, raising a hand to the others.

"Are you serious?" Basch'ra stepped forward and thrust a hand out toward what lay ahead. Three corridors led to three different directions. "This is ridiculous! We're in a damnable maze! And without proper IMTel readouts, how the blazes are we supposed to know where we're going?!"

"And how is this place even this big?" Zyler stepped forward to peer down one of the tunnels. "From the outside it barely looked bigger than a few yan. How are there so many paths that clearly stretch deeper?"

"We have been descending," Daveen's voice nearly caught Fenris off guard. The strange depth of it added to the mysticism of the labyrinth. "I've been tracking it on my rifle. Our depth has been declining at a staggering rate."

"Hmm, now that you mention it, you're right," Ethar nodded, his head slightly tilted as he checked the IMTel. "As far as we've been going in, we've sloped down at quite the rate. Perhaps it's whatever makes up this strange construction that has made it seem like we've been on a straight path."

Fenris scowled as he looked down the three ways. "Daveen, Ethar, any ideas on where to go?"

The sniper held up a hand but did not speak. It seemed he was communicating with the drone- rifle. After a few moments, he shook his head, a strange mix of sadness and annoyance coming from him through the shard.

"This... construction goes beyond anything I have encountered. We cannot scan or see anything through it. Normally, we would be able to detect life forms or even more specifically, this strange alien technology that it normally would not recognize. I see nothing but emptiness from the walls ahead and no way of knowing where the paths lead."

"Great," Tona growled. "If we can't detect other life forms, who knows what else is crawlin' around in here with us."

"The IMTel gave us this mission because it knew we would be successful," Fenris raised his plasma rifle as he started moving toward the eastern path. "And the IMTel is never wrong."

While the IMTel could not ascertain the inner passageways of the ancient settlement, it still felt as if it were leading

Fenris. The first path he chose took them down a long, winding hallway that split to another tri-fork. Choosing this time the left one, they soldiered on until they came to another fork, this time with only two paths. He chose the right, but before he was able to take more than a few steps, he felt the unease of the others.

"Boss, you know where you're going?" Tona stepped forward to walk beside him. "How can you so confidently pick paths without thinking on it?"

"To be honest, I don't know where I'm going. But we don't have much time. I just..."

Fenris's voice trailed off and he came to a slow stop. The narrow walls spread out several yan in both directions to reveal a wide room. There seemed to be an entirely different energy in this location, as if something was humming underneath their boots, breathing and pulsating. Small lines of green crawled like bugs across the walls in different paths. As Fenris stepped forward, he noticed a semi-circle set up near the far wall. Once he set his sights upon it, the IMTel registered that it was some sort of older technological receiver.

"A control panel!" There was excitement in Ethar's voice as he moved ahead of his leader. He paused and came to attention, the sheepish feeling hiding in the recesses of the shard as he fought the feelings back. "Sorry, sir. If I may?"

"Have at it, Ethar."

The savviest of the tech-warriors led them behind the console and they were washed in the blue glow of the displays coming to life. Ethar at first seemed too in awe to react, as he stood in front of it, his hands held out awkwardly at his sides. It was not until the others nudged him through the shard relaying their impatience that he cleared his throat and began to gently push buttons and issue commands on the displays.

"Oh, yes. This is definitely what we're looking for. It's certainly Fifth Age. Belonged to a group called the Mandolarees. They seemed to have been a lesser-known race that were more interested in studying the way that Antares worked rather than fighting against the various warring factions."

"Can you download everything to the shard?"

"Yes, and..."

Ethar pressed a button and there was a whooshing of air followed by a small cube rising from the internals of the machine. As Fenris studied it, it seemed to be of the exact same black, shiny material made up of the entirety of the ruins.

"And then there's this. It seems that whatever type of technology this is, the Mandolarees used this to both cloak themselves and jam outsider technology. While the IMTel is advanced enough to not be completely jammed, this explains why it was unable to get a read on the interior of the facility. While it may take some time to reproduce their efforts, this can at least be the building block to help us get started – both figuratively and literally."

"That sort of technology would definitely prove useful to our cause." Fenris nodded and Zyler reached out to grab the hand-sized cube. Using a carefully designed storage container they had brought specifically for this mission, he stored the strange artifact on the side of his suit. "Download as much of the data as you can salvage, and then we'll get out of here."

As Ethar connected the IMTel to the machine and began to transfer the information to his personal shard, Fenris almost felt like he could let his guard down. But something about the ominous ruins made him feel otherwise. It was not the Mandolarees ruins themselves, but the darkness, the oppression from the tight spaces, and of course the unknown factor of the two armies they had opposed to gain access.

Almost on cue, there was a faint rumbling emanating from the passageway they had come. Every moment it grew louder, and all members of the unit had their weapons trained and ready. Fenris kept trying to spot the red dots that symbolized enemies, but thanks to the Mandolarees' alien tech, that was not going to happen.

He had expected something big from the way the ground was rumbling, and thus Fenris was partly caught off guard when the outcasts came flooding in toward them. They screamed in howling terror as their slavemasters drove them forward. The narrow opening to the chamber proved a good choke point to shoot them down as the phase commander laid on the trigger, but the width of the large room proved to work against the Isorians as the few outcasts that got through spread out and made for harder targets.

The outcasts were fearless and fired back at the Isorians as they stormed inward, causing the phase troopers to have to duck or time their phases very carefully.   Fenris tried to get a read on where the slavemasters were, but the outcasts were overwhelming. How many did they have? How many more were focused on the Algoryn? Damn the Mandolarees and the death trap they set up.

"Boss, we need to stop playing the sitting duck game!" Basch'ra roared as he hammered down on five outcasts that came too close for Fenris's liking. "Look! There are other tunnels beside the one we came in!"

Fenris watched his second's finger and was surprised he had not noticed the other halls. Cutting down a swath of plasma on another few outcasts, he slammed back down next to Ethar.

"What's the status?"

"Sixty percent, sir. Almost all data this terminal has on the Mandolarees is completely transferred!"

"Alright, I need you to find us another way out! Download the schematic on this place and find us another exit!"

"Of course, sir! I'm queuing it to do simultaneously!"

Fenris sighted up and he recognized one of creatures the Ghar called their 'slavemasters'. This creature looked even more primitive than the half-naked, barely armored outcasts. He wore a mask fashioned out of metal, shaped like an Algoryn skull; his body covered in a mock-up of various different armors of those he killed. Disgusting battle trophies. His maglash whipped ferociously in one hand while a mag pistol barked in the other, firing wildly to match the roar coming from the creature.

Fenris wasted no time laying into the beast. Several of his shots sparked off the tattered armor and bone-metal helmet, causing the slavemaster to fire back at him. His shield dispersed the energy of the return fire, the percentage of energy dangerously low, and Fenris sighted up for another round of fire. That was, until, a vicious bolt struck through the slit of vision on the Ghar's helmet, causing him to spill to the ground, whip and gun limp.

"You're not too bad with that thing," Fenris breathed down the shard to the sniper.

"Thanks for keeping it occupied." Daveen answered, the slightest hint of a joke in his voice.

Fenris turned his attention back to the outcasts and held down the trigger as they rushed closer and closer. Just how many of the suicide runners were left? If this kept up...

A map schematic formed in the upper left corner of his vision. While it did not show positions of the enemies, it at least gave the Isorians an advantage of knowing which way to go. And there was indeed a back exit!

"On my mark, we move!"

Fenris checked the x-sling on his arm. There was only one grenade left. He stood and fired in the center of the oncoming Ghar, hoping that the explosion that rocked the room would not cause some sort of cave in. The assault seemed to become paralyzed with both the loss of one of the slavemasters and what seemed the bulk of the outcasts. Using the dust to obscure the enemies' sights, Fenris ran forward, out toward the highlighted route.

A red flashing warning displayed on his mind's eye, and this time, it flashed brighter and strobed more importantly than the last. Without thinking, Fenris phased out. He lost feeling across his whole body, as if his consciousness left the mortal flesh, except for that connection that had been trained between his brain and the trigger. He always found this experience strange, yet pleasing. The sensation made the PanHuman body feel like it wished to stay around in this strange feeling forever, but he knew better – he knew the dangers associated with that desire. Fenris released the phase command and felt like his brain was sucked back into his body from the strange slipstream of time; yet at the same time, it felt as if he simply blinked from the time he saw the red blip to that moment.

He looked at the wall behind him and noticed a dark char mark from an explosion. His head swiveled back around and brought his plasma rifle back to par against the Ghar battle suit – he knew there was something down with them beside the outcasts. The pilot on the inside of the hulking structure could not be seen, but the spider-like vehicle, as it crawled about on the four legs, clad in a dark purple armor with red beady eyes, made it seem all the more menacing. It raised the heavy scourer cannon on its arm as it prepared to fire once more.

Before either force could react, several heavy mag shots struck the side of the Ghar, rocking it to the point that it almost toppled over. Set up in the entrance to one of the tunnels on the other side of the room was an Algoryn light support mag cannon. It continued blasting into the Ghar machine, and the beast brought another arm up to shield itself before turning to address the more persistent foe.

"Go! Now!" Fenris led his phase troopers with all of the strength his legs could muster as they pounded down, pushing him forward. Several shots from the Algoryn mag cannon came in their direction and he was not sure if they were missed shots on the battle suit or purposeful attempts to remind the Isorians of the Algoryn presence.

Fenris followed the map, aware of the other members of his group tightly following him. Left, right, right, straight... The other exit was further than the entrance they had used. He just hoped it would take them out to safety.

"Fenris, when we get back, you owe me one hell of a stiff drink!"

Fenris grinned at Basch'ra's call. "When have I ever not treated the squad for a successful mission?"

"I expect double the usual. If we make it."

"We will."

"Boss, I have a rather pressing question." Fenris's optimism drew back from Tona's worry. "How in the blazes are we getting back to the ship? It was hard enough getting through the jungle in stealth, but without even that..."

Fenris could see the light just up ahead; they were almost out. And he had not stopped to consider that rather disturbing aspect.

"Oh!" Ethar called, causing them all to stop. He swung the drone around from his back, the lights blinking alive and filling their shard with great joy. "It's back on-line!"

They jogged out in the open air once more and Fenris reveled in reconnecting to the drone as he activated the veil over the phase troopers and their sniper ally. Not more than a few moments after the drone reactivated its stealth did a unit of Algoryn AI flush down into the ruins, from where they had just exited. The phase commander had to laugh at the irony.

"That... was too close," Zyler shook his head as he dropped his rifle to his side.

"It seems like the damn thing was saving its power until we needed it the most," Basch'ra shook his head, waving a tired arm toward the drone. "It's almost as if..."

"As if the IMTel knew all along what it was doing?" Fenris raised his thin brown eyebrows several times within his helmet. Even though Basch'ra could not see the motion, he made sure the sarcasm conveyed through the shard.

"Yeah, well, I'm just glad it gave us the damn silent sniper and not a NuHu. And I think I've seen enough of Pfytorus for one lifetime."

"I think you're right, Basch'ra." Fenris nodded, feeling the warmth of the IMTel in its entirety once more. He looked at the strange cube in storage on Zyler's side and hoped they would be able to unlock its mysteries. "We have a lot to bring back home. I think a stiff drink sounds good to me, too."

Into Darkness
By Andrew Tinney

Radiation. The whole planet was saturated in it. Vegetation had turned brown and wilted, the primitive cement blocks of outmoded settlements were corroded, and vast fields that once produced crops for outlying systems were scarred black with iridium poisoning. A crimson sky streaked with acidic gray clouds generated a dense atmosphere. The planet's single sea was mucus green, tainted beyond repair, glowing filth visible from orbit. The planet was once called Ylarys, before war had come and the inhabitants' pathetic resistance was wiped out in a single thermal battery assault. This desolate setting was where Argon Kale found herself.

"Miserable place," a voice said, sounding through Kale's combat interface. She glanced at Ghalris, her newest recruit, an un-blooded soldier prone to speaking his mind more often than necessary. His crimson Algoryn infantry armor was a flickering green through the tinted vision of her helmet. Kale raised a hand at Ghalris, beckoning him to continue moving. Even though her eyes were hidden, the gesture should have been enough to silence him. Annoyingly, it was not. "It's quiet too," he continued, indifferent to her command, "almost too quiet."

"Enough, Ghalris," she hissed down the interface. "Keep moving."

Despite her frustration, she knew the infuriating Ghalris was right. The whole landscape of Ylarys was eerily still. The only audible noise was the buzzing from the energy fields of their armor. The area that Kale led the six others through was dense with trees bereft of both leaf and life. A low hanging bough caught on Kale's mag gun. She pulled it free and it disintegrated in a shower of ash.

A new voice whispered in through an external shard. "Leader Kale, respond."

"Kale here," she replied, raising a hand to halt her squad.

"Commander Fantris awaits a report. Hold for contact."

There was silence, the dull hum of the shard establishing a connection, then yet another voice materialized; one that filled Kale with scorn.

"Kale, report."

"Commander Fantris," she said, forcing her tone to remain neutral. "The woods are quiet, as expected. Contact with Leader Jarg, seventh squad, has confirmed no life forms present in the villages south either. The planet is empty, sir."

Kale may as well have spoken to the trees around her, for Fantris ignored her completely. "Order, Kale," he continued, "there has been no report from Leader Drayus, fifteenth squad. Reconnaissance with Drayus and report back immediately as to their status."

"Drayus, sir? Drayus and his squad are six thousand yan west, toward the mountains."

"Did I give you cause for question, Leader Kale? You have your orders; I shall expect results within the hour. Fantris out." The connection made a rasping sound and then shut down.

"Six thousand yan?" Kale heard the sigh in the voice of Byris, her second in command, as he set the heavy mag support gun down. Her most trusted officer shrugged, and even though Kale could not see it, she sensed the annoyance the whole squad would undoubtedly share. Kale nodded and Byris ordered the rest of the squad to fall in. She watched as the keen-eyed Gestra, as well as J'ko, Maynn, and Usta, the three male veterans, came to attention before their commander. And then of course, there was Ghalris, languishing as always behind the rest.

Despite the silent grievances of her squad, coupled with the disdain with which she regarded her superior, Kale was a soldier, trained like all Algoryn from birth; which meant she followed her orders. "You heard the commander," she said, "six thousand yan east. Move out."

"Six thousand 'teheck'n yan," Ghalris said using the guttural swears of his homeworld.

"Ghalris, I won't warn you again."

They set out, Kale leading at a strong pace. She was tired, her body aching under the weight of her armor that she had worn without respite that past week; or whatever passed for a week on this planet. Her squad had slept rough too, sheltering in abandoned barns and under trees. They ate only the carbon sealed food from the ship's cantina they brought with them, which was running dangerously low, yet still Fantris urged them to go on. "There is a transmat here," he had said in his marshaling speech, "a way of safe passage back to the fleet. We will find it, and we will secure it, for the glory of the Prosperate!" Kale remembered the scattered, pathetic applause that had accompanied her commander's declaration.

"Don't see why we have to do it," Ghalris whined again. "Why are we even here?"

Kale stifled a sigh. Ghalris was new, a recruit fresh from Kah'uun, a world on the periphery of the Prosperate. He had not witnessed the destruction of Zyra, the homeworld of Kale and the rest of her squad. The catastrophic damage that the Algoryn had been forced to inflict upon their home, once a vast, lush troposphere, had torn their hearts asunder; but better that than have the Isorians taint it, bending the environment to their will.

So they set out, scouring the edges of this far flung solar system in search of a gate that could lead them to another world, one they could perhaps call their own once more. Kale had been assigned to Expeditionary Force Seven, positioned at the vanguard of the fleet proper, and tasked with scouting out worlds as potential colonies. Fantris had brought them to Ylaris, seeking glory for himself alone, and now due to what he was terming a 'technical' fault they were all cut off from the ships above them in orbit. Enviro scans had detected the presence of transmats, a means to regroup with the fleet proper. All they had to do now was find them in the vast ruin of a world, which was how Kale and her squad found themselves traversing a desolate wilderness.

Kale felt a twinge of sorrow as they marched east, armored footfalls kicking up a cloud of ash in their wake, reminding her of Zyra, of the ashen husk they had reduced it to. She looked up and prayed there would be a sanctuary out there, another world they could find and colonize to save them, and that no other world should have to suffer the cruel fate that was becoming all too familiar to her.

They cleared the woods, only to be met by a steep incline that rose into the foothills of an impressive mountain range. All remained quiet and the crunch of steps on ashen forest ground was replaced by the scrape of metal armor on stone. Kale programmed her sensor field to probe outward for any Algoryn presence, yet the scan returned void. Byris had noticed the irregularity also.

"Odd," he said through a private interface so the rest of the squad could not overhear them. "Do you think it's a trap?"

"Doubtful," she replied. "We've been here for fourteen suns and still no sign of any life on the planet."

Byris was silent for a moment. "Ylarys is a big place, and the expeditionary force was small enough to begin with. Maybe we shouldn't have separated our forces."

"Leader Kale, look," Gestra interrupted.

Kale turned to where the AI soldier was, thirty paces or so ahead, overlooking the crest of an incline of stone. She charged up the slope, fingers instinctively tracing the trigger of her mag gun.

The slope lowered into the vast expanse of a crater, formed no doubt by the massive impact of one of the immense thermal bombs that had ravaged the planet. Dust and toxic residue still floated skyward from the devastation. Kale scanned the scene, the view taking a few seconds to adjust and focus from her combat visor, until she saw what caused Gestra's alarm.

Red armor, mangled and scattered across the crater floor.

"Weapons ready," she ordered, raising her mag pistol. Her squad checked their weapons' compression chambers ensuring they were ready for whatever could come their way. "Move out. Byris, Gestra, set overlapping fire grid here. Watch our backs."

With the cover of the x-launcher behind her, Kale led the advance into the crater. The armor was Algoryn, of that there was no doubt. Shards of twisted crimson plate marked white with kill insignias lay scattered at their feet as they moved to investigate the scene.

"They get caught in the blast?" Ghalris wondered aloud.

"Have you seen any thermal blasts in the past suns?" Kale barked, shutting him up. Something didn't sit right with her about it all.

One hundred yan took them to the center of the colossal crater. A signal flickered up on her sensor screen, faint but nonetheless there.

"You see that, Byris?"

"Negative."

"Keep watching our backs." Kale glanced around. A rumbling sound broke the silence, like that of thunder in the distance. She checked the sky, which was clear, except for the wispy ash clouds. The rumbling continued. "I'm going to have a look around."

"Affirmative. Weapons ready."

Pacing slowly, she ordered her squad to spread out. She checked the scraps of armor, noting that they were bloodstained and warm, heat radiating through the padding of her combat gloves. Algoryn had been here, and now they were dead. The rumbling got louder.

"What is that?" Ghalris asked.

No sooner had the words sounded down their combat array, the earth exploded with a titanic surge. Fragments of rock blasted from the perimeter of the crater, followed swiftly by harsh gravelly grunts and the too familiar ripple of mag gun fire. Shots fizzled off Kale's energy shields, drawing her attention to the cloud of dust haze that obscured her primary vision. Her visor fed her distorted readings, faint dancing images of hulky forms advancing from all sides. Boromites. She leveled her gun.

"Open fire!"

Her squad regrouped and sent a volley into the new enemy. The ambush had claimed Maynn and Usta, warriors of numerous campaigns gone in a single volley; but those who remained enacted revenge with swift, practiced efficiency. Kale would mourn them later. Mag slivers pounded toward the exposed hides of the advancing Boromites. Some merely glanced off energy fields, but more found their mark and the torrent of fire brought the brutes to a halt. Kale ceased fire with her mag pistol and raised her right arm, sending a frag round from her x-sling into the relenting foe. It struck a Boromite square in the chest, exploding in black smoke, leaving nothing in its wake but gore and rock flesh. Seeing the Boromite cease, Kale ordered her squad into a counterattack formation.

Then the second explosion sounded.

"Fall back!" Kale ordered instinctively as dust rose from her flank and another squad of Boromite warriors appeared.

This time, plasma rounds accompanied mag shards. A lance of blue light seared close to Kale and struck Ghalris on his arm, severing it clean from the elbow down. His screams funneled through the monitor, and Kale rushed to his side, shoving him on.

"Back," she ordered. "Back!"

Byris covered their retreat with short bursts from the squad's deadly micro x-launcher, explosive rounds keeping the Boromites in check. Dragging Ghalris, Kale mounted the hill and slid down next to her second.

"Bastards," Byris swore, sending another volley into the Boromite ranks, felling one. "What now?"

Another explosion sounded, robbing Kale of her reply. Below, and behind them at the foothills of the mountain, another tunnel erupted, spewing forth yet another gang of Boromites who formed a line, taking cover behind rocks and trees. In their ranks, Kale could see the sinister silhouette of an x-launcher which would blow her squad into nanite particles if she didn't act fast. Byris turned to his rear and unleashed a torrent of fire from his side arm onto the enemy below.

"Maintain fire," Kale yelled, standing tall and pointing her weapon back toward the crater. A Boromite took aim at her but she downed him with one precision shot to the head before he could pull the trigger. A mag shot managed to penetrate her shields, yet it merely chipped her breastplate. Kale, ignoring the blow, charged down into the crater once more.

"Squad, with me!"

It was near suicide in theory, but this was no textbook maneuver. A score of Boromite warriors stood in the crater but were stunned by her sudden attack, expecting the five remaining Algoryn to remain pinned. Kale's charge had ground them to a premature halt, giving her time to launch another round from her x-sling and watch it decimate two brutes. Her mag pistol fired then, a steady stream of munitions that, though heavily inaccurate, forced the Boromites to keep their heads down. She howled, her squad echoing her cry through the combat array, and she knew those howls would not be heard by the Boromites. They came like silent crimson death, blasting their way through the stunned assembly.

Kale led the way, her gun sending a steady stream of fire toward the Boromites. She reached the mouth of one of the recently emerged caves and ordered her squad in. "Take cover," she barked and they obliged, maintaining a steady flow of covering fire as they hunched down behind rocky debris. Even Ghalris, blood oozing from his severed arm, charged into cover, using his free hand to discharge shots from a mag pistol. Byris had been behind her, but when she turned she now saw him in the center of the crater, wielding his heavy gun in both hands. Thick mag rounds were flung across the space, tearing tough Boromite energy shields to the hard flesh beneath, mangling the rocky hide. Kale hissed at him down their shard.

"Follow me, Byris, that's an order!"

He let his gun erupt explosive shots into the face of a Boromite who dared to charge too close. "Go," he replied, "I'll cover you."

"Byris," Kale snapped, "get over here!"

It was too late. The Boromites closed the gap and surrounded him. Kale watched in stunned silence as slivers of mag sliced through Byris' shields and seared into his armor, tearing strips from his flesh. Blood spilled, but Byris fought on, his support weapon laying into the brutes, dispatching three and pinning the rest. One Boromite weathered the torrent, the thick rounds that managed to reach him bouncing harmlessly off rock-gray flesh. He wielded a glowing blue pistol in one hand from which he discharged a single round that crippled Byris, bringing him to his knees. In the other, a crude, primitive drill whirred menacingly. With one mighty thrust, the Boromite brute drove it through armor and shield into Byris's chest, grinding armor, flesh, and bone into one gory mess.

"Hell," Ghalris breathed, just loud enough for Kale to hear.

She ignored him, wrenching her eyes from Byris's corpse to the swiftly regrouping enemy. She bolted back into the tunnel. "Run," she barked to her squad, "down into the tunnel, go!"

They ran, years of combat drills and training overriding any emotion they may have felt at the death of three of her longest serving squad members. Kale's squad sped ahead, and she leveled her x-slinger, firing two rounds at the roof of the cave, causing it to crash, sealing them inside darkness.

***

Through the darkness, Kale could just barely make out the ash that shifted around them, stirred by the cave in. Kale's visor flickered with static at the now sealed entrance that had shut them out from the Boromites and the desolated planet beyond. She switched to night vision and the darkness dissipated into an emerald glaze, flecked with the hazy outline of her remaining squad; Gestra, J'ko, and Ghalris whose severed arm was being cauterized by his armor, the dull hiss of the sealant masked by his groans. Just past the boulder, the antagonized shouts of the Boromite aggressors could still be heard. And Byris's blood would be soaking into the hard, radiated earth.

"Move out," Kale called, hefting her mag gun and turning toward the tunnel interior. She had scooped up the weapon from the dead body of Maynn, taking pleasure in the idea that she would avenge his death with his weapon.

"Move where?" Grunted Ghalris, his voice cracking as his armor finalized the sealing process. The bleeding had ebbed away, the sophisticated stemming system of his battle armor slowing circulation. He was alive, but Kale feared for him, for his blood had been exposed to a heavily irradiated atmosphere.

"Down the tunnel," she retorted. "Gestra, take point. Activate night vision. Go!"

They adjusted their visors to low light conditions, the scene turning from pitch black to a collage of grays and whites. Gestra took the lead, setting a cautious pace, treading down the tunnel which meandered deep into the mountainside. The crude rock had been meticulously carved away, support beams of HMC positioned at regular intervals. The Boromites had been there for some time, Kale surmised. But why...

"This stings like nothing else," Ghalris moaned.

"You'll be alright," Kale said. She approached him, glanced over his wounds, and, satisfied, grasped his shoulder firmly. "I've seen worse," she encouraged, "you'll live." As long as radiation hasn't seeped into his bloodstream, she wanted to add, but knew that would do no good. As much as Ghalris irritated her, he was a member of her squad, and it was her duty to keep him alive.

Just as she should have kept Byris alive.

She shook those thoughts from her head. Byris would be mourned, as would Maynn and Usta. They would be avenged, she vowed, drumming her fingers on the handle of the mag gun. Dust trickled down from the ceiling, a continuous torrent of gray cloud seen through their visors. Gestra slowed. Kale marched to her side.

"What is it?"

"Check your sensor probe, Leader," she whispered, her voice barely audible.

Kale calibrated her visor, a green flash scanning the area. Heat signals returned positive.

"More Boromites?" Gestra asked, raising her weapon.

Kale said nothing. The heat signals were odd, very odd. Instead of the normal human sized silhouettes of enemy soldiers, the signals returned as lumps of red, blipping briefly before flickering away, only to return after a series of seconds. They were moving, slowly and in random directions. Kale could discern four separate readings, each varying in size and stature.

"Could be a glitch," J'ko added, though he too held his weapon ready.

More dust fell from the ceiling and Kale was convinced she could hear the sound of digging behind her. "We need to move on," she said. It would not take the Boromites long to re-open the tunnel entrance and trap them within. Though where they were going, she had no idea. She only knew they had to keep moving.

They advanced forward, slower even than before. Shadows danced in the peripheral of Kale's visor. Fear gripped her for a reason unknown and she felt ashamed. Algoryn did not feel fear in battle, she reminded herself. The heat signals flagged up again.

"Wait," Ghalris breathed down the interface, his voice weakening. The squad halted, Kale keeping her eyes fixed ahead.

"Status?" She asked him.

"The rocks," he said quietly, "shoot them."

"The rocks?"

"Shoot them, now!"

Kale swerved angrily toward Ghalris, but before she could speak, a gout of flame spouted from the tunnel ahead. It engulfed Gestra, who shrieked, but Ghalris was there, mag pistol firing, drumming into the boulder that seemed to scuttle ponderously toward them.

"Aim for their mouths!" He shouted.

Kale saw it then. The heat signals were creatures, small and hunched and rock-like in appearance. There were four of them and they moved with swift purpose despite their bulky frames. Gestra was untouched, her sophisticated reflex armor protecting her from the flaming burst. The rock opened its mouth again and inside Kale could see a molten interior. Fire should have come from that gut of lava, but Ghalris discharged a furious number of compacted rounds into the gaping maw. The creature shuddered and slumping to the ground; the heat signal vanished.

Following Ghalris lead, Kale sent rounds from her pistol into the opening gullet of another rock creature. The beast reared onto its hind legs, spouting a torrent of flame. The burst came at Kale through her visor like the waves of a gray ocean. Akin to Gestra, her armor absorbed the inferno, energy shield sizzling, and she burst through unscathed, her shots firing down the monster's throat. It too shuddered wildly and keeled over, dying in a rising cloud of dust. The other two creatures were felled by J'ko and Ghalris, who stepped over one of the dead frames and kicked it.

"Lavamites," Ghalris said, wheezing.

"What are they? Boromite?" Kale had fought the worker gangs before but never had she encountered creatures that breathed fire.

"Boromite pets," Ghalris answered. "They use them to melt rock particularly hard to shift. Nasty buggers, especially in groups. They're usually herded by a Boromite soldier though. These ones must have broken free."

"Or this is him here," J'ko hailed.

Kale went to where J'ko was standing, thirty paces down the tunnel, standing over the body. He stood over the body of a fallen Boromite. Through the gray tint of her visor Kale could see the rock flesh was singed and bitten. The herder had been killed by his herd, and Kale harbored no sympathy. In the dead rock brute's hand was a glowing apparatus. Kale reached out for it.

It appeared to be some form of tech, Boromite in origin. It was square in shape, clumsy in design, and heavy. The single screen at its center whirred and blipped, foreign symbols flickering at sporadic intervals. Kale tried to decipher the wavering digits, but her interface found no match in its vast databank. "What is it, Leader?" J'ko asked.

Ghalris responded. "It's a map." He reached over to press a button on the device's flank, which locked the screen onto one sequence of symbols.

Kale was skeptical. "How do you know? There are only numbers and lines."

"That's how the Boromites read maps. The numbers down are the tunnels they have excavated, the series of digits beside them are the co-ordinates to the entrances, and these blocks that flash green are where they camp. They have multiple settings, dependent on which sector they are in, making it easier for gangs mining to find one another. It's made so their enemies can't track them." He sounded pleased with himself. "Quite clever really."

Kale pulled the device away. "You know how to read this?"

"It's simple, once you're shown," Ghalris said with growing enthusiasm.

"And who showed you?" J'ko asked. Like the rest of the squad, J'ko held disdain toward their newest member and his know-all attitude, even in moments like these where Ghalris's knowledge proved surprisingly useful.

Ghalris shrugged, holding his severed arm. "Back on Kah'uun, in my village, a Boromite gang was hired to blow through core rock to reach the minerals beneath. The Boromites were quiet, but liked to show us things, especially things to do with digging and blowing things up." He kicked the dead lavamite again. "Showed us how to deal with them too."

Kale had to admire her newest squad member, despite his supercilious demeanor. "Can you read it then?"

"Yes." He nodded, remaining still.

"Then read it," Kale barked, throwing the device at him, "and get us out of here."

Ghalris made what she could only imagine was a discontented groan. He struggled using only one arm, but after clicking a few buttons, seemed to manage it. Dust clouds cascaded from the ceiling again. A rumble sounded behind Kale. She turned to look back down the tunnel and saw glimmering light through the suit of her visor; the faint glow of daylight.

"Move," she called, lifting her weapon and charging back to her squad. "They're coming. Move out!"

"I'm nearly done," Ghalris started, but a sharp shove from J'ko soon silenced him.

"Do it running then," the veteran squad member said, "unless you want to wait see if the Boromites will help you."

They ran down the tunnel blind, taking the left route where a junction appeared. Ghalris was behind her, shouting.

"We've gone the wrong way! This leads deeper into the mountain."

"Then find another way," she shouted back.

They ran for a good five hundred yards, dust falling in a cloud behind them. Through the interface, Kale could hear her squad panting with fatigue and knew they could not maintain this pace much longer. They couldn't hide, for these were the Boromite tunnels and the brutes would know every nook and corner.

"Left here," Ghalris shouted.

They followed his command. Over the heavy pounding of their footfalls, Kale could hear the distinct yet unmistakable flurry of gunfire coming from beyond. The Boromites were swiftly closing the gap.

"Right," Ghalris shouted again, taking them down a steep decline. Kale skidded and dust clouded her vision. J'ko overtook her, his armor clanking on the earth. Kale got up and pounded on, her armor heavier with every furious step. Ghalris hailed them through the interface.

"Wait, something isn't right."

"What are you talking about, Ghalris?"

"This isn't...wait!"

Kale tried to skid to a halt, but it was useless. The ground below them disappeared and she flailed with her squad as they helplessly plummeted to the unknown below.

***

The engine of Ail Vagar's interceptor roared, an inspiring cacophony that rang like a lullaby in his ear. Beneath the ebony chassis, the blighted landscape of Ylaris was but a blur, melding into one continuous strip of radiated brown. Four other interceptors tailed him, flying in a 'v' formation with Vagar leading. He could feel the tingle of wind through the thick padding of his gloves, a sensation which made him smile. This was where he was born to be.

This was why they called him the Sky Raven.

"Three quadrants west, Leader," his second, Fannra, called through the combat interface. Vagar raised a fist in affirmation, and on his signal his squadron banked left, interceptors whirring. Before them, a vast forest spread itself out and the squad broke formation to traverse the barren trunks. Vagar did not slow his pace, nor did his squadron. They were Ravens all, denoted by the distinct black armor they wore in favor of the traditional crimson of the Algoryn. They were elites, chosen to undertake this special mission by Commander Fantris himself. The best of the best.

"Signal, Leader," Fannra voiced once more, his voice crackling through Vagar's helmet. Vagar saw it too, the faint blip flickering in his visor's area relay. It was faint, slow, and it was Algoryn. Vagar kicked his interceptor into a higher speed and headed for the source, allowing himself a smile. This is how glory is attained, he mused.

This is how legends are born.

***

Kale, accustomed to the rigors of combat and campaign, opened her eyes slowly and, for the first time in many years, felt uncontrollably weak. Her visor crackled with energy, the screen splintered, distorting the image of her surroundings. A murky river flowed behind her, trickling along the edges of her combat boots. She hoisted herself up, groaning with pain. Further north, she could see the immense waterfall that had spewed her and her squad from the false mountain tunnels; the trap laid by the Boromites.

She was alone. Scrambling around, she discovered her weapon gone, lost in the mire of the radiated river. Ponderously, Kale crawled forward, jerking her head as her visor whined and whirred, attempting to regulate the damaged image feed. "Leader Kale to squad," she croaked, tapping into an open communication shard. "Leader to squad. Leader Kale, distress signal," she called again and was greeted by the harsh echo of silence.

Kale managed to free herself of the muddy riverbank, propping against a tree. The river gurgled softly and above her head she could hear the distinctive call of an avian creature. The planet was no longer still, and Kale was alone.

Slowly she lifted herself onto her feet, each step a new sensation of pain; broken ribs and a fractured hip, she suspected. Without her armor, however, the fall onto the rocks below would have shattered her like splint. For that, at least, she was grateful. Calibrating her sensor field, Kale sent out a distress call through her shard, searching for any sign of her squad. The sensor beeped twice then flickered off as the results returned void. She wondered if any of them had survived the fall, if they were nearby, and struggling to find her as she was sourcing them.

Kale shook herself. She needed to keep moving; she was lost, alone, and weaponless on a planet filled with hostile forces. Re-programing her communication shard, Kale opened a wider channel and sent out a distress call.

"Kale to Command, come in. Distress call 8-0-9-2, squad down, request immediate assistance."

Again, there was no reply. Kale grunted. The riverbank led into yet more trees, bereft of limb and leaf, the bark torn and warped. Her footfalls generated a low cloud of dust that snaked along her feet. She would have been exposed to the planet's radiation she knew, her body no doubt afflicted by the sheer mass of irradiated water that had crushed down upon her. She may not even survive the night, yet she would endeavor, survival instinct embedded in her psyche.

Shelter appeared ahead, flickering faintly in her cracked visor. An old ruin. It appeared to resemble a primitive temple, circular in shape, its sun-faded stone the color of bone. Fragments of timber-framed dwellings littered the area as the trees dissipated. A religious settlement, Kale surmised, devastated by the onslaught of the thermal assault. At that moment, she cared little. She headed for the stone ruin, convinced only that she need to rest and hide.

The steps rose and led to a pointed archway where once a door had no doubt been. Inside was mostly intact, surprisingly, though Kale garnered that the building had never contained much in the way of physical articles. It was without a roof, blasted away by an external explosion, and in the center was a stone altar, round and surrounded by rubble. A small room to her left seemed the best option, a primitive door still hinged. She pulled it, and after a few attempts it came loose and swung open to reveal a tiny chamber. The interior too was littered with rubble, stone fragments blocking the door, but Kale squeezed and set herself down on the floor. Her breathing was ragged, her body aching. Vison began to fail her.

"Kale to command, distress call 8-0-9-2. Call 8-0-9-2, come in command. Anyone? Please."

The interface crackled, returning no response and Kale let fatigue wash over her, drifting off into a low slumber.

***

The ore was of poor quality. Grun-Dar growled as he examined the paltry sample the Isorian messenger had supplied him with. It was light in his hands, and crumbled easily. Fickle, just like the Isorians.

"Where did they say we'd get the rest?"

Grun-Dar turned to Kullek, his second who had spoken. The rest of Grun-Dar's squad examined the poor specimens they had been given with the same scorn. The mood was foul.

234 Beyond the Gates of Antares

Grun-Dar's squad now numbered only five, the rest having been wiped out by the Algoryn forces that escaped into the tunnels. Grun-Dar had made the one that fell behind pay though, churning the reptilian's insides into mulch with his drill. It had been a deserved death, and Grun-Dar wanted to enact it upon the remainder of the tenacious Alorgyn squadron that had eluded his grasp.

"The temple," he replied, tossing the ore into the paltry pile they had been given. "She said the rest would be there."

"I don't trust them," Kullek grunted. "Those Isorians are a rare sort. And those tentacles aren't natural."

Grun-Dar spat a mass of dirt-ridden phlegm onto the dusty ground. The air was heavy, and even Grun-Dar, an experienced miner accustomed to the hazardous environs of bio-drilling, found it harder to breathe on Ylaris. The planet was irradiated beyond hope, but the Boromites had a high resilience to any and all kinds of chemicals, centuries of mining in toxic environments warping their biological make up. "They said they'd pay us, and after the past few days, we deserve it."

"We do," Kullek replied, "we've done enough of their dirty work." He kicked at an ore sample near his foot and it crumbled into fragments. "Digging those transmats free, that was the easy part. They never told us the Algoryn would show."

"We'll get them too," Grun-Dar reassured his companion. "The Guild Mother forgets nothing."

"Let's just hope it's soon." Kullek cast the specimen in his hand aside wantonly. "Pathetic," he murmured. "Sooner we get off this rock the better."

"And where would we go then?"
Kullek shrugged. "There's a nice contract going in the Xavian system. Harvesting planetary lava streams. Wouldn't mind an easy job like that for a time."

"We'll get this one over with first." Grun-Dar tossed the useless ore away. Time to get paid properly, he decided. "Squad, move out."

They left the caves, entering into the twilight of the planet. Days were long on Ylaris, the orbit around the planet's one remaining sun taking the better part of forty-six hours. The atmosphere was odd, the air thick with more than just radiation, and Grun-Dar wondered how such a desolate, backward world had ever been so close to the outskirts of a Gate and yet advanced so little. They descended the slopes, their heavy footfalls echoing in the small valleys. In the distance, Grun-Dar could see the vague outlines of the planet's former settlements, darkened silhouettes that invaded the horizon. A planet of darkness. It almost made him shudder.

"How far is this place again?" Kullek rasped.

"Not far." Grun-Dar pointed a massive finger ahead. "In the middle of those trees somewhere. She said they would send out a signal. We should pick it up soon."

"I don't like it," Kullek reinforced.

Neither did Grun-Dar, but he remained stoic. The Isorians troubled him too, with or without their ominous armor affixed with spindly tentacles. They were an odd breed, a collaboration of alien and human tech that was as disconcerting as it was frightening in power. Their language was forebodingly delicate, spoken in hurried whispers and through riddle. They must have been persuasive in their jitterings, for Grun-Dar's Guild Mother had accepted the contract and so Grun-Dar found himself on Ylaris, doing what he and his diggers did best. Only something set him ill at ease.

"That it?" Kullek piped.

They had been walking for some time, time that had passed unexpectedly swiftly for Grun-Dar. His gang was separated out, the hulking Scukkar taking point. Kullek was beside him, and ahead the towering ruin waited.

"Any signal?" Grun-Dar asked Scukkar, who reached into his pouch with a massive gnarled hand to reveal his surface detector. Two bleeps later and he nodded back to his commander. "The ore should be here then," Grun-Dar said, but readied his mag gun all the same, advancing cautiously. "Keep your eyes open. I don't trust those tentacled bastards one bit."

They advanced through the gloom, entering the ruined structure with caution, each one of the bulky soldiers alert and uncertain.

***

A thundering roar roused Kale from her slumber. Instinctively she reached for her holster to draw her gun, but all too late remembered it was gone. A crash sounded seconds later, followed by guttural voices. Boromites.

Drawing her combat dagger, Kale adopted a stealth position on her haunches, crawling breathlessly toward the ruined door. Her ribs still stung and her head throbbed mercilessly. The soldier in her overrode those mere physical trifles however, and Kale took in her surroundings. The mutterings ceased, and she could hear heavy footfalls marching away. Carefully, she leaned her head against the door, peering through the cracks, seeing through her hazed visor the muscled forms of Boromite warriors stomp away.

"Responding Leader Kale, call 8-0-9-2, what's your status?"

The call took her by surprise. Not that it had been sent, but because it was on an open interface, an open shard.
A shard that the Boromites heard.

As one, the brutes turned and headed straight for Kale's door.

Combat adrenaline kicked in. Drawing her combat blade, Kale sliced futilely at the granite hide of the closest Boromite, the thin weapon sizzling off his active reflex shielding. The brute swiped left in fury, but Kale dodged his clumsy blow easily, lancing up with her weapon again, this time penetrating his energy field and drawing blood on the softer flesh of the Boromites forearm. He grunted in pain. Next to him another Boromites opened fire with a mag gun. The shots glanced off Kale's armor, who spun rapidly to assault the shooter with a flurry of blows. The Boromite ceased fire and used his gun as a club to swat away the crimson soldier's strikes, which despite the fury of Kale's sudden assault were becoming laborious. She was tiring. Behind the brute she was futilely stabbing, Kale could see an opening; a low hole in the wall where she could escape.

A heavy blow landed on her back, sending her crashing forward. Dust and ash rose as she fell. Kale turned to face her attackers, who advanced on her, followed by the menacing hum of a combat drill. With horror, Kale watched the volatile mechanism shriek into life. Kale struggled to her feet, a few paces separating them, her feeble blade raised in defiance of her impending death.

And the night that had been encased in the wan illumination of twilight erupted with the magnificent glory of gun fire.

***

She didn't know where they'd come from, nor at that moment did she care. In the half dark of Ylaris, four interceptors surrounded her foes and peppered them with compact mag rounds from their under-slung armament. The rounds were not enough to fell the Boromites she had so desperately charged, but they drove them back, seeking shelter in the cover of the ruined structure. Kale kept her knife poised, anticipating a counterattack, but none was forthcoming. She felt a tug on her shoulder. A hand materialized, and she was hoisted onto the saddle of a roaring interceptor, which after showering one last hail of mag fire, reared into the night sky and fled the temple, leaving in its wake a trail of dust. Kale held tight to the rider before her, desperately fighting to remain awake. She was free. She would live.

She closed her eyes and let fatigue claim her consciousness.

***

Blip. She woke. Blip. A cold table. Blip. Her body was light. Blip. Free of armor. Blip. Vision blurred, white, no distinction in shapes. Blip. A harsh, overwhelming click. Blip.

A voice hollered, sounding so very distant, yet something told her it was much closer than she realized. "This one's finally awake. Call the medic, stat." Footfalls followed the voice, hard steps pounding on cement flooring. Blip. She was planetside. Ylaris? Blip.

"What happened?" She croaked and discovered her voice was but a mere gasp. No one answered. Blip. She spoke again, attempting to force her vocal cords louder. Blip. Nothing. Kale tried to rise but binding at her arms, chest, and ankles held her in place. Her heart pounded faster. Blip. Blip. Blip. She felt trapped.

Her eyes closed and Kale passed into oblivion.

***

Sight returned in a harsh light, drawing her out of unconsciousness. The insistent bleeping of the monitors had ceased. Kale felt stronger, and she discovered her muscles responded to her commands. She sat up in the straight, uncomfortable bed upon which she found herself.

"You're awake at last," a medical assistant who was checking serum levels of a patient next to Kale hailed. "Good. Let me check your focus levels." Before Kale could argue, a refractor was shone into her eyes, the minute apparatus whirring as it took a reading. The assistant smiled, his reptilian face sliced with a fake grin. "Good, good. Looks like you're free to go, Leader Kale. Thought we'd lost you for a while there."

"How long have I been here?"

"Three days," he said, filling out a chart and not looking up. "You took a beating."

She checked her surroundings, confused. "Where are we? Orbit?"

The assistant frowned. "No," he said with an air of exasperation, "we are planet side. Commander Fantris set base camp here, three quadrants from combat zone G."

"Combat zone? I thought we were an expeditionary force." She thought of the three cruisers that had taken them this far, equipped only with provisions for a short skirmish. Now Fantris had set up base camp on Ylaris and declared combat zones.

The assistant sighed. "The Commander had other ideas," he said, drawing a monitor from one of his many coat pockets and tapping it furiously. "He says we cannot afford to allow the Boromites to hold this rock and we must do all we can to push them out." The assistant paused a moment, his eyes cast to the ceiling of the small room. Finally, revelation dawned on his face and he clicked his fingers. "I've just remembered. The Commander wanted you to report to him as soon as you recovered." There was a look of unmasked relief on his face. "I'll let my superiors know you're on the way." He turned away.

"Wait," she called after him. Ponderously, the assistant halted and turned. "My squad, did they make it?"

The assistant shrugged and resumed walking. "Not that I saw, but we have dozens of casualties flooding in each hour. It looks like a hard fight out there." And with that he was gone.

Kale rose, finding her body slightly stiff, but after she took a few paces, her muscles loosened. The medical ward she was in was filled with whirrs and beeps of machinery, punctuated by the low moans of the inhabitants. Dozens of steel medical beds lined the walls holding wounded Algoryn. Some were still in battle attire, armor and flesh merged in bloody fusion, a consequence of heavy incoming fire. Kale was dressed in linen robes and felt naked without her armor's weight on her shoulders.

Two soldiers dressed in full battle armor littered with ivory kill markings, mag guns held at attention, greeted her at the exit.

"Leader Kale," one said, his voice distorted though his visor. "Glad to see you up again. The commander requests your presence."

"Do I have time to dress first?" She asked, holding the robes tightly shut. "I don't feel myself, out of armor."

"Your presence is requested immediately, Leader. I'm sorry."

Typical Fantris, Kale thought. The impatient commander would no doubt be in a foul mood that she had kept him waiting through being unconscious.

She followed the soldiers, striding through the Algoryn camp. Above her head, she could see the shimmering encasement of a status field that was purifying the air and keeping radiation as well as any stray bombardments from affecting the area. The camp itself was nondescript. It had been erected in the ruins of a settlement, straddled on one flank by the mountains and to the other a vast valley that led to the outskirts of a city. They had only one armory, a series of tents to serve as the barracks, and the med center which had been dropped from orbit by a carrier shuttle. Sensor arrays had been set up on the highest intact structure, an ancient tower now crested orbital relay probes. Power generators stripped from the cruisers engines and brought planet side hummed low, the earth below them vibrating softly.

Kale approached the crimson command tent topped with streaming banners depicting the sigil of the Prosperate, guarded by four Algoryn in their elaborate command armor, shoulder pads thick and also, like the guards that accompanied her, littered with white kill markings. They pushed the flap aside and let Kale enter.

Inside, three figures were assembled around a table, on which the flicker of an enviro map wavered. All three turned to face her. One was Leader Nyai, second in command to Commander Fantris, a sharp warrior who had lost an eye in the Caylus campaign. She nodded silently to Kale in greeting.

The second figure held himself high, a haughty demeanor surrounding him. His armor was ebony in color, and Kale recognized him as one of the Ravens who had rescued her. He raised his eyebrows expectantly.

The third and final figure was Commander Fantris, a man who owed his position to his ancestors and nothing else. Fantris was dressed in his usual battle attire, untouched by bullet or plasma round since the day of its crafting. Medals adorned his chest, welded into his armor; all of them belonging to Fantris' father. What troubled Kale the most about her commander's appearance were the kill markings that were delicately painted onto his crimson suit; all lies and not earned in blood as hers had been.

"You kept me waiting," Fantris said quietly.

"Forgive me, Commander," she answered keeping her tone flat. "I was indisposed."

"There is no excuse for tardiness," Fantris piped. "A soldier that does not arrive when summoned borders on the insubordinate. Be thankful I made allowances for your wounds, Leader."

Both Nyai and the Raven commander looked uncomfortable.

Kale bowed. "Again, Commander, I beg forgiveness."

"No matter," Fantris piped, dismissing her words. "Did you rendezvous with Squad Drayus, as ordered?" He looked at her expectantly.

"Commander?" She said, perplexed.

"Well, don't keep me waiting any longer. Report on their status."

Kale felt the need to speak slowly to her senior officer. "We were ambushed, Commander. Surely you received the distress signals?"

Fantris snorted. "Leader Vagar, you told me something about distress signals didn't you?"

"I did, Commander," Vagar said, "and I responded swiftly, as you ordered. We embarked and rescued Leader Kale from the Boromites."

Fantris smiled. "Ah, yes, I recall I dispatched you and you responded to my command immediately. Commendable action, Vagar, most commendable. I shall mention you to high command once we have achieved our victory. Now, Kale," he said turning back to her, "why did you send out distress signals?"

"I was surrounded, sir, and cut off from my squad."

He slammed a finger down on the table. "You disobeyed orders, Kale. Protocol dictates that distress signals are only to be sent in areas designated as combat zones. You were not in a combat zone, yet you proceeded nonetheless. You disobeyed protocol. And you failed to carry out the orders you had been given. As consequence, Squad Drayus remains lost. Have you anything to say for your insubordinate conduct?"

Kale stifled a sigh. "None. Forgive me, Commander."

Fantris appeared oblivious. "Be thankful Vagar is as noble as he is, otherwise you would not be here for me to accept your apology."

Forcefully, Kale saluted the Raven. "Thank you, Leader Vagar."

Vagar raised a hand, smiling. "Truly, no need," he said.

"See, Kale? Vagar needs no thanks. A true soldier. Most commendable."

Nyai spoke for the first time, interrupting the scene. "If we could, Commander, return to the task at hand."

"Ah, yes," Fantris said, as if waking from a dream, "our imminent victory. Look here, Kale. What do you see?"

Kale approached and looked down on the map arrayed before her. A battle grid was laid out, on it the depiction of a ruined city, neon green. Concentrated heat signals signified where the Algoryn forces were. Kale saw they were scarce and badly separated. "I see a battle, Commander."

"You see the victorious assertion of our military might over our enemies," Fantris corrected her. Ever the poet, Kale thought, every word in her mind laden with sarcasm.

"The Boromite attack has been pushed back to the city, Kale," Nyai said. "Commander Fantris has overseen the battle thus far. We owe where we are now to his tactical mind." She spoke monotone, her expression deadpan, and Kale saw she did not believe her own words. On looking at the map, Kale could see the Boromites were drawing the Algoryn in, letting them overstretch their lines while they reinforced their own. A counterattack would come and it would be devastating. Kale wondered how Nyai could keep such a taciturn manner in the face of such blatant stupidity. She wondered how they could allow such disasters to proceed this far.

"What's more," Fantris continued, "we have located the transmats!"

"The transmats?" Kale said. "Where?"

"In the city," Vagar said, "one of my squadrons discovered it on a scout run."

"It's located here," Nyai confirmed, pointing at the center of the Boromite position. "It's protected by the Boromites, but so far they have not seemed to have activated it."

Fantris was smiling. "Now we are on the cusp of victory. Tell her my plan."

"An all-out assault on the Boromite command position here," Nyai said pointing at the image of a well-fortified position located in the center of the city. "Push them back, and we secure the means of accessing the transmats on this system."

"Cut off the head of the snake and the body dies," Fantris piped. He stared at Kale, his smile widening. "And you, Kale, you will lead the vanguard."

"The vanguard?" That meant death. Kale glanced again at the supposed location of the Boromite base. A small rise, littered with buildings that could hide turrets, mines, and other vicious implements of destruction. After the rise, she could see a stretch of open ground before the high walls of a reinforced bunker. Killing ground where there would be no cover from the oncoming fire. It was madness. It was just what Fantris would do in his attempts to rid himself of her. She had to tread carefully. "I fear you place too much honor on me, Commander. I am not yet fully recovered and the position should go to someone more deserving of your favor."

"This is not an order that pleases me, Kale. I would rather the position go to a warrior worthier of the task. Yet Leader Nyai has convinced me otherwise."

Nyai kept her head down as Kale looked at her.

Fantris continued. "This is an opportunity for you to redeem yourself of past errors."

An opportunity for me to die, Kale thought. "My own squad then, sir, they are waiting for me?"

Fantris laughed, mockingly. "Your squad is dead or lost, Kale, and you have only yourself to blame for that."

"One of your squad remains alive, Kale," Nyai said. "A youngling, without an arm."

"Ghalris," Kale said, amazed that he had survived. "Will he be assigned to my command?"

"Negative," Nyai replied. "He has been assigned to the communications division. His knowledge of the Boromite tech and language has proved most useful."

"Then where am I to go?" Kale asked.

Fantris took over. "I am assigning you to Infiltrator Squad Cais. I cannot afford to give you another AI unit."

Demotion as well as death, Kale thought. "Yes, Commander," she replied.

"Good. You will report to your new second, Daesto, in the barracks. She is waiting for you. Dismissed, Leader Kale."

"Commanders," Kale said and marched away, wishing that a stray artillery round would crash through the barrier and into the encampment to blow Fantris, Nyai, and that pompous Raven into oblivion.

***

"Keep your head down!"

Kale bit her tongue. She was keeping her head down, but nothing seemed to satisfy her new overly cautious second, Daesto. Nonetheless she hunkered down closer to the ground, feeling uneasy in her new ebony armor. It was light, delicate, and after years of wearing the heavy combat armor of an AI, Kale felt exposed in the skin of an infiltrator.

A blast ricocheted off a building overhead, spilling a torrent of dust and stone onto Kale's new squad below. Beyond her second, Kale hadn't cared to learn the names of the others in her squad. They would be dead soon, just as she would be.

They stalked through the maze of ruins that littered the cityscape. The squad had advanced into what had once been a meeting house of some description, with cracked benches scattered across the space. The ceiling was gone, exposing the bleak night sky above. One solitary moon shone in Kale's view. She knew the other moon that orbited the planet could be seen also, yet now it was hidden behind the vast constructions that towered into the night sky. It was serenely somber. This would be the last time Kale would see the wan glow of moon. The squad approached the assembly point.

More blasts sounded, followed by more insignificant showers of scree trickling down. The Boromites knew the Algoryn were here, yet they waited. Kale could not fault them. Why waste time and troops when the Algoryn were going to present themselves as targets anyway? She could see the terrain ahead, the abrupt end to the cover, and a vast three hundred yard stretch of open ground. It was an ominous sight to behold.

That stretch of ground was where she would die.

"Squad halt," Daesto ordered. Even though their communication shard was secure, the Infiltrators used a hidden frequency, adding to the covert role. They were supposed to outflank the enemy, distract them with bursts of sporadic mag fire while the heavier AI squads advanced. Instead, Fantris had them charging the enemy head on, facing mag fire and whatever else the Boromites would send their way with only their thin armor and flickering shields to protect them. Yet those were Kale's orders, and despite all her hatred for Fantris, she had never disobeyed a command and would not start now.

If she was going out, she would go with a clean slate.

"Area secure," Daesto confirmed after a brief check with her proximity scanner. "Orders, Leader?" She used a blunt tone with Kale, no doubt discontented with her new leader. Daesto had more than likely wanted the squad for herself and Kale supposed she had earned it. Fantris had a way of aggravating all those under his command.

"Signal the other squads to advance," Kale ordered. Daesto did so. Ahead, the way was still, save for the infrequent bursts of mag launchers sending shells high into the air. The Boromites were targeting higher levels, she noticed, a wise move to keep the Algoryn from gaining height advantage. She wished they had their own artillery, longing to witness crimson blasts rippling down the Boromite lines. Yet Fantris, in his wisdom, had ordered the artillery to remain in camp. He had used the transmats' protection as a thin veil of an excuse. He was a fool.

Two Al Squads, led by Leaders Be'uc and Lytar, advanced up to Kale's position. Kale had fought with Be'uc before and knew him as a capable soldier, who shared her reservations toward Fantris, and his inability to command. The armored leader approached her, keeping himself low, his crimson battle gear littered with kill ivory markings.

"Kale," he greeted, "good to see you. Heard you took a pounding in the mountains."

"Be'uc," she said in cordial greeting. "It was nothing we couldn't handle."

He chuckled in his armor, tongue clicking through the interface. "Indeed," he said, then after a pause his tone turned somber. "I was sorry to hear about Byris. Good soldier."

"My thanks," was all Kale said, keeping her eyes fixed on the area before her. Nothing moved.

"What do you make of this madness?" Be'uc probed.

"It is just that - madness," she said forcefully.

The AI leader chuckled again. "That it is. Those are our orders all the same," he said almost remorsefully. He lifted his head slightly, scanning the area ahead. "Mines?"

"No," Kale said, noticing the undisturbed ground before them. "They're content enough to shoot us to bits."

Be'uc shrugged, his armor clanking as he moved his massive shoulders. "I've faced worse odds and lived. Remember the Huuj system?"

"The jungle," Kale recalled, images of the humid tropical climate and the heavily defended Concord outpost both her and Be'uc had assaulted and taken. "I remember that was a close call."

"No closer than this." He sighed, and then reached out to pat her on the shoulder. "Good luck, Kale. We wait for your order."

"Good luck, Be'uc. It's been an honor." The big Algoryn shuffled away, easing through debris clumsily in his hefty armor. Daesto approached Kale, her voice as low as always.

"It's almost time for the attack. The other squads are in position."

Kale nodded, drawing her attention back to the killing ground ahead. It was eerie, watching the still area, knowing that was where she would be spending the last seconds of her life in agony. "Are you afraid, Daesto?" Kale asked, her eyes still fixed on where she knew the enemy would be waiting.

"I'd be lying if I said no," her second replied.

Kale smiled. "I wish I had longer to get to know you, Soldier."

"Yes, Leader," Daesto said flatly.

Kale nodded and readied her mag repeater. She lifted her hand, ready to signal.

The Boromite lines erupted with the sound of gunfire.

***

"Repeat order?" Vagar asked through the communication monitor in his helmet.

A unfamiliar yet authoritative voice hissed through his combat interface. "Ravens to engage Boromite position K, gridlock 82-9. Execute attack formation."

"Our last orders were to await further instruction from the commander," Fannra reminded Vagar.

The ebony clad Interceptor leader supposed that was true. "Our orders are to wait here," he told the voice, "and not disrupt the attack on the Boromites."

"Your orders come from the High Command. You are to scour that position and neutralize those mag launchers."

"The High Command?" Vagar whispered, flattered that the masters of Algoryn strategy had contacted him. "Who is this?"

The voice sounded severely antagonized. "Does it matter who this is? Get in there now, that's an order. Communications out."

The interface crackled dead. Vagar attempted to re-open it, desperate to receive confirmation that the High Command had chosen him for such a task, but it remained unresponsive. Fannra was by his side.

"What should we do, Leader?" He asked. His squadron was around him too, waiting.

Vagar didn't know what to do. Fantris had expressly ordered him to hold position until further notice. It was getting too close for his liking out there anyway, and Vagar was glad to keep his perfect squadron out of the line of fire. Yet that recent communication had provided new orders which came from High Command, which meant they would supersede Fantris' orders. It was possible that the Algoryn Command had finally arrived and assumed control of the assault, yet Vagar did not wish to go against Fantris, who had praised him so highly. Praised and rewarded him for his heroism.

Yet... How much more would he be rewarded for his heroism by the High Commanders themselves...

"We follow our orders," he addressed his squad. "Mount up. We're going to join the attack."

***

The Boromite line was in chaos. Kale watched the scene with awe. The enemy rose from their fortified position, scurrying about in disarray. Boromite brutes jerked and fell upon broken pavements and shattered walls, blood misting in the night air. Behind them, illuminating the dark with repeated fire, were Interceptor squadrons.

Among them, Kale noted, the Sky Ravens.

"How is that for a distraction?" A familiar voice crackled through her interface.

"Ghalris?" Kale responded.

"Yes, Leader. I heard you were in a bit of a tight spot so I did what I could to help."

"You did this?" She looked at the devastation occurring before her and wondered that Ghalris was even capable of such things.

"In light of a thermal strike, it was all I could do," he said. "I haven't long, Leader, these channels aren't the best."

"Go," she said. "And thank you Ghalris."

His response was muted and lost as the monitor whirred and went dead.

"What now?" Daesto asked at Kale's side, watching the scene unfold with uncertainty.

"What do you think? We attack." Kale stood, up, raising her arm to signal the rest of her attack force. "Open fire," she called out, "Forward!"

"About time," Be'uc called behind her.

They charged, AI and Infiltrators screaming as they brought their weapons to bear on the Boromite lines. Kale felt alive, the sound of battle echoing around her. The Boromites were in disarray and she felt a rising sense of satisfaction as shots from her mag repeater felled a fleeing brute. To her left, Be'uc bellowed with joy, his x-slinger erupting with fragmentation bursts along the enemy lines. Some return fire came, and Kale felt her body shudder slightly as shots broke through her thin energy field and rattled down her light armor. She shook it off and pressed on, advancing with her new squad, whom she noted hugged cover and skirted forward dexterously. Daesto was ahead, sending sporadic bursts into the Boromite positions, keeping them pinned while the AI squads moved in to finish them off.

A bellow sounded to Kale's right and a huge Boromite warrior shot out of cover, heading straight for their lines. Kale opened fire, her shots ineffective, bouncing off the Boromite's shielding, nodes on the warriors back fizzling. The brute grabbed a hold of a nearby Algoryn and crushed his skull in his armor with one squeeze of a massive hand. The Boromite cast the corpse away, shrugging off more penetrating fire with his huge form before firing his own weapon, keeping those that tried to advance at bay. He was the biggest soldier Kale had ever seen, and despite her battle anger, she could admire his bravery.

Then, the Boromite disappeared in a shroud of fog. Kale halted, her vision straining through her visor as she attempted to discern what had happened. When the fog subsided she saw the Boromite had fallen, his arm severed from his now still form. Be'uc approached, his x-slinger smoking.

"That's how it's done, eh?"

Kale nodded and together they advanced, effective co-ordinated fire dispatching the last of the scattered enemy. Kale mounted the edge of the Boromite line, firing down on already dead bodies, her mind lost in the whirl of battle.

And in a brief moment it was all silent once more. Voices rattled through combat interfaces, filling the air with a cacophony of battle orders.

"The Boromites are falling back, the entire force is retreating. We've secured the city. The transmats are ours."

Kale sighed, and slumped onto her knees, exhausted with exhilaration. Around her, more Algoryn advanced, relishing in dispatching their fleeing foes. Kale remained still, for now she could rest. The battle was over, and the Algoryn had won.

Yet her eyes strayed to the corpse of a nearby AI soldier, blood oozing from an open wound in his back. The battle was done, she knew, but the fighting would never stop. There would always be war.

She rose to her feet, hefting her weapon to her shoulder and moved out, because war was what she was made for.

War was where she belonged.

Lightning Source UK Ltd.
Milton Keynes UK
UKOW04f1004180717

305534UK00002B/44/P